MW01615325

GARRETT'S DESTINY (SPECIAL FORCES: OPERATION ALPHA)

TACTICAL OPERATIONS SERIES, BOOK 1

ANNA BLAKELY

Dear Readers,

Welcome to the Special Forces: Operation Alpha Fan-Fiction world!

If you are new to this amazing world, in a nutshell the author wrote a story using one or more of my characters in it. Sometimes that character has a major role in the story, and other times they are only mentioned briefly. This is perfectly legal and allowable because they are going through Aces Press to publish the story.

This book is entirely the work of the author who wrote it. While I might have assisted with brainstorming and other ideas about which of my characters to use, I didn't have any part in the process or writing or editing the story.

I'm proud and excited that so many authors loved my characters enough that they wanted to write them into their own story. Thank you for supporting them, and me!

READ ON!
   Xoxo
   Susan Stoker

For you, my fellow Susan Stoker fans. Like you, I fell hard and fast for her heroes, and with every book she writes, I fall a little more. To be able to incorporate them into my own stories for this amazing world is a dream come true. Knowing you've chosen to spend time with my characters means more to me than you'll ever know.

XOXO ~

Anna

PROLOGUE

"Wait!" Salvador's heart thudded with fear as he stared down the barrel of the gun. "Please, Emilio. I have a plan! We can still make this work!"

He couldn't die. Not like this. Not in this musty-smelling forgotten hole where no one would ever find him.

I don't want to die.

The thought was naïve…and pointless. What he wanted didn't matter. Not anymore. And deep down, Sal knew this was exactly what he deserved.

After all, how many times had he heard others beg for their own lives? How many times had he, himself, turned a blind eye while their desperate pleas went unanswered?

But still, he wasn't ready to meet his maker. Not yet. Not when he had a plan to finally be free.

The thought of his impending death impaled Sal to his very core, filling his pores with such terror and anguish he was willing to sell his soul—and anyone else's—in order to survive.

All he had to do was make the most powerful man in the country reconsider his decision to kill him.

With his knees digging into the cool dirt floor and his insides burning with fear, he silently prayed to a god who'd long ago forgotten him. Sal prayed for mercy. That his ruthless boss would find it in his cold, emotionless heart to show mercy and spare him.

And finally, after what felt like a torturous eternity, the man in charge gave the silent order to stand down. Felix— the mass of muscle holding the weapon—paused. His trigger finger easing only slightly as he awaited further instructions.

Sal's shoulders sank, his chest heaving with relief. The sound of his rugged breaths echoed through the dank cellar as a rush of saliva filled his mouth.

A sure sign that his stomach was seconds away from emptying its contents all over the dirt in front of him.

Knowing his boss loathed signs of weakness, Sal pushed back the need to vomit, somehow managing to keep his trembling under control.

"Thank you." The rushed words were directed at the man standing a few feet behind Felix.

Positioned close enough to get a front-row seat to the show while also keeping a safe distance from any blood splatter that may occur, Emilio Garcia stared back at Sal with an unreadable expression.

It was because of this man that life as Sal knew it had completely changed.

No. Your life is fucked up because you chose to crawl into bed with the Devil.

Like he'd had much of a choice.

When Emilio first approached him, Sal had been

begging on the streets. Money, food, pussy...if he wanted it, he had to beg, borrow, and steal to get it.

In the beginning, accepting a job working for the El Sur cartel had been like a dream come true. In less than two years' time, Sal went from struggling to survive to living a life of luxury.

He'd purchased a lavish home. Paid cash for the sports car he'd admired from afar. And for the first time in his pathetic existence, he had women falling over themselves just for the chance to share his bed.

Yes, for Sal, becoming an intricate part of the El Sur cartel meant having everything he'd ever desired...and then some.

But in this very moment, with his life weighing in the balance of Emilio's hands, more than *anything*, Sal wished he'd never met the murdering son of a bitch.

"Do not thank me, Mr. Cruz," his boss spoke for the first time since entering the dingy cellar. "I've only delayed the inevitable."

Despite their seedy location, Emilio looked every bit the politician he pretended to be.

Tall. Dark. Handsome and well-groomed. Hell, the shoes on the man's feet and the shiny watch on his wrist combined cost more than most people in this country made in an entire year.

Yet Emilio Garcia claimed to be a man of the people.

More like destroyer of the people.

"There's another way," Sal rushed to offer Emilio—and himself—a way out of the mess he'd made. "Please. I'm begging you, just hear me out."

The intimidating man considered this before sliding his dark gaze to Felix. Once again, Sal was overcome with relief as he watched the gun lower. Felix took a single step back.

"Talk fast." Emilio brushed some imaginary dust from his expensive jacket. "There are places I need to be."

In the beginning, running drugs for the Dominican cartel leader had seemed like the best idea Sal had ever had. Not only did everyone in the country know who Emilio Garcia was...they *feared* him.

Two years ago, that same fear had been the driving force behind Emilio's landslide election to one of the country's thirty-two senatorial seats. It was also the reason he was weeks away from becoming the country's next president.

The fact that Emilio Garcia was a monster meant nothing. His crimes were rarely brought into question, and when they were, those behind the inquiries seemed to meet an untimely yet unquestionable end.

Unquestionable because no one was brave enough—or stupid enough—*to* ask questions.

Most of the country's law enforcement was on Emilio's payroll. Those who didn't work for him directly were too afraid to consider going against him.

Instead, they all chose to turn a blind eye to his illegal dealings.

For Sal, becoming a member of the El Sur Cartel—or ESC, as most called it—meant inheriting a fraction of that power for himself. It was like a fantasy...until it wasn't.

"My cousin called this morning." Sal spoke quickly, just as he'd been instructed. "He has something in the works. Something huge."

Literally.

"I don't have time for this." His boss started to turn away.

"Please, Emilio!" Sal made a move to stand, but Felix instinctively raised the gun once more.

With his hands held up showing he meant no harm, Sal kept his submissive position and continued with his desperate plea.

"Look, I get that I screwed this last job up for you." He swallowed, risking a sideways glance in Felix's direction. "For *all* of us. But you know me, Emilio. You *know* I can make this right. Please, just give me the chance to make it right!"

It wouldn't be an easy task, thanks to his screw-up. Sal had been given one job—to find the leak within the organization—and he'd failed miserably.

Not only had he identified the wrong El Sur member as the organization's mole, he'd also inadvertently cost the cartel a substantial amount of money when their last deal blew up in their faces.

Even so, Emilio had to know Sal's loyalty was unwavering. He *had* to. Sal just needed a little more time to prove it.

The senator spoke his next words with careful consideration. "Your cousin. He has done work for us before, yes?"

"Yes!" Sal's desperation nearly caused him to leap forward again. Keeping an eye on Felix and his gun, he licked his dry lips and composed himself. "Marcus has helped me on numerous occasions. And he's always come through for us. *Always.* There's no reason for me to think the outcome won't be the same this time."

"Come on, Boss." Felix gave Emilio an incredulous look.

"You're not really buying into this bullshit, are you? We've seen this same thing a million times. They always make empty promises when they realize they're about to die."

Sal tried not to think about the 'they' in question. Men who'd been in this exact same position. On their knees begging for their lives.

He also refused to think about how his ruthless leader had never spared any of them a stay of execution. No matter how much they pleaded.

Why lie to yourself, Salvador? You know how this is going to end.

"I know what you're thinking." He locked eyes with Emilio. "But I swear, this isn't just some kind of stunt to save my own skin. This is legit."

"Nice try, Sally Boy." Felix rolled his soulless eyes as he uttered the nickname he knew Sal hated. "But this isn't something stealing a bunch of tourist's ID's and credit card information can fix."

"Those jobs brought in a lot of money." Sal couldn't keep from reminding the asshole.

"Not three million dollars," Felix spouted off the exact amount Sal's screw-up had caused the organization. "Besides, tourists are getting smarter. We try a job like that again, those cards will most likely be cancelled the second you and your men walk away."

Seemingly accepting of this, Emilio gave his right-hand man a look before turning to leave. Once again, Felix raised the gun in Sal's direction.

Fear filled every cavity of Sal's core. It was no longer a concept or simple emotion. It was a living, breathing entity in and of itself.

This was it. He had seconds left to convince them he could salvage what he'd lost. If he couldn't...

"What if we don't walk away?" Sal blurted, his question echoing off the cellar's stone walls.

Emilio's movements halted. With his weight on his expensive heels, he turned and faced Sal once more. "What are you suggesting?"

"What if we take them?"

"The cards?" Felix's dark brows bunched together. "Are you deaf or just stupid?"

"I'm not talking about taking the cards." Sal kept his eyes on the man in charge. "I'm talking about taking the tourists."

Felix released a low curse. "Just let me shoot him, Emilio," he grumbled. The gun was still pointed directly at Sal's head. "This idiot's wasted enough of our ti—"

"Wait." Their boss raised his left hand. "I want to hear him out."

"He probably doesn't even have a plan. This is all just some lame attempt to save his own ass. Why allow him to manipulate you like this?"

"Why?" Emilio's narrowed gaze slid in Felix's direction. "Because I'm still the one in charge." With the intense reminder still hanging in the air, the dangerous man turned his attention back to Sal. "Go on."

"There's another ship planning to arrive a week from tomorrow," Sal informed him. "Very upscale."

Felix snorted. "And you plan to what? Board the ship and take everyone hostage?"

"Not everyone." Sal kept his tone steady despite the desperation turning his blood to ice. "A small group."

15

Emilio stared back at him. His expression was unreadable. "Explain."

"Marcus said registration for the river hike and dune buggy combo excursion was nearly full. I've helped my cousin run that exact tour more times than I can count. I know the route, and I know the perfect spot to strike. We ambush the group and hold them hostage until their families have paid."

Was it risky? Sure. But it wouldn't be the first time a group of unsuspecting tourists got caught up in such a situation. If others could pull it off, Sal was confident he could, too.

"I've researched dozens of incidents just like what I'm suggesting. Nearly every time, the families of the hostages, or the hostages' governments, paid the demanded ransom. We're talking twenty people, Emilio. We demand a million for each person, we'll bring in more than six times the amount of money we lost."

"You mean, the money *you* lost by wasting our time going after the wrong guy." Felix, the bastard, brought his fuck-up back into the equation. "Not to mention you're talking twenty tourists against you and your cousin. Will you and Marcus be prepared if those people fight back?"

Still down in his humiliating position, Sal shot the arrogant man a look. "Fight back with what? The tourists won't be armed, Felix. They *can't* be. Customs would never allow them through."

And even if someone did manage to make it past Customs, ship security would catch up to them when they attempted to board.

"And it wouldn't only be my cousin and me," Sal explained. "There are others. Men I trust with my life."

"That's good, considering your life is, in fact, on the line." Emilio took a step toward him as he mulled over the idea. "Let's say I agreed to this plan of yours. Where would we hold the hostages?"

"Same place we hold our other merchandise."

"The old warehouse?" Felix huffed out a loud breath. "This is insane, Emilio. He's talking about deliberately bringing a bunch of witnesses into the heart of our operation. What happens if one of them gets free and—"

"It's no greater risk than using that same warehouse to hold our other product before moving it," Sal quickly assured both men. "Marcus and I will personally keep the hostages secured in the north side until we get the money."

Marcus was the only member of his family he was still in contact with. He was also the only one he'd ever been able to count on.

"And after?" Emilio's interest gave Sal hope when he'd thought all was lost.

He looked up at his boss with earnest. "After payment is made, we see to it that the hostages disappear." Just like all the others.

Only these captives wouldn't be sold as sex slaves like the others. Unless…

Another idea struck. A brilliant, potentially ass-saving idea.

"There's more." He rushed his attempt to sweeten the plan. "Big ship like that, there's bound to be at least one or two women on the excursion that will fit our customers' tastes. We keep those women separated from the other hostages until our ransom demands are met. Then we add them to our inventory."

Second after endless second passed. For Sal, the

silence that followed his suggestion felt as if it stretched on for days.

The force with which his heart pounded against his ribs was proof of his unprecedented despair. But he refused to let the other men see it.

On his knees, Sal's breath remained frozen in his lungs as he awaited his fate.

Just when he was certain Emilio would disregard his plan and move forward with his execution, the powerful man surprised him with a slow forming smile.

"This is your last chance, Salvador," Emilio warned. "Rest assured, there will not be another."

Tears of the unexpected solace pricked at the corners of Sal's eyes. "Thank you, Emilio." His voice was thick. "You won't regret this."

Turning away, the powerful man stopped at the bottom of the steps for a final, parting glance. His cold eyes reached deep inside, laying claim to what was left of Sal's soul.

"Make sure that I don't."

CHAPTER 1

"Sonofabitch!"

Garrett Morgan ducked his head, rolling onto his back as a bullet whizzed past. Warmth from the projectile's heat kissed his cheek a fraction of a second before he found himself lying safely behind a large boulder.

His heart pumped a massive shot of adrenaline into his veins.

"You good, Falcon?"

Beckett "Bones" Stone's southern drawl hit Garrett's ear through the state-of-the-art coms provided to each of the Tac-Ops teams.

"Yeah," Garrett huffed out a quick response to let the former Marine know he hadn't taken a hit. From his hidden position, Garrett—Falcon to his teammates—closed his eyes and took a moment to regroup.

The back of his shirt stuck to him like some sort of grotesque second skin. Dust and grime filled his nostrils, and the night's hot, humid air continued to draw sweat from every pore in his body.

God, I hate it here.

That same thought had been rolling through his mind since he'd stepped off the plane a few hours ago. Not surprising, given the fact that his previous times in Syria held very few good memories, and those he did have stemmed from his time on base with his former unit.

Before leaving the military, Garrett had been a special operations sniper for the 75th Regiment—more specifically the Army's 3rd Ranger Battalion. During that time, he'd grown as close to his fellow soldiers as he was his own family.

In the years since leaving the Army behind, Garrett had found a new extended family. One he cared for and trusted as much as his last.

Though he'd only been employed by Tactical Operations for three years, he'd formed the same type of unbreakable bond with the team he was on now. Bones, Apollo, Digger…they were all former military and tough SOBs. And he trusted each and every one of them with his life.

Speaking of…

From both sides where Garrett lay, his team fired back at the enemy. Clearing the way for him to do his thing.

Waiting for the signal telling him it was safe to move, Garrett silently cursed his still-racing heart. And though it was impossible, the heat from that damn bullet still seemed to warm his cheek.

Fuck me. He'd had close calls before, but none like that one. Still, he needed to get his head on straight and concentrate on the task at hand, or he'd be useless to the men fighting beside him.

Eyes still shut, he focused on the job he was here to do.

Using techniques he'd learned back in his Army days, Garrett slowed his breathing. Working to get his racing heartrate back to a normal pace.

Soon his pulse became steady, and his body slowly lowered its elevated adrenaline levels. The physical reaction he'd experienced was more than a little intense. And confusing as hell.

This wasn't the first time he'd come close to being hit. He *had* been hit before. Both in the Army and since taking the job with Tac-Ops.

What the fuck, Morgan? You should be used to this shit by now.

On paper, Garrett and his teammates were senior travel insurance agents for a company known as Travel Assurance Coverage and Operations.

The company's headquarters was in the heart of Charlotte, North Carolina, though there were offices located around the globe.

What the public saw when they drove past their highrise office building was exactly what their boss wanted everyone to see... A high-end company that sold personal protection and extraction insurance to those traveling abroad.

What the public didn't see—what they *couldn't* see— was that Garrett and his team actually worked for a clandestine group of operators known as Tactical Operations, or Tac-Ops for short.

The acronym happened to work for both their cover jobs as insurance agents and their true reason for employment. A brilliant move on their boss's part.

While Garrett and the other members of Tac-Ops One *were* licensed travel protection insurance agents, they were also specialized, below-the-grid operatives who took on government-sanctioned jobs.

Jobs that very few people knew about. Ones that included, but were not limited to, hostage location and rescue.

In short, the multi-million-dollar insurance agency was a legitimate front for what they'd *really* been hired to do...

Help rid the world of the worst mankind had to offer.

Thanks to the United States' long standing and unwavering stance on negotiating with terrorists—they *don't*—it was up to companies like Tac-Ops to step in when Uncle Sam refused.

Not that anyone within the American government would ever acknowledge their existence. Each team member was well aware of the ramifications should they be caught and captured on foreign soil.

To put it simply, if Garrett and his team screwed up, they'd be ass out.

But despite the risks, they'd signed the dotted line without hesitation. Just because they got out of the military didn't mean their loyalty to their country's citizens had waned.

It didn't matter if it was one innocent or one hundred... if someone fucked with the United States, the men of Tac-Ops would do whatever they had to in order to take them down.

Case in point.

More than ready to get the job done and leave this Godforsaken place, Garrett spoke into his coms once more.

"Please tell me you have the bastard in your sights." The comment was directed toward Bones.

"Just...about...there." The former Marine Raider let

his words linger. A whisper of a shot followed and then, "Got 'em!"

With his movements instant and fluid, Garrett wasted no time rolling back onto his stomach and repositioning his weapon. Using the night optics mounted atop his SR 25 rifle, he found his next target.

Releasing a slow, controlled breath, he did what he'd been trained to do. With a precision he took pride in, Garrett began the countdown in his head.

Three...two...

His lungs deflated with a slow exhale. His hot breath feathered past his parted lips as it brushed over them.

He pulled the trigger.

Bitter sulfur and smoke warred with the sweet smell of gun oil as the lethal round was released through the weapon's chamber. The combination of scents provided Garrett with a feeling of comfort he'd only ever found on the battlefield.

Through his lens he watched the man crumble to the ground like a deflated balloon. One Garrett had popped with less than five pounds of trigger pull.

"Party's started, boys." Bones' Texas accent was laced with anticipation. "Time to drink up."

Garrett's lips curved upward. The other man's good looks, charismatic personality, and laid-back demeanor allowed him to thrive in just about any situation. Right now, the former Marine's tone gave away his desire to finish this and get the hell home.

I feel ya, brother.

Over the next several minutes, the sound of crackling gunfire filled the night air as they continued with the first phase of their plan. One by one, the team systematically took out each of the tangos standing between them and their objective.

With all visible threats neutralized, they began closing in on the building currently housing the hostages. A dozen barely qualified private contractors hired by the U.S. government to help train local military and other security agencies.

Despite the contractors' own lack of sufficient training and experience.

For the past three weeks, the group of men had been held against their will after being ambushed by Syrian insurgents unwilling to accept the positive changes happening in their country.

It was Tac-Ops' job to locate, rescue, and return the hostages to safety.

They'd found them. Now they just needed to get them out alive and transport them back home to their families.

Let's do this.

"Keep your eyes peeled, gentlemen." Digger's deep voice commanded as their boots whispered over the dry dirt. "No mistakes."

As their team leader, it was Digger's job to make sure they were at the top of their game. But Garrett was tempted to tell the man that his order was unnecessary.

They all knew what was at stake.

Experience had taught them that one fuckup was all it took to change—or end—a life forever. Or in this particular case, *twelve* lives.

With their weapons held securely in front of them, Garrett and the others moved shoulder-to-shoulder as they crossed the dry stretch of land between the hillside and the decrepit building.

Their steps were precise and purposeful. Their boots marching swiftly across dirt and rocks as they stayed alert, ready to pull the trigger at the first sign of danger.

"Tac-Ops One, do you copy?"

The familiar voice reached the ears of every team member. As usual, Garrett, Apollo, and Bones remained quiet so Digger could respond.

"Affirmative, Shadow. What do we know?"

"Your perimeter's clear. Hostages are still in the same location, northeast corner of the building. There are seven tangos inside. Two with the hostages, three standing guard in the main area, and two more moving around inside the building's entrance. They know you're coming, so be ready."

No shit. Garrett smirked. He was tempted to point out the fact that the gunfire had been a dead giveaway but kept his smartass comment to himself. This wasn't the time or place for their usual, friendly banter.

"Copy that," Digger mumbled. With his night vision goggles focused on the door they were inching toward, their leader addressed the team once more. "All right, boys. You heard the woman. Let's take care of these assholes and get those people home."

Letting out a low "Hooah", Garrett once again forced his breathing to remain steady as they reached the large, stone structure. With Shadow serving as overwatch, he felt confident in their approach.

Using her mad skills on the keyboard, the mysterious woman was the team's eye in the sky, so-to-speak. Shadow saw everything...and missed nothing.

No matter where Garrett and his team found themselves, she was always there. Watching over them from the start of each mission to the end.

She'd inform the team of any and all threats her high-tech system detected, doing all she could to warn them of possible menacing forces in their vicinity.

Yes, Shadow was brilliant, to say the least. She was also something of an enigma.

Always working from an undisclosed location, her voice provided a touch of calm in the midst of chaos.

Everyone on the team trusted her. Every piece of intel...every suggestion she offered...they all took her at face value. Despite having never met her in person.

Other than their boss, no one knew her real name or how she'd come to work for Tac-Ops. What the team did know—the only thing they *needed* to know—was that the woman they all called Shadow had their backs. Always.

"Breaching the building's entrance now."

Digger's hushed voice broke through Garrett's thoughts. Positioning himself to the right of the rusted metal door, he watched as Apollo pressed the breach strip onto the door above the handle.

On Digger's order, the other man pressed the remote detonator. A fraction of a second later, the device exploded.

With a burst of smoke and minimal debris, the locking mechanism was destroyed. Using the sliver of space between the jarred door's edge and its frame as a pathway for their bullets to travel, the men inside wasted no time in their attempts to neutralize Garrett and the others.

Anticipating the tangos' reaction, the team waited for a break between gunshots to return fire. Just as they had countless times before, each member took his assigned infiltration position and began moving in on their targets.

Garrett stayed low while Digger took the upper stance. Both men's shots were synced as they simultaneously took out the first two targets. With the entrance cleared, Bones and Apollo followed as the four men moved deeper into the moonlit warehouse.

"Your location's been compromised." Shadow's announcement came as no surprise. "Three tangos are headed your way."

Weapons secured, the team moved past the two bodies through the industrial space. Another rush of adrenaline spiked through Garrett's veins as he steeled himself for a fight he knew was coming.

Shadow had given them invaluable intel on their opponents' general locations and movement, but no one could accurately predict the last-minute decisions the remaining tangos might make. For this reason, the men of Tac-Ops kept their guard up and their trigger fingers ready.

In a wave of movements, each team member did as they'd been trained to do.

Bones reached for the door's handle. Apollo withdrew an M18 smoke grenade from his vest and waited. After another silent countdown courtesy of Digger, Bones curled his fingers around the knob as Apollo inserted his gloved index finger into the thin metal circle at the top of the grenade.

Pulling the pin, Apollo waited for Bones to open the door before releasing the grenade's safety lever and tossing the metal cannister through the door's opening. The bursting charge was released, its telltale hiss preluding a billowing stream of thick red smoke.

The instant cover allowed the team to enter the space unseen while their infrared goggles attached to their combat helmets made it possible to locate their targets with ease.

Through the thick, swirling smoke, the team brought the three bastards into their sights. Garrett dropped the first tango to fill his vision.

Almost simultaneously, Bones and Apollo took down the other two while Digger covered the team, sweeping the space for additional threats.

Thirty seconds later, the smoke had all but cleared as Garrett and the others crossed the expansive space toward the room where the remaining hostage takers, or HTs, were presumably located.

According to Shadow's intel, there were only two tangos left. Both holed up in the same enclosed area as the twelve men Garrett and his teammates had come here to save.

.

"Shadow, tell me what you see," Digger ordered as they covered the distance toward their final targets.

"I'm still picking up fourteen heat signatures in the room to your left."

Twelve hostages. Two tangos. Exactly what they were anticipating.

"Perimeter?" Digger double-checked.

"Clear."

"Copy that."

Positioning themselves by the door—Digger and Bones on the left, and Apollo and Garrett on the right—the four men readied themselves for what they hoped to be their last confrontation on this particular op.

Just as he'd done for the initial breach, Digger used hand signals to count down from three. When he curled his fingers inward to form a tight fist, the team sprang into action.

Using the same type of low-impact explosive as before, Apollo blew the locks. The door popped open, a smoke grenade was thrown, and the team took out the final two HTs with relative ease.

It had all gone exactly as planned.

Blowing out a breath, Garrett lifted his goggles and lowered his weapon, relaxing for the first time since coming here.

He had no way of knowing what a grave mistake he was making.

The threats had all been neutralized, but what they didn't expect—what he, Shadow, or the others couldn't possibly have predicted—was for one of the hostages to pick up a dead HTs gun and aim it directly at Garrett.

"Wait!" Garrett threw up a hand to show the man they were the good guys. But it was too late.

The terrified hostage pulled the trigger, releasing a round of ammunition through the automatic rifle's barrel. The single projectile tore through the stale air, the heated metal heading straight in Garrett's direction.

Traveling at 3,300 feet per second, there was no way to avoid being hit.

The bullet slammed into the center of Garrett's chest, forcing him off his feet. He landed with a hard thud, his back and head bouncing off the room's cool concrete floor.

Chaos ensued as his teammates yelled at the man to drop the weapon. Their voices and Garrett's vision faded in and out as he fought to remain conscious.

The shock to his system stalled his breathing. His lungs failed to follow the command his brain was sending.

Breathe, damnit. You need to fucking breathe!

Pain ratcheted throughout his entire torso, grabbing hold of his heart and clamping down. Garrett's lungs burned with their need for oxygen, so he opened his mouth in search of the air his body needed to survive.

It didn't work.

Jesus. He'd been hurt

before, but not like this. Never like this.

The pain was indescribable. He could actually *feel* his organs beginning to shut down. Or at least he thought that's what he was feeling.

As he lay there, Garrett's faltering brain screamed to understand what was happening. One quick glance at the man who'd shot him, and he knew.

You're dying.

The pain in his chest remained. His lungs still refusing to open. A dark cloud framed his blurred vision, and little by little, it began closing in around him.

Garrett felt himself fading away.

"Falcon!"

Someone yelled his Tac-Ops nickname, but he couldn't respond. Rough hands pulled at his vest and shirt.

"Come on, man. Stay with me!"

More discussion erupted between his team and the hostages. Garrett could hear his men assuring the captives that they were safe. Someone—Bones maybe?—announced that they were American operatives sent to rescue them.

Some hostages cried with relief. Others cheered. The

man standing beside him kept repeating how sorry he was for having shot him.

Though he tried again, Garrett couldn't formulate a response. He wanted to tell the distraught hostage to stop. That he understood why the guy had done it.

The man was scared. Desperate to find a way out of this hell hole. And Garrett and the others hadn't been able to identify themselves before the shitstorm had broken loose.

For all the poor bastard knew, Garrett and his team were just another set of bad guys coming to take them to a secondary location. Or worse.

But he couldn't tell the remorseful man that or anything else. All he could do was lay there. Praying for air that refused to come and wondering if his luck had finally run out.

Cold from the concrete penetrated the back of Garrett's vest and sweat-drenched shirt. Or maybe it wasn't. Maybe it was just his injured body knocking on death's door.

As he began to lose consciousness, Garrett thought about his dad. His brother, Colt. The mom they'd lost years before.

Garrett missed her like crazy, but at thirty-five, he wasn't quite ready to see her again. There was still too damn much he wanted to do with his life.

Not ready to fucking die.

"Quit being so dramatic." Apollo's deep voice traveled through the fog. "You're not fucking dying, so stop with that shit."

What the...

Had he said those words out loud? Garrett somehow

managed to peel his eyes open and stare up at his olive-skinned teammate.

"Welcome back." Apollo gave him a wink.

Well shit. Maybe he wasn't dying after all.

Putting conscious effort into speaking again, Garrett managed to rasp out a strained, "V-vest?"

"Did its job." Hands pressed along his sternum and ribs as Apollo checked for fractures or other signs of injury. "Bullet tore through the first protective layer but didn't penetrate the ceramic plate." His teammate's fingers continued with their poking and prodding. "Doesn't feel like anything's broken. No obvious signs of internal injuries, but you'll need to be checked out as soon as possible, just in case."

Thank Christ.

Now that Apollo mentioned it, the horrific pain Garrett had felt seconds before *was* finally beginning to let up. More of a dull, bruising ache than the suffocating burn, he was able to focus on the people around him better. Their images becoming clearer.

Garrett's chest expanded slowly as he tested his lungs. Filling them at a cautious, hesitant rate, he used the same controlled pace to release the air he'd just pulled in.

Garrett repeated the action. Once. Twice. Three times.

"There ya go, buddy." Apollo spoke again. "That's it. Nice and easy."

"How is he?" Digger's large, hovering form came into Garrett's view.

"He'll live."

"Help me up." Garrett grunted. He raised a hand, which Apollo immediately took.

With his teammate's help, he got back onto his feet.

The tender pull in his chest made him wince. He'd no doubt be feeling the effects of being shot at close range for the foreseeable future.

"You good?" Digger squeezed one of his shoulders.

Garrett nodded, looking at the twelve strangers anxiously staring back at him. "Let's get these guys out of here and get the hell home."

"I second that motion," Bones chimed in. "Don't know about the rest of you, but I'm damn glad Owens is giving us the next two weeks off. My ass needs a vacation from all this shit."

Two close calls on a single op?

A vacation's exactly what I need.

CHAPTER 2

"What about him?"

Hearing her sister's low question, Avery Webb looked up from the drink she was stirring to follow the other woman's gaze. When she realized what—or rather who—her sister was referring to, she couldn't keep her face from betraying her thoughts.

"Ronald?" Avery blurted loudly. With a quick glance to make sure the man standing at the bar a few yards away hadn't heard her, she leaned toward her sister and lowered her voice. "Are you crazy or just drunk?"

Layers of Alex's long, dark locks bounced atop her shoulders as she laughed. "Neither. Well, I'm not crazy. I might be a tad tipsy, but that's not the point."

"Oh, you have a point?" Sarcasm oozed from Avery's tone as she straightened herself back up. "I know I'm going to regret this, but I'll bite. What's your point, dear sister?" She put her straw between her lips, sucking in more of the delicious Amaretto-based drink.

"That you need to get laid."

The cool liquid Avery had yet to swallow flew out of her mouth, spraying their small, round table…and Alex.

"*Alex!*" She reached for the napkin dispenser, pulling several of the absorbent paper squares loose.

Unaffected by the sudden alcohol shower, Alex casually wiped down the front of her Black strapless dress. "What?"

"What do you mean, what?" Avery hissed. Scowling, she moved her glass and blotted at the mess she'd made. "I can't believe you said that."

"Why?" Alex shrugged. "It's the truth."

"It is not!" Okay, so maybe it *had* been a really, *really* long time since she'd been with a man. Almost two years, but who was counting, anyway? Not Avery.

Liar, Liar.

"You should try one of those online dating apps. If you aren't looking for anything serious, you could even sign up with the ones designed for casual hookups."

"I'll pass." Avery cringed just thinking about it. The thought of having sex with someone she barely knew didn't appeal to her in the least.

"Come on, Aves." Alex signaled their waitress to bring another round. "You've got to learn to loosen up a little. You're an adult; you're single…and as long as you're smart about it and take precautions, there's nothing wrong with having a casual sexual relationship."

"Says the woman who has nothing *but* casual relationships." *More like a running list of one-offs.* "You're lecturing me about my lack of a social life when you're the one too scared to settle down."

Avery regretted the sharp words as soon as they flew from her mouth.

"I'm sorry." She attempted to smooth things over. "I didn't mean to—"

"No, you're right." Alex cut her off. "After what I went through with Evan, I can't seem to let myself get close to anyone. Not yet anyway."

The vulnerability shimmering behind her tough-as-nails sister broke Avery's heart. It also made her want to hunt down that lying, cheating bastard, Evan, and beat his skanky side pieces' asses.

"You will." She tried to sound reassuring.

"I know." Alex smiled with a confidence Avery wasn't sure her sister possessed. "And so will you. *If* you ever let yourself have a little fun, that is."

She knew what the other woman was doing. Alex hadn't really talked about what went down with her ex, other than the fact that she'd caught him in a pack of lies.

It was clear she still didn't want to talk about it. Instead, tonight's conversation was apparently going to revolve around Avery's non-existent personal life.

"Look, Aves." Alex's expression softened. "I don't mean to get all up in your business. I'm just saying you could use a little excitement in your life. That's all."

Avery snorted. "And you think Ronald the accountant is the man to give it to me?"

Not only no, but hell no.

She'd spotted Ronald Schwimmer the second he'd walked through the door. He worked for one of the local loan companies she was contracted with just down the street from where they were, and the guy was not her type. At. All.

He'd asked her out a few times over the past two

months, but thankfully the persistent fellow finally took the hint after she continued turning him down.

Ronald was nice enough, she supposed. But despite his tall stature and fit runner's build, he wasn't attractive in the least. Not that Avery judged a man solely on his outward appearance, but there had to be some semblance of attraction there.

When she looked at Ronald, she felt...nothing.

No electricity. No lightning bolt. Nada.

I want lightning. Or at the very least, a small spark.

Giving the man in question a second glance, Alex scrunched her face and shook her head. "Okay, you're right. Good call on the accountant."

Avery chuckled. "Thank you."

"But still..." Her relentless sister continued pushing. "You spend all day, every day staring at a computer. And your nights aren't any better."

This made Avery frown. "How do you know what I do at night?"

"Please." Alex rolled her pretty brown eyes. "You go home, feed your cat, eat some takeout, and spend the rest of the night with your nose stuck in those romance novels you're so obsessed with." When Avery opened her mouth to deny her sister's claim, Alex arched one of her perfectly plucked brows. "Tell me I'm wrong."

"That's not fair, and you know it."

Okay, so maybe she *did* spend her days in front of a computer, but only because it was her job. At twenty-eight, Avery was the youngest leading financial software designer in the country. So yeah, computers were kind of her thing.

As for the other...

"Lots of women enjoy getting lost in an enthralling story."

With an unladylike scoff, Alex lifted her glass to her smug lips and muttered, "You mean you enjoy reading *smut*."

"It is not smut!" Alex blurted loud enough to draw attention from some of the nearby tables. Damn it, she really needed to stop doing that.

"Is there sex in those books of yours?" her sister challenged.

"Yes, but—"

"There ya have it." Alex grinned. "Smut."

Her sister had a point. Though the books Avery read weren't filled with cover-to-cover hot monkey sex, there *was* a certain level of steam mixed into her beloved stories.

Some leaving her so hot and bothered, she was thankful her batteries were the rechargeable kind.

"There's also plenty of action and adventure in them," Avery defended her choice of reading. "And suspense... and romance." Stories of happily ever after that left her toes curling and her heart hopeful.

Hopeful because she'd read way too many amazing books for that sort of thing to not be real. Sure, the stories themselves were fictional. And of course, the drama and suspense weren't true to life. But boy when Avery found herself caught up in a good story...

What I wouldn't give to feel that same sort of passion for real.

And the men...God. Just the *idea* of an alpha hero risking it all for the woman he loves made Avery's heart believe those stories could happen. That they had to have stemmed from someplace *real*.

Her logical brain couldn't accept anything else. Because to her, it made perfect sense.

If her favorite authors could create such visceral, physical reactions from words alone, then surely that meant those emotions and experiences existed *outside* the pages.

Apparently just not in Avery's world.

"I like my books." She turned to Alex once more. "And I don't judge *you* for how you spend your nights."

If anything, Avery was envious of her older sister's outgoing personality. Alex was a social butterfly. Her, not so much.

Even as a kid, Avery preferred the solace of her bedroom. She spent most of her time solving puzzles or playing intellectually challenging video games. Placing that last piece with the others or reaching the next level in a game filled her with a sense of accomplishment and pride.

Those same traits had followed her into adulthood. Only now, instead of jigsaw puzzles or brain teasers, Avery created accounting programs and financial software used by several Fortune 500 companies.

Alex, on the other hand, was beyond horrible with math and computers, but great with people.

Growing up, she was always the popular one. The cheerleader who dated the quarterback. The prom queen who stole the hearts of all the boys in school. Star of the school play.

Avery didn't begrudge her sister any of those things. She was truly happy for each and every award and prize Alex had ever earned.

Even now, as they spent the evening celebrating her sister's upcoming show at the most prestigious art gallery in town, she was filled with nothing but excitement and pride for the woman sitting across from her.

Which reminded her…

"Enough about me. Tonight is supposed to be about *you*." Avery lifted her almost-empty glass in the air. "So, here's to you, your amazing talent, and to what I know will be the best damn art show this city has ever seen."

Smiling wide, her gorgeous sister lifted her own glass. Clinking the rim with hers, Alex downed what was left of her mixed drink. "Thanks, Aves. Your support means a lot." Alex's smile wavered, a touch of bittersweet sadness filling the woman's dark eyes. "I wish Mom and Dad could be here to see it."

Reaching across the table, Avery covered one of her sister's hands with hers. "They are, Alex." Tears pricked the corners of her eyes, but she blinked them away. "They're always here."

With a gentle squeeze, the two sisters let the moment linger before Alex sniffled and straightened her shoulders. "So." She cleared the thick emotion from her voice. "Back to your boring, predictable life."

"Really?" Avery's gaze narrowed. "I may not be the most sought-after artist in town, but that doesn't mean my life is boring and predictable"

"You go to work; you go home to an empty apartment."

"It's not empty. I have Gus."

"A cat doesn't count."

Avery's jaw dropped. "Gus does *to* count. He's a sweetheart."

"He's a cat, Avery. Sweetie, I love you to bits. You know this. But I swear one of these days, you're going to wake up and realize you've become the quintessential crazy cat lady. And it would be one thing if you spent your weekend cuddled up to him, but even those are filled with extra programming jobs on the side. Which I don't understand at all. It's not like you need the money."

It was true. Software design was an extremely lucrative career. Especially for a single woman living alone.

Avery managed her money wisely and never went overboard with any expenditures. In fact, she had everything she needed.

Well, almost everything.

"I take those jobs because I enjoy what I do." She didn't add that she also took them because she had nothing better to do.

Alex's expression softened. "It's great that you love your work, Aves. It truly is. Not many people can say that and mean it. But don't you want more out of life?"

No. Yes. Maybe. "I'll get more. Just not right now."

"If not now, then when?"

"Well, I don't have an exact date marked on my calendar." Avery's smart mouth flared to life.

"Maybe it should be."

"Ha, ha." She rolled her eyes. "Very funny."

"No, I think you're on to something." Alex leaned forward, resting her elbows on the table. A few seconds passed before her face lit up with a Cheshire grin. "Pick a date. Or better yet, a week."

"A week?" Avery couldn't remember the last time she'd gone an entire week without working. "To do what exactly?"

Confusion sent her sister's brows inward. "Uh...have *fun*."

"Alex—"

"No, this is perfect, actually. It's so obvious; I don't know why I didn't think about this before."

The excitement in the woman's voice made Avery nervous.

"Think about what?" She stared at her sister, wondering just how strong their drinks had been.

Playful arrogance lit Alex's face as she declared, "I dare you to take an entire week off from work and do something adventurous."

Avery started to laugh but stopped short when she caught her sister's expression. "You're serious."

"You said you read those books for the adventure, so… I want you to go have one of your own."

"You're *daring* me to have fun? What are we, twelve?"

"Nope. You're almost thirty, and I'm already there plus a couple of years. Which proves my point even more. It's high time you crawled out of your shell and started living. And to make sure you know just how serious I am…" Alex leaned in closer. "I'm not just daring you to do this. I *double-stuff* dare you."

Flashes of childhood memories entered Avery's mind. She and Alex used to do what they coined as double-stuff dares; whoever lost the bet had to use their allowance money to buy the other a package of double-stuffed Oreos.

And no matter what the task was, neither sister had ever backed down from a double-stuff dare. Ever.

There's a first time for everything.

"This is ridiculous." Avery shook her head. "We're adults, Al. Not a couple of kids vying for a package of cookies."

Disappointment filtered through Alex's dark eyes.

"You're right." She settled back into her chair. "I should've known better. Forget I ever brought it up."

A nagging feeling tugged at Avery's gut. Though it was beyond silly, she couldn't help but feel as though she was letting her sister down in a big way.

Crap. "Let's say, for argument's sake, I accept the dare. What happens if I don't follow through?"

Back in the day, in addition to the purchase of cookies, they'd come up with all sorts of additional punishments for failing. Cleaning the other's room for a month. Backrubs every night for a week. That sort of thing.

But now that they were grown, Avery couldn't help but wonder what sort of *payment* her sister would come up with.

"If you accept the challenge and fail…" Alex's voice trailed as she mulled it over. With a quick glance at the man they'd discussed earlier, she looked back at Avery with a sly grin. "You have to go on a date with Ronald."

Ronald. Had anyone ever screamed that name during a mind-blowing orgasm? She bet not.

Her eyes shot to the man still standing at the bar. A man she had absolutely *no* desire to spend any time with—work related or otherwise.

"Fine." She agreed to her sister's terms. "I'll go home right now and look at my calendar. But if I do this, then you have to…" It took her a moment to formulate her own brilliant punishment. Avery grinned. "You have to *stop* dating…and having sex. For six months."

Alex's jaw dropped. "Six *months*?"

That should be enough time for the commitment-phobe woman to finally deal with the heartache she'd suffered, rather than hiding from it by becoming a serial dater.

"Six. Months." Avery held her hand out across the table, pinky raised. "That's the deal. Take it or leave it."

You're totally in the clear. There's no way Alex will agree to this.

The thought had barely entered Avery's mind when her sister reached over and curled their pinkies together.

"Fine." Alex initiated the same finger shake they used to do as kids. "If you actually go through with this, I'll stop dating for six months."

Son of a...

"And no sex!" Avery blurted.

Her sister sighed and mumbled, "And no sex."

Well, crap. That plan sure backfired. But, if her taking a few days off work meant forcing Alex to realize all wasn't lost in the world of love and happiness, then it would be worth it.

Releasing her sister's hand, Avery smiled at the waitress who'd finally gotten around to bringing them more drinks.

An hour later, as her ride was pulling to a stop near her apartment building, the confidence she'd felt earlier had begun to fade.

Why had she agreed to such a stupid, childish bet? She *read* about adventures. She didn't participate in them.

Flashing lights up ahead caught her eye, pulling her from her sea of regret. A slew of emergency vehicles was parked directly in front of the building.

Two police cars, a firetruck, and an ambulance.

What the...

Avery spun her head toward the brick structure, expecting to see smoke rolling from the windows or flames shooting out from the roof. But there was neither.

"Must be some sort of medical emergency," her driver stated the obvious. "Hope whoever it is, is okay."

"Yeah." Avery nodded as she opened the door. "Me, too. Thanks for the ride."

"No problem. And if you would, I'd really appreciate a good review. Helps with business."

"Of course." She shot the man a smile. "Have a good night."

"You, too."

Shutting the door, Avery began walking toward the entrance. Like the kind driver, she hoped whoever had called for help was okay. Mostly keeping to herself, she didn't really know many of the people in the building. Only two, really.

Stephen, a guy around her age, and Ms. Wilson. In her eighties, *she* was a tried-and-true crazy cat lady.

They both lived on her floor, but each in a different hallway than hers. And since the building was enormous— it was an old paper factory that had been converted into apartments—Avery only saw Stephen and Joan occasionally, as they came and went.

The other tenants she encountered throughout her days pretty much kept to themselves, which was perfectly fine with her. In fact, Stephen and Ms. Wilson were the only ones who'd ever gone out of their way to speak to her.

Holding her key fob up to the electronic pad, Avery waited for the green light before reaching for one of the glass double doors. As she made her way into the entrance and over to her assigned mailbox, she was surprised to find it quiet.

No emergency personnel or out-of-the-ordinary activity. Just her and her junk mail. But then…

"Avery!"

Closing the small metal door to her mailbox, she turned to see Stephen exiting the elevator and walking toward her. In his late twenties, the guy was tall, somewhat fit, and had dark brown hair and eyes.

He'd asked her out once, right after she'd first moved in. But even if he didn't give off the whole player vibe—which he totally did—Avery had never pictured the two of them dating.

Like Ronald, Stephen wasn't *un*attractive. Just not the breath-stealing *wow* she hoped to someday find.

"Hey, Stephen." She greeted him with a polite smile.

"Did you hear?"

"Hear what?"

"Joan's dead."

Avery sucked in a shocked breath. *"What?"*

"I know." The man's dark brows rose as he blinked. "Crazy, right?"

That explained the police and other first responders.

"Yeah. Apparently, she's been dead a while," Stephen filled her in. "The people in the apartment across the hall from her noticed a rancid smell and called maintenance. That's who found her."

"Oh my gosh, that's awful." Avery frowned. She didn't know Ms. Wilson—*Joan*—well, and while the woman was a bit on the quirky side, she'd always been kind to Avery. "What happened?"

"So, get this. I overheard two of the cops who are up there talking in the hall. They're assuming it was natural causes, but that's not all. Since she'd been gone a while, her cats ran out of food."

"Nooo…" Avery shook her head, praying he wasn't about to tell her what she was already imagining to be true.

"Yep." Stephen nodded. "They ate her face clean off."

Her hand flew to her mouth. "Oh, god."

"I know." He pretended to gag. "Disgusting, right? But I mean, you can't really blame 'em. With no one around to feed them, they did what any animal would do and found their own food."

Avery closed her eyes, the alcohol present in her stomach churning. *Poor Joan.*

A loud ding signaled the opening of the elevator doors. On reflex, she opened her eyes to find two paramedics pushing a gurney into the lobby.

Though the form beneath the white sheet was hidden —*thank God*—Avery was fully aware of the horror it covered.

Both nauseated and sad, she waited for Joan's remains to exit the building before bidding Stephen a quiet 'good-night' and heading for the stairs. Her apartment was on the fourth floor, but she occasionally chose to walk up, rather than taking the elevator.

When she did, it was for exercise. Tonight, it was to avoid being in the same place where her dead neighbor had just been.

She opened the door to her floor; her shocked and scattered mind having forgotten it was located just a few feet from Joan's apartment. Avery caught a very distinct whiff of what she could only describe as death.

Not that she was experienced in that area, but there was no mistaking the smell of decomposing flesh.

Picking up the pace, she covered her mouth and nose as she rushed down the hallway and into her own apartment. Once inside, Avery slammed the door shut, fell back against it, and sucked in a long, cleansing breath.

After a few extra inhales, she went straight to her bathroom and splashed some cool water over her face. Patting her skin dry, she clutched the small towel in one fist as she rested her hands on the porcelain countertop.

Against her will, the image of Ms. Wilson's body on that gurney resurfaced. Seconds later, Alex's words from the bar rang through her head.

One of these days, you're going to wake up and realize you've become the quintessential crazy cat lady.

Avery lifted her head, staring at her reflection. "No." She shook her head. "I'm not."

Leaving the towel in a ball on the sink, she flipped off her bathroom light and marched down the narrow hallway into her kitchen. Plopping down onto the barstool she typically used, she fired up her computer and began searching for the adventure her sister had dared her to find.

For the next forty-five minutes, Avery read about cave explorations, skydiving, and mountain climbing. But she was mildly claustrophobic and deathly afraid of heights, so all three of those options were out.

Fifteen minutes later, she was about to give up when she came across an ad for a last-minute cruise special.

Despite knowing she'd never go on a cruise by herself, Avery clicked on the link. Her screen was instantly filled with gorgeous pictures of clear, turquoise water and heart-stopping sunset views.

The site described it as a six-day, five-night seascape into paradise, and if the few images provided were to be believed, that was exactly what it appeared to be.

A tab labeled *excursions* in the top right corner caught

her eye. With her sister's voice echoing in her head, Avery clicked on the link to the cruise's available offshore adventures.

Just as when she'd begun her initial search, Avery was inundated with choices. Everything from an all-inclusive day at the beach to dolphin swims and snorkeling adventures.

One activity allowed participants to swim with wild stingrays…and even *hold* them.

Hard pass, thank you very much!

Feeling as though this whole thing was a giant waste of time, Avery started to click out of the site when she saw another excursion that piqued her interest.

"Waterfalls of Damajagua and off-road buggy combo," she read the bold heading to herself.

Promising herself that this was the last one she'd look at before taking a shower and calling it a night, she clicked on the link.

Avery wasn't sure what she expected to see, but images of down and dirty dune buggy drivers and riders splashing through a creek bed wasn't it. Even she had to admit, it looked like fun.

As she scrolled through the different pictures and read the excursion details, she became more and more interested.

Not only did those who registered for the six-hour adventure get to ride through the Dominican countryside and villages, they were then led on a forty-minute hike through the gorgeous landscape.

The day ended with a river walk and trips down several small, naturally formed waterfalls.

Avery couldn't help but notice how happy everyone

seemed. Even in the pictures uploaded by individuals who'd gone back to the site after their day of fun to leave reviews, each person was smiling from ear to ear.

But then she sighed, noticing how everyone in the pictures were with other people. Happy couples. Parents and kids. Friends.

She'd probably be the first person in history to sign up for something like that alone.

Baby steps, Aves. Baby steps.

Exiting out of the excursion tab, she went back to the cruise line's main page.

The thought of being stuck on a giant ship in the middle of the ocean for an entire week...by herself...was mildly terrifying. On the other hand, it would force her to follow-through with the crazy idea.

After all, it wasn't like she'd be able to change her mind after a day or two and Uber back home.

But the more she thought about it, having to spend even one night with Ronald made her cringe even more than being a loner on an exciting cruise vacation.

Realistically, Avery knew she could get out of the bet either way. She was an adult. No one could *make* her do anything she didn't really want to do.

But—and though she'd never admit it to Alex—her sister was right. She *did* want more out of life. And if she didn't take the first step and make it happen now, would she ever?

You know the answer to that.

With thoughts of crazy cat ladies and their meat-eating felines swirling around in her head, Avery grabbed her wallet, chose the type of room and location on the ship she wanted, and began entering the required information.

GARRETT'S DESTINY (SPECIAL FORCES: OPERATION ALP...

A few short minutes later, the only thing left to do was confirm the order.

Before she could talk herself out of it, Avery clicked her mouse one final time. Her email dinged with a confirmation from the Sunset Adventure Cruise Line, along with her vacation itinerary.

Holy shit. She was going on a cruise. By. Herself!

"Take that, Sis," she whispered aloud.

Let's see how predictable you think I am when I'm sending you pictures from the Eastern Caribbean.

Closing her laptop, Avery felt an unexpected pep in her step as she proceeded to shower and change into her favorite comfy PJs. Crawling into bed, she set her alarm before plugging her phone into its charger and placing it on the nightstand.

Settling into her pillow, Avery closed her eyes with the thought that she'd text her sister tomorrow with a screenshot of her trip confirmation and itinerary.

An unusual sense of excitement and confidence made her smile as she fell asleep.

A week later, as Avery stepped off the shuttle bus and onto the platform adjacent to the cruise ship's boarding area, that confidence hadn't merely wavered.

It had shriveled up into a tiny ball and thrown itself far, *far* away.

Still standing in front of the bus, she caught her first sight of the enormous vessel. With a crowd of fellow passengers and workers bustling all around her, her stomach tightened, and a giant ball of dread began to form at its center.

What the hell were you thinking?

CHAPTER 3

What the hell were you thinking?

The question had been rolling through Garrett's mind ever since he'd woken up at the ass crack of dawn to head to the airport. But deep down, he knew the answer.

You were thinking you're tired of a life filled with nothing but work, guns, and death.

It was true, even if he was having a hard time admitting it to himself.

When his team left Syria last week, Garrett had made a clear plan. Go home, lock himself away, and try to forget about that last job and the fact that it had almost been… well…his last everything.

But when his brother had called and discovered he had some free time, he'd *insisted* they take a vacation together. Garrett had surprised them both by accepting the offer.

They almost never had the same stretch of time off, so Coulter—or Colt, as Garrett had always called him— had taken advantage of the rare opportunity and purchased two tickets for a six-day cruise to the Eastern Caribbean.

Quality brother bonding time, he'd called it.

Though a part of him wanted to keep wallowing in the self-pity hole he'd just started digging for himself, a nagging feeling had led Garrett to agreeing to Colt's generous and unexpected offer.

Probably the fact that he'd seen too many of his friends fall into that same hole over the years. Most of them never found their way out.

Garrett didn't want to be like those other guys. He loved his job and his teammates, and couldn't imagine doing anything else. But lately, he'd been feeling as though something was missing.

Like he needed something more.

To add to his frustration, he had this nagging feeling that if he didn't find whatever it was soon, he never would.

Balance.

That's what he needed in his life. Strong, solid balance between work *and* pleasure.

Not an easy thing for guys like him to come by. Impossible, if most of the guys he'd served with in the Army—and those he worked with now—were to be believed.

But Garrett wasn't sure he did believe that. Not anymore. Because though he'd seen many relationships crash and burn throughout his years as a door kicker, he'd also witnessed a few that stood the test of time.

So no, it wasn't impossible. Hard, maybe. *Really* fucking hard. It took a special woman to put up with all the baggage black ops guys carried around. That was for damn sure.

Crazy schedules. All the secrecy that came with working classified missions. The time spent at home wondering when—or if—their loved ones would make it back in one piece.

But if he did somehow manage to find a woman willing to accept him for who and what he was? He'd hold onto her with both hands and never let go.

"Sorry," a man apologized for bumping into him.

The contact forced Garrett back to the task at hand.

Leaving his melancholy thoughts behind, he began writing his name on a special luggage tag the cruise line required.

Another man brushed against him, making Garrett's back teeth grind together. He may want more out of life, but he was fairly certain he wasn't going to find it here.

Colt had shocked the hell out of him with the offer of the all-expense paid trip. The second he'd agreed, his brother had gone online and bought their tickets.

Tickets that included all the food they could eat for the next six days, as well as twenty adult beverages each. After that, their account would be billed for any additional drinks.

Good thing I have plenty of money in the bank. I have a feeling I'm going to need it.

He glanced over at Colt who was chatting it up with one of the couples who'd been on their shuttle. Unlike Garrett, who's entire adult life had depended on carefully detailed planning, Colt was like a damn nomad.

The guy never stayed in one place for more than a few months at a time. A year, at the very most. And he never, ever took himself or anyone else too seriously.

Of course, having bypassed the military for the whole college experience—including sorority girls and fraternity parties—it was no wonder Colt's outlook on life was so vastly different than his own.

Regular phone calls and the rare, in-person appearance…those were the staples of their sibling relationship.

Garrett knew his younger brother loved both him and their dad, and the feeling was mutual. But between Garrett's day job and Tac-Ops' other assignments, and Colt's fly-by-night way of life, the two barely spent any time together anymore.

Something else Garrett wanted to change, hence his agreement to go on this trip.

"Isn't she gorgeous?"

Turning, he found Colt ogling the cruise ship as if it were the most beautiful woman the man had ever laid eyes on.

"If you say so," Garrett mumbled, barely giving the big boat a passing glance.

With a giant smile and a loud clap of his hands, his brother let out an excited whoop before pointing his phone at The Majestic—the largest and most elaborate ship in the Sunset Adventures cruise line.

Shaking his head, Garrett barely resisted rolling his eyes. Even at thirty, Colt had never quite grown up. At this point, Garrett was beginning to wonder if he ever would.

Like now. While *he* stood in the hot, humid air filling out the ship's required luggage tags with their names and stateroom information, Colt was standing off to the side in a ridiculously loud, yellow, and hot pink Hawaiian style shirt.

The guy was taking selfies like a social media queen and grinning like a kid at Christmas.

"You gonna help me with this or just stand there lookin' like a damn idiot?"

Completely unaffected by the insult, Coulter's smile grew impossibly bigger as he adjusted his baseball cap and grabbed a pen from the provided pile on a long folding table beside them. Yanking a tag from Garrett's hand, he *finally* began pulling his weight.

"Dude, we are going to have *so* much fun this week."

Garrett secured the tag he'd been working on and immediately began writing on another. "Not if we don't get our luggage checked in with the crew and end up having to wear the clothes on our backs for the entire trip."

"Nope." Colt shook his head. With a raised brow and a pointed finger, his brother's blue eyes which matched his exactly lasered into a stern look that would rivel their father's. "I've put up with your grumpy ass all week. I don't even know what happened to put you in such a pissy fucking mood, and at this point, I don't even care. You are hereby notified that any and all grouchy ass comments or foul moods are strictly prohibited for the next six days."

Shit. His brother was right. He *had* been grumpier than normal since coming back from that last job.

Almost dying could do that to you.

Not that Colt would know anything about that, thank God. The last thing Garrett ever wanted for his family or anyone he cared about was to be touched by the evils of his world.

That was a weight he was more than happy to bear alone.

Even if he wanted to share what had happened—which he didn't—he couldn't. Just like when he was with the Rangers, all Tac-Ops missions were classified.

Without responding to his brother's scolding, Garrett finished attaching the tag to the bigger of his two bags and placed it into a large metal cage as they'd been instructed to do.

He ignored the slight soreness still present in his chest. It had been seven days exactly since he and his team had returned home, and as of this morning, the bruise had turned from a dark blue and red tint to a nasty greenish yellow.

Given its location, hiding it up to this point had been effortless. But that wasn't going to last for long, and Garrett had yet to come up with a story to explain what had caused it.

Better figure that out before Colt drags your ass to the pool.

Given the multitude of activities available that didn't require him to be shirtless, he planned to steer Colt in a different direction. At least for the first couple of days. By that time the bruise should be all but healed.

He hoped.

"There." Colt tossed his pen back onto the rectangular table next to them. "Done."

"They go in here." Garrett dropped his second bag into the cage. Bending at the waist, he grabbed the strap connected to his carryon duffle and slid it over his shoulder.

"Why don't you put that one in, too? That way you don't have to mess with it once we're on board."

"I'd rather not," he kept his answer vague. Colt would probably shit his pants if he knew there was a government-issued weapon secured snuggly inside.

Each member of Tac-Ops held special TSA and

Customs' clearance. Whether they were traveling in the air or on the sea—or in this case, both—all they had to do was show their White House issued ID, and they were good to go.

In both the airport and customs, Garrett had maneuvered things a bit to ensure he went through a separate line from Colt. Otherwise, his brother would've seen the ID which served as an all-access pass to carry both in the air and on the water. Then he would've started asking questions.

Questions Garrett couldn't answer.

"Suit yourself." Colt let the duffle bag conversation go. "Come on, bro. Looks like they're starting to board."

Seeing that his brother was right, Garrett fell in line beside him. Following the crowd, the two men made their way out of the platform's covered portion and onto the wide, concrete walkway leading to the ship's boarding area.

Really taking in the ship for the first time since arriving, he had to admit…it was bigger than he'd expected.

"Damn."

"Right?" Colt gave him a blatant, *I told you so* look. "You really need to get out of your own head and start appreciating the beauty of your surroundings. Like that pretty little thing right over there."

At his brother's low, appreciative whistle, Garrett followed the other man's gaze to a woman walking up ahead.

A floppy, wide brimmed hat, like the ones he'd seen women wear to the beach, rested atop thick layers of long, dark brown locks that fell over her shoulders in waves. The gorgeous hair stopped in the middle of her back, and

Garrett's hands twitched with a sudden urge to run his fingers through it.

The dress's loose fit hid what he instinctively knew to be luscious curves. His gaze dropped to the delicate bare ankles brushing against the ruffled hem. Fuck, even the woman's feet, encased in a pair of strappy white sandals, turned him on.

Jesus. Had it really been so long since he'd spent time with a woman he was becoming obsessed with a pair of *feet*?

Quickly doing the mental math, Garrett begrudgingly admitted to himself that yes...it *had* been that long.

Christ, I need to get a life.

"Helloo... Earth to Garrett."

A waving hand appeared in front of his face. Blinking at its back-and-forth motion, Garrett realized Colt had been talking to him.

"Sorry. What?" His focus shifted from the woman he'd been admiring to his brother.

"I asked what you wanted to do first. You know, once we're on board."

"Check out our rooms." They each had their own. "Make sure all of our luggage makes it back to us like it's supposed to."

"Bro." Colt's face went deadpan. "You seriously need to relax."

Garrett frowned. "I *am* relaxed." Or...he was starting to be, at least.

"Right. Well, we have a limited amount of fun-in-the-sun time, and I for one am not wasting a second of it waiting for bags I know will be coming."

The man had a point. "Fine. We'll find our rooms so I

can put this inside, and then we'll head up to the main deck for the welcome party. Happy?"

Colt slid his Ray-Bans over his blue eyes and smiled. "Very."

Forty minutes later, they'd finally made it through security and onto the ship without incident. The cruise line didn't fuck around when it came to the safety of its passengers. Something he could appreciate.

As the pair made their way up to their ocean-level staterooms, Garrett found himself searching for the woman in the sundress. Which was ridiculous since he'd only seen her once, not to mention she was probably here with someone.

A husband. Fiancé. Boyfriend. Someone who could give a woman like that the life she deserved.

Jesus, man. You know nothing about her, and you're making assumptions as to what she does or doesn't deserve? The woman could be a hoity toity bitch for all you know.

But his gut said she wasn't, which was yet another ridiculous assumption. Again, he'd seen her once. From behind.

Garrett gave the strap on his shoulder a tight squeeze then forced the muscles in his hand to relax. Damn it, Colt was right. He needed to let shit go and start enjoying their current situation.

Starting with the woman in the hat. She was just one of over four thousand passengers aboard the giant ship, and chances were he'd probably go the entire rest of the trip without ever seeing her again.

After finding their rooms—each next to the other's— the two men headed up to the main deck for the welcome party. Once there, Garrett planned to grab one of those fruity drinks with an umbrella in it then spend the next six days chilling the fuck out.

Ten minutes later, he'd implemented the first part of the plan.

"This." Colt stood with his elbows leaning on the tiki-style bar behind them. "This right here is what I'm talking about."

With his flamingo shorts and brightly flowered shirt, the man looked like the stereotypical Caribbean cruise passenger.

From behind his dark lenses, Garrett bit his tongue to keep from razzing Colt about his attire and looked out over the crowd. For the first time since stepping foot on the ship, he drew in a deep breath and soaked in the scenery.

Songs he could only describe as tropical island music blared through the speakers. People dressed in everything from bikinis to Bermuda shorts—and everything in between—were spread out over the expansive wooden deck.

Some were talking. Several had already begun drinking. One group had even come together in the center, dancing to the uplifting beat of the steel drums.

A cooling breeze blew in from the Atlantic, making the humid Florida air more bearable. Still taking everything in, Garrett noted that everywhere he looked, he found smiles.

Not the small, polite kind. No, these were toothy grins accompanied by loud, boisterous laughs.

An odd feeling settled in his gut. He honestly couldn't remember the last time he'd laughed like that.

"Yeah, okay." He took a sip of his frozen strawberry

and rum concoction. Something the bartender had called a Miami Vice.

"Okay, what?"

"You were right."

"Of course, I was right." Colt snorted.

Garrett felt his lips curve. "At least you're modest about it."

"Why hide the truth?" His brother chuckled.

A stretch of silence passed and then, "In case I haven't said it. Thanks."

His brother shrugged. "Consider this an early Christmas present."

"Damn." Garrett licked a drop of cold, sugary sweetness from his bottom lip. "All I'd planned to get you was a pair of socks and a new tie."

With a barked laugh Colt said, "Skip the socks and tie, man. Just promise to enjoy yourself this week, and we'll call it even."

Hardly. "You've got yourself a deal. From here on out, it's nothing but fun."

Lifting his glass in the air, Colt turned the declaration into a toast. "To nothing but fun."

Both men clinked their drinks together before drinking from their straws. Seconds later, Colt spotted a food cart with complimentary appetizers.

"Mini crab cakes?" He stood straight and started in that direction. "Hell yeah!"

"Grab some for me!" Garrett hollered after him. With a shake of his head, he smiled as he watched his brother interact with a couple of women he passed by.

Definitely going to be an interesting week.

The thought had no more entered his brain when two

giggling women—or girls, rather—came up to the bar. One was blonde, the other brunette. And both were dressed in matching barely-there bikini tops and cut-off shorts that showed the entire bottom half of their asses.

Jesus.

Knowing they couldn't be more than twenty-one, *maybe* twenty-two, Garrett kept his gaze glued on his brother who was standing near the end of a fairly long line.

"Hey, there." One of the girls nudged his arm. "You look a little lone...ly."

The ship hadn't even started moving yet, and these two were already sloshed.

"Just waiting for my brother," he spoke without looking at her.

"Brother?" The other's ears perked up. "Well, that works out perfectly, then. One for me and one for my friend."

The high-pitched laugh that escaped both girls' throats made Garrett physically cringe. Doing his best to make his non-interest clear, he lied and said, "Thanks, but I don't think our wives would appreciate that."

Neither he nor Colt had ever been married. But these two didn't need to know that.

The brunette slapped the blonde on the ass. "I told you a guy who looked like him would be taken."

"How was I supposed to know?" The blonde whined. "He's not wearing a ring." She looked up at him. "Why aren't you wearing a ring?"

"Didn't want to lose it in the ocean." The second lie rolled off his lips as if it were the God's honest truth.

It was a skill he found useful in his line of work.

"Fine." The young woman pouted. Words slurring, she added, "Tell your wife, she's one lucky lady."

"Oh, she knows." He gave them a polite grin. "You two be safe out here."

"Safe shmafe." The brunette waved him off as if he was stupid. "We're here to par-tay!"

Belting out identical, ear-piercing squeals, the two girls forgot all about him and disappeared into the crowd.

Behind him, the bartender—Shawn, according to his name tag—laughed. Garrett didn't crack a smile.

All he could think of was how vulnerable those two young women were, and how easily someone could take advantage of that…or worse. He'd seen it happen far too often.

Forget the job and focus on the fun.

Doing his best to ignore the numerous potential dangers around him, the unspoken words became his mantra for the next several minutes while he waited for Colt to return.

There wasn't any danger to him. Just a lot of unaware partygoers oblivious to the fact that they could fall prey to the same type of bastards he and his team had recently taken down.

These people are all just here to have a good time. You promised Colt you'd do the same. Now get your head out of your ass and follow the fuck through.

Realizing this whole fun and relaxation gig was going to be harder than expected, Garrett had just taken a step in his brother's direction when a rolling breeze carried with it a new scent he didn't recognize but was impossible to ignore.

A mixture of coconuts and vanilla. And something else he couldn't quite put a name to.

The sweet scent compelled him to stop. Turning in search of the source, his lungs froze inside his chest when he saw her.

It was the woman in the hat. She'd just walked up beside him, and from this angle, he could finally see her face.

Perfect, bow-shaped lips with a natural rosy tint. An adorable button nose he could imagine himself pressing his lips against. And huge, milk-chocolate eyes he knew he could get lost in...if she let him.

Goddamn, she's beautiful.

And like his, her left ring finger was bare.

"What'll you have?" Shawn asked over the loud music.

"I...I don't know." Her soft voice was like a balm to his hardened soul. "What do you suggest?"

"Depends." The man behind the bar eyed the line that had begun to form. "What do you like?"

"Um..." The woman scanned the various bottles of liquor lining the hut's back wall. Glancing over to the three frozen drink machines constantiy stirring their contents, she bit her bottom lip as she tried to decide.

"Do you want me to come back to you?" The bartender motioned to the people behind her.

"Oh, uh..."

Sensing the woman was overwhelmed by her choices, Garrett leaned a bit closer and asked, "You like strawberries?"

Her eyes lifted to his, and Christ if he didn't feel her gaze to the depths of his soul. One second, he was fine, and the next...he couldn't fucking breathe.

Hell, if she'd asked his name, he wouldn't have been able to tell her. All Garrett knew was that he was staring at the most breathtaking woman he'd ever seen.

For one, crazy moment in time, he considered asking her if she'd like to go back to his room with him.

"I do."

Garrett blinked. Fuck, had he said those words out loud?

Strawberries, asshole. You asked if she liked strawberries.

"Oh, right." He cleared his throat. "This is called a Miami Vice. It's a mixture of rum, piñā colada, and strawberry margarita. It's really good."

Another second passed before the woman nodded. "Okay. I'll try one of those." She started to remove the plastic card held by the lanyard around her neck, but Garrett stopped her.

"Just put it on mine." He quickly removed his own cruise ID and handed it to the bartender.

Each passenger had been given an ID card connected to their individual cruise accounts. Every time they ate or drank, their cards were scanned. Since their food and non-alcoholic drinks were included with their initial tickets, the scans were simply to keep track of selection data for the cruise line.

But they could also transfer money from their bank accounts to their cards for purchases made in the gift shops and at the ship's many bars.

It was smart, really. Doing it this way knocked down the need for passengers to carry around a bunch of cash or their debit and credit cards. This in turn helped ward off criminal activity such as petty theft and robbery.

"That wasn't necessary but thank you." The woman smiled up at him.

He'd buy her as many drinks as she wanted if it meant getting to know her better.

Garrett returned her smile with one of his own. "You're welcome."

"Here ya go." Shawn handed him back the card and the woman her drink.

Slipping the lanyard back over his neck, he watched as the beauty beside him took her first sip. Those mesmerizing eyes grew wide, and her entire face lit up with excitement.

"You're right." She took another sip and closed her eyes, moaning as she licked her lips. "That's really good."

Ah, fuck. Garrett's dick began to swell behind his zipper. Thank God he was wearing baggy shorts and an untucked shirt.

Wait. Had she said something? If she had, he'd missed it. Probably because he was too busy watching the tip of her tongue peak out and run along her full, bottom lip to notice.

"Thanks again." The woman started to walk off.

Say something, dumbass. Say. Something.

"Garrett Morgan," he blurted his name.

His real name, not *Falcon*. That was only used by his teammates either behind closed doors or on a mission.

He wasn't even sure why he'd given her his name at all, really. It wasn't like she'd remember it after she walked away.

Another strong breeze blew past as she turned back around. Moving quickly, she shot a hand to the top of her head, barely managing to keep her hat from flying off with the wind.

"Should I know who that is?"

With anyone else, he would've taken the question as a sarcastic quip. But the confusion on her pretty face struck him as genuine.

"Me." His lips twitched as he held out a hand. "I'm Garrett Morgan."

The warmth from her sweet smile heated him from the inside out. "Avery Webb. And I'd shake your hand, but…" Her eyes motioned upward toward her hat.

"Of course." He lowered his arm. "Wouldn't want you losing that."

Actually, I'd rather enjoy you losing a lot more than that hat.

"I'm not so sure." Her cute as fuck nose scrunched up. "It was my sister's idea. In fact, this whole trip was her idea."

"Really?" That sure sounded familiar. "My brother talked me into coming." Garrett pointed to Colt who was getting cozy with the woman standing behind him in line. "He's the one flirting his a…uh…butt off."

"I can see the resemblance." Avery's smile grew a tiny bit more. "That's quite an outfit he's wearing."

Unable to tell if she truly liked it or was poking fun, Garrett was glad he'd chosen a white linen button-up with short sleeves and khaki shorts. Simple. Classy. And cooling in the sun's blaring heat.

Although he had a feeling it could be snowing, and he'd still feel warm and toasty as long as Avery Webb was near.

"I don't want to keep you from your sister," he lied.

"You're not. She didn't come with me."

"She talked you into taking a cruise and then ditched you?" Seemed like a shitty thing to do to anyone, especially a sister.

"No." Avery shook her head. "She was never coming."

"Oh." Garrett made it sound like he understood completely, though he was confused as hell.

What's confusing? Her sister talked her into taking a vacation, and she did. With someone else.

"Well, I'm sure whoever you're with is missing you." He sure as hell would be.

"I'm...by myself." She glanced away as if she were embarrassed.

Garrett blinked. No way he'd heard her right. This gorgeous woman was on this huge ass ship...alone?

"It was a dare." The blurted admission caused Avery's skin to become flushed. "A really stupid dare that I never should've agreed to."

"So why did you?"

"I don't know. No, that's a lie. I do know."

She began talking a bit faster, and he couldn't help but wonder if it was the alcohol or her nerves. *Probably both.*

"I wasn't going to come," Avery continued, "But my sister and I have always had this thing where we used to dare each other to do stuff. Nothing bad or illegal. Just crazy stuff we wouldn't normally do. And we're both too stubborn to back down, so I accepted the challenge. But then I changed my mind, and then later when I got home, I found out this lady in my building....Joan... She died, and her cat ate her face, and I didn't...I didn't want to end up like that."

Garrett had no idea what she was rambling on about, and he didn't care.

When she'd first approached the tiki bar, she'd been quiet. Reserved. But now that she was loosening up a bit, it was like a dam had burst free.

She was going on and on about her sister, and cats, and a dead woman. Shit, did she say the cat had *eaten* her neighbor?

It didn't even matter. Garrett was standing there, staring while Avery held her drink with one hand and that damn hat with the other, and all he could think was…

She's fucking amazing.

"Fucking amazing!" Colt's voice parroted his thoughts.

"What?" Garrett tore his gaze from Avery just in time to see his brother approaching with a plate piled full of food.

"These crab cakes. They're so freakin' good."

Crab cakes. Right.

"I see you've made a friend while I was gone." Colt gave him a sly look before shoving the overfilled plate in his direction. When Garrett took it, his brother switched his drink into his left hand and held out his right. "Coulter Morgan. My friends call me Colt."

"Avery Webb." Noticing the wind had died down, Avery let go of her hat and took Colt's hand.

Garrett's chest tightened with an unexpected rush of jealousy. The reaction was crazy. It was just a handshake, for shit's sake. But still…

I want to be the one to touch her.

"Webb, huh?" Colt's voice took on what Garrett referred to as his *get-a-woman-into-bed* tone. "Guess I'll have to watch myself around you. Wouldn't want to get caught up in your...*web*." With a wink and a grin, the idiot then said, "Get it? 'Cause your last name's Webb?"

"Yeah, Colt." Garrett slapped his brother on the shoulder and squeezed. "Pretty sure she gets it."

"Easy, man!" Colt narrowly avoided spilling his drink.

Garrett shot Avery an apologetic look. "Sorry about him. I swear, he's harmless."

"I'm not so sure about that." Her lips curved in the same, almost timid smile she'd worn before.

The one that made him want to strip away all her inhibitions and make her deepest, darkest desires come true.

"But those crab cakes do look pretty tasty. I think I'll go get some for myself."

Garrett wanted to offer theirs up to her, but something told him he needed to go slow with her.

"Maybe I'll see you around this week." He did his best to sound casual.

Her growing smile gave him hope. "Maybe. It was nice to meet you both."

"Nice meeting you." Colt's words were barely audible due to his crab-filled mouth.

Garrett shook his head but smiled. "It was nice to meet you, too, Avery."

With a slight tip of her head, Avery turned away and headed for the food cart line. Garrett's gaze followed her the entire way.

"Wow." Colt swallowed another bite. "She's totally—"

"Off limits."

His brother arched a brow. "You callin' dibs?"

"She's a human being, asshole." Garrett reached for a crab cake. "I'm not calling fucking dibs. I'm just saying you've got an entire ship full of women to choose from."

"So basically...I need to choose someone else?"

"Exactly."

Colt chuckled then began to cough as some of the bite he'd just taken went down the wrong pipe. It would've been funny as hell if Garrett wasn't still completely enthralled with the angel in the floppy hat.

It made no sense for him to warn his brother away from her. Hell, he'd just met the woman. In no way, shape, or form did he have the right to call dibs or anything else where she was concerned.

But if he did, Garrett knew...

Avery Webb would be mine.

CHAPTER 4

Avery leaned on the door behind her and blew out a breath. She'd done it. She was on a cruise ship. By herself. And she didn't totally hate it.

You should probably check your phone for a breaking news alert because hell has most definitely frozen over.

The internal thought made her smile. Not only did Avery not hate it here...she'd actually *enjoyed* her time up on the main deck.

The frozen Miami Vice concoction had been to die for. The sweet combination of coconuts and strawberries was one she already planned to consume again. As an added bonus, the alcohol had helped to ease her anxiety levels a bit.

Of course, the smokin' hot man in the white shirt had raised her heartrate to alarming levels.

Even now, as flashes of Garrett Morgan's gorgeous face filled her mind's eye, Avery felt her insides tingle and flutter. The man was hands down the most gorgeous male specimen she'd ever laid eyes on.

Standing at least a foot taller than her five-three frame, the intriguing man had towered over her. Something she found both intimidating and sexy.

His light brown hair was shorter on the sides and back than it was on top. Streaks of natural highlights had glimmered in the sunlight, and Avery had found herself itching to touch it.

Even now, just thinking about the possibility made her cheeks feel hot and flushed.

Still leaning against her door, Avery pictured Garrett's strong jaw and kissable lips. And then there was his voice.

Not once in all her twenty-eight years had she heard such a deep, sultry voice like the one coming from the man she'd just met.

When Garrett Morgan spoke, it was as if every word he uttered was specifically designed with the purpose of drawing her deep into his spell.

No, not you. Women. Plural.

Her subconscious was right. This was insane. She knew absolutely nothing about the man, other than his name. *If* that was even his real name.

For all she knew, Garrett was a total player. His brother clearly was. Not that it mattered now, anyway.

On the off-chance Garrett *wasn't* just a hot guy looking to score, he'd probably avoid her like the plague, now that she'd rambled on and on about her dead neighbor's flesh-eating cat.

See? This is exactly why I keep to myself as much as humanly possible.

A frustrated growl bubbled up inside her throat. "Since when do you care what some random guy thinks about you?"

Since now, apparently.

Giving herself a mental smack on the head, Avery pushed off the door and made her way further into her stateroom. Forcing thoughts of sexy strangers away, she made note of the tiny bathroom on her right and even tinier closet to her left.

Passing through the narrow entryway, she stepped into the bedroom area that made her smile.

There was a built-in dresser to her left which wasn't huge but offered plenty of space for her things. The long mirror above it running the entire length, and at the mirror's end was a small T.V. mounted high on the wall.

A loveseat and coffee table were directly across from the dresser, and in front of where she stood was the room's queen-sized bed.

Her luggage had been placed between the bed and the table.

The room was small, less than two hundred square feet and basic in décor and function. But with the large window overlooking the water and a small, private balcony, it was perfect.

Avery's smile grew as her eyes fell onto the bed. An elephant made from white towels stared up at her from the center of the mattress. It had gold, foil-wrapped chocolates for eyes, and was one of the cutest things she'd ever seen.

Pulling her phone from her purse, she snapped a quick picture. "Alex is going to love you," she spoke to the inanimate object.

Turning in a slow circle, she proceeded to take several more snapshots before sending them all with a text to her sister. Alex responded immediately.

· · ·

Avery: *I'm not saying you were right, but it's off to a good start.*

Alex: *Yay! And OMG, the elephant! I want!*

Avery: *I'll see if I can buy one. Not sure what kind of service I'll have, but I'll try to text/call when I can.*

Alex: *Can't wait for more pics. P. S.... did u find my note?*

Avery: *What note?*

Alex: *Front pocket of your purse. Read then do. Gotta run. Heading to the gallery for a prelim run-thru for the show. Love u and have fun!*

Avery: *Love you, too. And no dating while I'm gone!*

Curious as to what Alex was referring to, Avery set her phone on the bed before removing her hat and placing it on the coffee table behind her. Lifting her crossbody up over her head, she unzipped the front pocket and looked inside.

Sure enough, there was a small piece of paper folded neatly inside.

Pulling it out, Avery unfolded the note to find it wasn't really a note at all. It was a list. One Alex had compiled with the heading '20 Things to Do on My Cruise'.

Seriously?

Starting at the top and working her way down, Avery began reading each one aloud.

"Number one... Get on the damn ship." Laughing, Avery grabbed a pen from her purse and crossed it off with a smile. "Number two... Try one of those fruity drinks with an umbrella in it." *Check again.* And number three? "Talk to someone I don't know."

Not really a stretch since I don't know anyone here, but okay.

Forcing herself not to think of Garrett in all his tall, dark, and handsomeness, Avery drew a line through that one, too.

With a quick glance at the other seventeen things her meddling sister had felt the need to pen, she wondered just how many would be crossed off by the end of the cruise.

Some were simple, such as the talking to someone she didn't know thing and try something new to eat each day. But others made her wonder if Alex had been drunk when she'd compiled the list. Number twenty was a prime example.

"Kiss a hot guy?" Avery snorted. "Yeah, right."

Leave it to Alex to come up with something so ridiculously impossible.

Refusing to think of the hot guy she'd already met, Avery folded the paper and put both it and the pen back into her purse then walked over to the sliding door. Unlocking it, she pulled it open and stepped onto the balcony.

Her hair flew across her face as the warm, salty air whipped around her. Tucking the wayward strands behind one ear, she moved closer to the chest-high railing.

A hint of fuel filled her nostrils as she cautiously peeked over the edge. Not too far. Just enough to see the ocean's water sloshing lazily against the ship's hull.

She'd purposely chosen a room on the balcony level closest to the water. But it was still a long way down.

The low hum of a motor purred to life from somewhere far below. Glancing at her watch, she noted they still had an hour before the ship was scheduled to depart.

Must be getting things warmed up and ready to go.

Avery took a moment to gaze at the endless ocean to her left. Her heart beat a little harder as she wondered what the next few days would have in store.

Glancing back to the land on her right, she had to admit the view was less than desirable.

Shipping crates lined up in a row on a concrete slab. Two giant cranes she assumed were for loading supplies onto the ship.

Because her room was located on the starboard side, she couldn't see the U.S. Customs building she and the other passengers had gone through prior to boarding, but she spotted several other industrial-type buildings that seemed to stretch on for miles.

But it was land, and to Avery, it was safe.

Take a good, long look, Aves. Once this sucker takes off, there's no going back.

The realization sent her heart racing. Her chest tightened and breathing became more and more difficult.

Recognizing the telltale signs of an anxiety attack beginning to unfold, she went back inside and slid the door shut. With a sideways glance, she focused on her luggage which had been delivered prior to her coming into the room.

There's still time. You could find one of the staff. Tell them there's an emergency and you have to get off the ship so you can get back home.

They'd have to believe her, right? They'd have to let her off the ship.

For a second, Avery seriously considered grabbing her bags and getting the hell out of there.

But then what?

She'd be forced to go home and prove her sister right. Admit that she was every bit the boring, predictable woman Alex had accused her of being.

No. That was *not* how this was going to play out.

It was just a short trip. A dream vacation for most. And no matter how uncomfortable this coming week may be, Avery was determined to see it through to the end.

If she didn't, if she walked away now, she had a gnawing feeling she'd regret it for the rest of her life.

Straightening her spine, she marched back over to where her purse lay. Yanking the list free once more, she flattened its seams and studied the contents closer. Not only was she *not* going home...she was going to do every damn thing on the list.

Even number twenty.

"Attention passengers." A boisterous voice laced with a heavy Australian accent came over the speaker located in the room's ceiling, making her jump. "This is Martin, your friendly cruise director. On behalf of Sunset Adventures, I'd like to welcome you all to the Majestic. The largest and most lavish passenger cruise ship on the sea. Your tropical adventure will begin in less than an hour, and for the next six days, you will enjoy the most incredible vacation you've ever experienced. However, before that can happen, all passengers must attend the mandatory safety meeting that begins in ten minutes. I repeat, all passengers are required to attend the mandatory safety meeting before the ship can depart the port."

Avery remembered reading something about that, but she had no idea where said meeting would be taking place.

As if Martin could read her mind, he added, "All passengers have been divided up into separate meeting areas based on your room's location. You will find your assigned area on today's personalized itinerary located inside the welcome folder. This should be on the small table next to your bed.

Turning her head, Avery saw her folder exactly where Martin said it would be. As the energetic cruise director continued informing passengers of various activities the ship had to offer on their first night at sea, she opened the folder and found where she was supposed to report.

Dining Room A.

"Shouldn't be too hard to find."

Nine and a half minutes later, Avery was nearly breathless as she rushed toward the crew member waiting at the door.

"Sorry I'm late. I got turned around."

"No worries." The woman gave her a polite smile. "Still happens to me on occasion." Doubtful, but Avery appreciated the effort to make her feel less embarrassed. "Here you are."

She was handed back her cruise card.

"Thank you." Avery gave the woman a small smile.

Hoping to join the others without being noticed, she walked through the short entry located behind a curved, split staircase. Following another almost-late passenger who'd chosen to go right, Avery stepped into the most gorgeous, elaborate room she'd ever seen.

The far wall was made entirely of windows offering a stunning view of the North Atlantic. Countless round tables filled the main seating area, some piled with clean dishes and silverware that was snuggled inside pristine linen napkins.

Preparations for this evening's dinner.

The place was packed with passengers, their conversing voices coming together to form a dull roar as they waited for the mandatory meeting to commence.

As she moved through the dense crowd in search of an open place to stand, Avery couldn't help but be in awe of the gorgeous turquoise chandeliers running along the ceiling's center, or the rose gold décor scattered throughout the entire space. And the split staircase leading to the second level...

"Wow."

"Pretty impressive, isn't it?"

The male voice behind her made her jump. She turned, disappointment rushing through her when she found a man she'd never met before staring down at her.

"It is." Avery nodded politely.

There are over four thousand passengers on this ship. Did you really expect it to be Garrett?

Though she hated admitting it, yes. She had.

"I've been on a lot of cruise ships, but I have to say, this one's the best."

Unsure of how she should respond to the man's slightly slurred comment, Avery simply nodded and looked away.

"I'm Jack." He held out a hand.

She stared at it a full two seconds before deciding to take it. With a tight smile forming on her pressed lips, she returned the gesture. "Avery."

"Avery." Interest filled the man's dark eyes. "I like that."

A strong, nauseating whiff of whisky filled her nostrils, which she assumed derived from the near-empty glass in the man's free hand.

Another quick glance at Jack's pupils revealed he'd drank more than his fair share.

Fabulous.

Slipping her hand free, Avery remained silent as she fought the urge to wipe it clean. She wasn't sure what it was, but something about this guy sent her Creep-O-Meter buzzing.

Jack opened his mouth to say something else, but thankfully the speakers chose that time to start blaring fun, upbeat music. Crew members wearing identical uniforms entered from every direction—down the stairs, through both doors, and around the sides toward the area where Avery was standing.

Singing along with the music, they showed off their dancing skills as they got into their assigned positions. As the music died down, a very attractive woman stood at the top of the stairs and addressed the crowd using a microphone.

"Hello, everyone!" She smiled down on them. "I'm Savannah, and I just have one question for you. Are you ready to have some fun?"

The room filled with cheers, Jack clapping his hands and nudging Avery's shoulder. She gave him a tight smile, praying he'd decide to move on.

Of course, she couldn't be that lucky.

As the woman on the stairs went over the safety rules and procedures—where the lifeboats were located, where to find the emergency evacuation route for each section of the ship, and so on—Jack would periodically lean down to comment on one thing or another.

The man clearly felt he knew everything there was to know about cruise ships.

By the time the meeting was coming to an end, Jack was seriously getting on her last nerve.

"Wanna go for a drink?" he asked the second they were released.

Not a chance. "Thanks, but I'm good."

"Just one." He pouted, giving her heavy-lidded, drunken puppy dog eyes. "Please?"

Avery turned to leave, her heartrate spiking when he followed her.

"Hey, wait up!" Jack hollered after her. "I wasn't done talking to you."

But I'm done talking to you.

Picking up the pace, Avery's heart was in her throat as she closed in on the dining room's exit.

"You know, you don't have to be so rude." He caught up with her. "I was just trying to be friendly. Pretty lady like yourself shouldn't be alone. Hey!"

From the corner of her eye, Avery saw that Jack, or rather Jack*ass,* was reaching for her.

His fingers brushed against her arm as he started to grab her. Avery opened her mouth to yell for help when another large hand shot between them.

One attached to a taut, sinewy arm that made her heart race for a completely different reason.

"She's not alone, asshole." Garrett's voice blanketed her with a sense of relief and safety. "She's with me."

Not really accurate, but Avery wasn't about to correct him.

"Oh." Jack looked up at Garrett and blinked. "I-I didn't—"

"Understand the word 'no'?"

A smile tugged at her lips. She rather enjoyed seeing Garrett put the guy in his place.

"No." The idiot shook his head then frowned. "I-I mean, yes. I mean…I understood. I just—"

"Need to apologize." Garrett growled. "Now."

Warmth seeped through Avery's veins as she realized why she felt such a pull toward a man she'd just met.

Garrett was the type of guy who'd stand up for a woman. Not because he wanted to get into her pants, but because it was the right thing to do.

How do you know he doesn't want to get into your pants?

Avery nearly choked at the thought. She didn't attract guys like him. Computer geeks or accountants…those were the types of guys who asked her out.

Not hot, muscular men with lethal smiles and a body made for sin.

"I'm sorry." Jack's forced apology broke through her thoughts.

Unsure of what she should say, she crossed her arms at her chest and gave the man a curt nod. "Apology accepted."

Garrett leaned toward Jack with a final warning. "I see you near her again, you and I are going to have issues. We clear?"

"Yeah, man. Sure." Jack's head bobbled up and down quickly. "Whatever you say."

"Glad we understand each other." Garrett released Jack's arm with a slight push and motioned for the door.

Rolling her lips inward to keep from smiling, Avery watched as the idiot tripped over his own feet and fell to the carpet, spilling his drink before jumping back up and taking off.

The crowd behind them—one she hadn't even realized had formed—began clapping and whistling with approval. A couple of guys even taunted Jack as he disappeared around the corner.

"Thanks for that." She lifted her gaze. A sharp intake of air became caught in her throat when she got her first look at his ocean blue eyes.

Wow.

She already knew the man had a handsome face and mouthwatering body. But those *eyes...*

He stared down at her. It was probably her imagination, but when their eyes met, Avery could've sworn she felt a type of charge traveling throughout her entire body.

A powerful, magnificent, electrical charge. And it felt a lot like...

Lightning.

This was it. *This* is what she'd always read about. What she'd always dreamed of finding.

She thought she'd felt it earlier but had blown it off as overzealous nerves and wishful thinking. But now, as Garrett's gaze remained locked with hers, Avery couldn't deny there was a connection.

One unlike any she'd ever felt before.

Clearing his throat, his low voice reached past her thoughts. "Hope I didn't overstep. I saw that idiot start to get stupid with you and thought I could help."

"I'm pretty sure he was already stupid long before he met me," Avery teased.

Garrett's wide shoulders shook with a deep chuckle. "Pretty sure you're right. Anyway, I figured if he thought you were with someone else, then maybe he'd steer clear of you for the rest of the trip. Hope that was okay."

"I appreciate you stepping in." She was unable to tear her gaze away. "Thank you."

"No thanks necessary."

Lost in his seas of blue, Avery suddenly found herself wondering what it would be like to stare into those same eyes every day for the rest of her life.

Whoa, Aves. Slow it down a bit.

Her subconscious was right. She'd just met Garrett. Hell, she really didn't know any more about him than she did Jackass Jack.

Except for reasons she didn't understand, her instincts were telling her this was a man she could trust.

"There you are!" Garrett's brother appeared beside them. "What the hell, G? One minute, you're standing next to me, and then I looked up and *poof.* You were gone."

Like Garrett, Colt had his sunglasses resting on the top of his head. With a clear view of his eyes, too, Avery noticed they were identical to Garrett's in every way but one.

No lightning.

"It's my fault." She jumped to Garrett's defense. "This guy was bothering me, and your brother stepped in to help."

A throaty noise escaped the back of Garrett's throat. "Some dickhead tries to manhandle you, that's not your fault."

"What the hell?" Colt's playful expression hardened. To her, he asked, "You okay?"

"I'm fine," she assured both men. "The guy just got a little pushy when I turned him down. That's all."

Jack hadn't even touched her, and these guys looked like they were ready to draw blood.

The muscles in Garrett's strong jaw bulged, but he gave Colt a nod as if to say the situation had been handled. It must've been enough because the tension in Colt's shoulders eased almost instantly.

"I was going to head up to the casino. See if I can get lucky. You coming?"

"Actually, I'm getting a little hungry. Thought about grabbing a couple slices of pizza at the twenty-four-hour place." Avery was surprised when Garrett's gaze slid to hers. "Feel like grabbing a bite?"

Her stomach *was* feeling a bit empty. And it might not hurt to be seen sharing a meal with Garrett. Just in case Jack was still lingering around somewhere.

Nice excuse, Aves. You keep telling yourself that's why you're about to say—

"Sure. Pizza sounds good."

"Suit yourself, big brother." Colt slapped Garrett on the shoulder. "I'll come find you later to show you all my winnings."

With his eyes still on Avery's, Garrett's lips curled into another half-grin. "He'll come find me later when he loses all his money and needs more."

"Not true." The other man shook his head and started to leave. From over his shoulder, he gave them a quick wave and a loud, "Have fun you two. Don't do anything I wouldn't do."

"Something tells me that list is pretty short."

Garrett laughed. "Try non-existent. Come on." He rested his hand on her lower back and led her out of the dining hall. "I know a shortcut to the pizza."

Heat from his palm seared her skin through her thin dress. Normally, Avery wasn't a fan of people randomly touching her, but nothing about Garrett felt random.

In fact, as crazy as it seemed, she felt almost comfortable around him. Safe. As if they'd known each other for much longer than an hour.

Thirty minutes later, Avery found herself sitting with Garrett, finishing their pizza, and talking. He'd chosen a small table on the upper level of the main deck.

Looking out over the water, Avery took in the incredible view through the glass wall that kept passengers from falling over the edge.

She made the mistake of leaning closer to the glass and looking down. She nearly fell out of her chair trying to sit back up.

"You should've told me you were afraid of heights," Garrett rumbled. "I would've chosen a table down below."

"It's okay," Avery lied. Her heart still felt like it was trying to claw its way out of her chest. "I'm trying new things this week."

Instead of smiling, his brows turned inward, causing the skin between them to bunch. "You can do that without scaring yourself half to death."

"I know." She sighed. "But this trip is about breaking out of my shell. Figured the sooner I get started, the easier it'll become."

I hope.

"Is that the reason your sister dared you to take this cruise?"

With a nod, Avery confirmed his suspicions. "She thinks I need more excitement in my life. And she's right. I do need to get out more. But I work from home most days, and I guess it's just easier to *stay* home."

"What do you do?" He took another bite of his pizza.

"I design financial and accounting software for large businesses."

"Wow." Garrett's dark brows arched in surprise as he swallowed. "That's impressive."

It was also nice to hear a man acknowledge it. "Most guys I date think it's nerdy or boring." As if realizing what she'd just said, Avery rushed to correct herself. "Not that we're dating. Of course, we're not dating. We just met. I didn't mean to imply that we're—"

"I know." He gave her the kind of lazy smile that made her body tingle and her mind think of unspeakable things.

"Sorry. I'm usually pretty quiet. Until I get nervous, and then I tend to ramble."

"I noticed."

"Sorry." She repeated herself then cringed.

"Never apologize for being who you are, sweetheart."

Sweetheart?

Avery's heart did some sort of fluttering thing. No man had ever called her that. Not even her dad. He'd always called her Avey Baby. But never sweetheart.

"So, where are you from?" he continued with the routine getting-to-know-you line of questioning.

"I grew up in a small town in North Carolina."

"Really?" This seemed to interest Garrett. "Where?"

"Nowhere you've ever heard of." Avery snorted. "Trust me."

"Try me."

"Okay." She sat her water bottle down. "I grew up in Lillington. It's—"

"About forty minutes north of Fayetteville, in Harnett County. There's a trail near there. I can't remember the name, but it's in Raven Rock State Park."

Holy shit.

Avery felt her jaw drop. "You're talking about the Loop Trail."

Garrett snapped his fingers. "That's it! It takes you to the Overlook on the—"

"Cape Fear River," Avery finished for him. "My sister and I used to go there all the time when we were younger." They still did whenever they got the chance. "But... Lillington's a tiny blip on the map. Last I checked, the population was only up to something like thirty-five hundred people. How on earth do you know where that is?"

Grinning, Garrett dropped a massive bomb. One with the potential to change everything. "I live two and a half hours west of there. In Charlotte."

Avery's jaw dropped for the second time, her disbelieving gaze locking with his. "You're joking, right?"

He has to be joking.

"Nope." Garrett shook his head. "The company I work for is based out of Charlotte. I've lived there going on five years, now."

"You *really* live in Charlotte? Charlotte, North Carolina?" Avery couldn't wrap her mind around that fact.

"Yeah." He chuckled. "Why? You got something against the Queen City?"

"Only the traffic," she scoffed. Then she dropped a bomb of her own. "Garrett, I've lived in Charlotte for the past seven years."

"You're shitting me." He sat up a little straighter. "Seriously?"

"I swear."

"Well, I'll be damned." Humor and something else she couldn't quite place shone from his eyes. "Okay, so I know you said you work from home. Do you live downtown, or..."

"I have an apartment in Camden Grandview," she shared. "It's on Morehead."

"I know exactly where that is." Recognition flickered across Garrett's face. "I work two minutes from there."

"No, you don't."

"I swear!" Garrett threw up a hand as if to take an oath. "The company I work for has an office on south Tyron. It's in the TAC Center, across the street from—"

"Duke Energy." Avery nodded. "Duke switched over to my accounting program last fall. I spent a week there, helping their IT people set it up and then training their accounting department on how to run it." Disbelief had her shaking her head. "This is crazy, right? I mean, what are the chances?"

Garrett sat back in his chair and chuckled. "I'd say slim to none."

Several seconds of silence passed as they both processed the interesting turn of events. They lived in the same city, had worked across the street from each other for a week. And it had taken them both flying to Florida and boarding a cruise ship to the Eastern Caribbean to meet.

Suddenly wanting to know everything about this man, Avery took a sip of water and switched the conversation back to him.

"You said you work in the TAC Center. What is it you do there?"

"Insurance."

She nearly choked. Coughing, she managed to ask, "You sell insurance?"

His lips formed a slight smirk. "Something wrong with that?"

"Of course not." She coughed again. "You just don't strike me as the insurance type."

"No?" Humor flashed behind his gorgeous eyes "And what do I strike you as?"

Hot. Sexy. An alpha male badass who makes me want to reach across this table and—

"Wait a minute." She cut her simmering thought short. "You said you work in the TAC Center, right? And you sell insurance? You don't by chance work for Travel Assurance, do you?"

Surprise flickered across his face. "As a matter of fact, I do."

"They use my program, too." Avery laughed. "I was just there last week updating all the systems. We could've walked right past each other."

Granted, Travel Assurance took up multiple floors of the expensive high-rise. But still.

"One, if I'd walked past you, I would've remembered it." He shot her a panty-dropping smile. "And two, I was off last week. The first of my two-week vacation."

"Oh." Avery nodded. "Still, I can't believe how close we've been to each other this whole time."

"Me, neither."

The low humming she'd heard earlier grew exponentially louder and the ship gave a slight lurch forward as it prepared to leave.

Inappropriate thoughts interrupted; Avery's head spun toward the rippling water. Drawing in a deep breath, she was still trying to keep her bludgeoning nerves at bay when a warm, strong hand covered hers.

"You're going to be fine." Garrett's deep voice rolled through her like a calming wave. "I promise."

Glancing down at their joined hands, Avery felt a sense of peace that made her want to believe him.

"Come on." He pulled his hand away, the move leaving a much bigger void than it should have. "You'll see that we're perfectly safe. I'll even buy you another drink to celebrate our departure."

With a wink that made her lower belly tighten with lust, Garrett stood and began clearing the table.

"Fine." Avery rose to her feet. "But only because I really liked that drink. And if I go overboard and get eaten by a shark, just know...I'm coming back to haunt you."

CHAPTER 5

Two days later…

FROM BEHIND HIS DARK LENSES, Garrett glanced at the cabana-style lounges and other beach chairs lining the water's edge. He told himself he wasn't looking for Avery, but his subconscious knew he was full of shit.

Just admit it. You were hoping to see her again.

Hell yeah, he was. Especially after last night's dream.

He'd survived the first two nights on the water, falling asleep to the ship's rhythmic beat as it moved across the Northern Atlantic. The recurring nightmare plaguing him since his return from Syria had only woken him once these last two days.

A definite improvement from previous nights.

Even better was the dream Garrett had after falling back to sleep last night. One that included Avery.

He hadn't seen her since their shared pizza and drinks to toast their departure. Yesterday, during their first full day at sea, Garrett had caught himself looking for her within the ship's bustling crowd. Everywhere he and Colt went, he'd hoped to find her.

But he hadn't.

Asking for her room number had crossed his mind more than once that first night. Especially after learning they lived in the same damn city. But he hadn't wanted to come off as a pushy bastard, so he'd held back.

Now here he was, kicking himself for not growing a pair and asking.

Flashes of last night's dream replayed through his mind as he continued walking the length of the beach.

It had started with a knock on his door. When he opened it, Avery was there. The beautiful brunette had come to *his* room. And she'd been wearing a black dress and fuck-me heels.

In the dream, he'd reached for her hand. The two hadn't spoken a single word, communicating solely through touch.

His hands on her soft skin. Her lips pressing whispering kisses along his jaw and neck.

Even now, fully conscious and aware, Garrett could almost *feel* the way Avery's body had fit perfectly with his. As if he were an unfinished puzzle, and she was his final piece.

It was by far, the best dream he'd ever had. And it had left him with a raging hard-on, and Avery's sultry smile burned into his mind.

So here he was, searching the beach like a heartsick teenager desperate to find his first crush.

What is it about this woman?

Garrett wished he had the answer. All he knew was the

connection he'd felt with her had been instant and fierce. That they lived mere miles from each other only added fuel to his need to see her again. He may not understand it, but he sure as hell wasn't going to fight it.

Garrett scanned the tropical area again.

Sunset Cay, the private island owned by the Sunset Adventures cruise line, was the first of their ship's two scheduled stops for the week.

In addition to the white sandy beach and incredible turquoise water, the tiny strip of land housed gift shops, jet ski and snorkel rentals, and a handful of two-story houses that passengers could rent for the day.

There was also a bar in the shape of a pirate ship at the top of the hill. Of course, Colt had taken off in its direction the second they'd stepped foot onto the beach.

Garrett, on the other hand, had immediately began his search of the crowd for the brown-haired beauty he couldn't stop thinking about.

Five minutes later and still no luck. Maybe they'd missed each other in passing.

Or maybe she'd had enough of the crowds and decided to stay on the ship.

It didn't take a genius to realize Avery was a bit of an introvert. Hell, she'd admitted as much when they'd had dinner together. But when they'd parted ways after the ship had set sail, she'd mentioned looking forward to having a day at the beach.

Maybe it's for the best.

For once, the voice in his head—the fucker—was wrong.

After damn near getting his ass shot off, Garrett spent

several days rethinking his life choices. Things he wanted. Things he didn't.

And Avery Webb was something he most definitely wanted.

"Look who I found!" Colt's raised voice filled his ears.

Turning his head, Garrett spotted his brother…and Avery…walking toward him. For the second time in as many days, Garrett couldn't seem to catch his breath.

Holy Mother of…

Avery was wearing the same floppy hat she had on when they'd first met. The sundress, however, had been replaced with the most mouthwatering bikini he'd ever seen.

Or maybe it was the woman *wearing* it who had his eyes bugging out from behind his sunglasses.

The two-piece she had on was white with bright pink flowers. Keeping her most intimate parts hidden—damn his luck—the silky-smooth material molded perfectly to her luscious curves.

God, what he wouldn't give to see what was underneath.

Laced together in the center and secured with a bow, the top's triangular cups hugged a set of perky breasts exquisitely proportioned to her petite body.

Garrett's fingers twitched at his sides as he imagined himself reaching up and pulling that bow loose. He envisioned her breasts spilling out, filling his palms while he—

"Hi." She smiled up at him from beneath her tortoise-shell frames.

"Hey."

Hey? That's it? That's all you've got?

"I was heading down here with our drinks when we ran into each other," Colt explained. "Literally."

Avery's cheeks turned a deep shade of pink. "I may have been texting my sister and not paying attention to where I was walking."

"Lucky for you, big brother"—Colt handed him a frozen drink in a yard party cup—"I have cat-like reflexes and was able to salvage these."

"Lucky me." Garrett studied the ridiculously tall beverage. "What's the matter? Didn't they have a bigger size?"

His brother rolled his eyes. "You're hilarious."

An adorable snorting sound escaped the back of Avery's throat, making him smile. Christ, everything about this woman set him on fire.

At the risk of sounding like a psycho stalker, Garrett kept his tone aloof. "I didn't see you around yesterday."

"I spent a lot of time in my room. Not hiding out," she quickly assured him. "I just got caught up in a book I've been wanting to read and couldn't put it down. So I sat on my balcony most of the day."

"Sounds nice." He took a drink of the concoction Colt bought for him. It wasn't as good as the ones on the ship, but it was okay. "You enjoying it here?"

"Oh, yeah." She glanced out over the swimming area. "This place is incredible. I mean, I've seen water like this in pictures, but I always assumed the photographers photoshopped the color to make it look bluer and more vibrant. I had no idea it would really look this way in person."

Her awe-struck tone made him smile. "You been in yet?"

"Figured I should get some water since it's so hot out."

He nodded. "Staying hydrated is important on days like today."

Garrett wanted to roll his own eyes at that one. Jesus, he really needed to step up his game.

Colt's low cough and hidden smirk emphasized that very point. "I'm, uh...gonna go find a chair to relax in. Or maybe I'll check out the jet skis." He tipped his ball cap as he walked off. "Nice to see you again, Avery."

"You, too."

Subtle, little brother. Really fucking subtle.

"So, what are you—"

"Would you like to—"

Garrett and Avery laughed as they began speaking at the same time. With a smile, he motioned for her to continue. "Ladies first."

"No, you go."

"I was just going to ask if you wanted to go for a swim."

"Oh, uh..." She bit her bottom lip and glanced out at the water. "Sure."

Doing his damnedest not to think about how badly *he* wanted to bite that lip, Garrett grinned. "Great. I'll find a chair to set my towel and shoes on, and then we can—"

"You can put them on mine."

"Okay, then. Lead the way."

It turned out to be one of the best requests Garrett had ever uttered.

With Avery walking in front of him, he had the perfect opportunity to appreciate all of her other...assets.

Christ Almighty.

Thicker at the bottom, her heart-shaped ass tapered upward into a small, svelte waistline. She was petite, but not too thin. Which was perfect, since Garrett preferred women with a little meat on their bones.

From what he could see, Avery's body was soft in all the right places.

Just like in my dream.

His cock jerked and swelled inside his shorts. Remembering the crowd around them, Garrett inconspicuously positioned the tall plastic cup in front of his crotch.

As he continued following Avery to her chair, he prayed the boxer briefs beneath his trunks were tight enough to keep his raging hard-on at bay. Yes, he was physically attracted to the enchanting woman. But what he felt went much deeper than that.

It made no sense. Like, at all. He barely knew anything about her. But rational or not, the connection he felt with this woman was real.

"This is me."

Avery set her half-empty bottle of water onto the towel folded neatly on the lounger. Removing her hat, small purse, and sunglasses, she placed the purse with the other items, laying the hat over all to help keep it hidden.

"You can set your stuff wherever."

After taking a big gulp of the watered-down drink, Garrett set the cup in the sand next to the chair. Dropping his towel next to Avery's, he removed the black slides off his feet, nudging them under the chair. Next came his ballcap and sunglasses.

Grabbing the hem of his shirt, Garrett pulled the t-shirt up over his head, tossing it with the rest of his things. Avery sucked in a sharp breath.

"Oh my gosh!" Her wide eyes zeroed in on his chest. "What did you do?"

Fuck. He'd been so focused on her fine ass and luscious curves, he'd forgotten all about his bruise.

Quick on his feet, he didn't skip a beat when he rolled out the first excuse that came to his mind.

"I'm on our company's softball team. Took a line drive to the chest at our last game."

"Ouch." Her face scrunched together in an adorable-as-fuck way.

"Yeah." He laughed it off. "Hurt like a bitch, but it looks worse now than it feels."

"That's good, at least."

She bought it!

"Yeah," he agreed. Removing his glasses, Garrett bent over to tuck them under his towel. "You ready?" He stood and turned around in time to see her eyes flying back up to his.

"Yep." Avery spun on her bare heels, facing the water while she waited.

Her stiffened spine and tight voice sent Garrett's lips curving upward. She'd been checking out his ass, and from the tension in her body, he was confident she liked what she saw.

I'd be happy to show you the rest.

Garrett stepped closer to her. So close he could feel her body's heat. Avery's breathing picked up, and the pulse point on her neck thumped harder than before.

At first, he thought maybe he was scaring her. Needing to be sure, he lifted his eyes for a glimpse at her beautiful face.

Her lips were parted slightly. Her soft cheeks flushed. And when he glanced down at the pointed peaks of her hidden breasts, he knew she felt it, too.

"Garrett..." His name escaped with a low rasp.

Leaning inward, he was about to kiss the side of her neck when he remembered where they were.

Not wanting to embarrass or make Avery feel uncomfortable in any way, Garrett forced his raging need for this woman down and repositioned the angle of his head.

Letting his lips whisper across her ear, he told her, "Last one in's a rotten egg."

Then he smiled and ran toward the water.

"Wha...hey!" Avery took off after him. "That's cheating!"

Reaching the water before her, he stopped when he was ankle deep. *Jesus, that's cold.* With the slow, lazy waves caressing his feet, he turned and waited as Avery closed the distance between them.

Garrett's cock twitched again when he saw her breasts bouncing with every step. If she wasn't careful, she'd fall right out of the skimpy top.

If they were alone, he'd be all for it. But the idea of all these *other* people seeing his woman's breasts made him want to grab the nearest towel and wrap her up like a fucking burrito.

She's not yours, dickhead. Not even close.

No, Avery wasn't his. Not yet. He still had a few more days to change that.

Garrett was standing there, thinking of all the ways he could achieve that goal when Avery ran straight past him in a blur.

"I win!" She wore a smug smile, splashing him as she moved deeper into the swimming area.

The cold water left his breath hitching. "No way. I got here first!"

Avery kept running. "You said last one *in*."

"I *am* in!" He hollered after her.

"Feet don't count!"

Since when?

Garrett opened his mouth to ask the question, but he was too late. As if it were nothing, Avery had braved the frigid water, diving head-first beneath its clear blue surface.

"I'll be damned."

Not wanting to come off as a pussy, he did the same. Then he came back up, shivering and sucking in air.

"Holy shit!" He rubbed a hand down his face. "I wasn't expecting the water to be so cold."

With her long, wet hair cemented to her head, Avery laughed as she rubbed her arms and bobbed up and down. "It is a bit chilly."

"You think?" He frowned. "And since when do feet not count?"

"Since always." Her expression became serious. "For you to be the first one *in*, your entire body must be completely submerged before the other person's."

For a second, Garrett wasn't sure how to respond. Then he saw her lips twitch and realized she'd pulled one over on him.

"You tricked me into going under."

"Yep." She didn't look the least bit sorry.

Then it hit him. "You've already been in the water today, haven't you?"

"Maybe." She pressed her lips together to keep from smiling.

"So *you're* the cheater!" With a playful swipe at the water, Garrett splashed her.

Avery screamed and turned her head, her arm flailing in a blind attempt to get him back.

After a few lucky shots, he decided to take things a bit further. Diving under the water, Garrett reached out and wrapped his arm around her center.

He could hear Avery's high-pitched scream as he lifted her in the air and tossed her a few feet away. She landed with a giant splash.

Garrett laughed, but when Avery came back up, she was coughing and struggling to breathe.

"Oh, shit." Garrett swam over to her. "I'm so sorry! I didn't mean to—"

He got a face full of salt water.

"Two can play at that game." An arched brow topped off her defiant expression. "It's game on."

Avery splashed him again. Wiping his face, Garrett watched her swim gracefully away.

Oh, it's definitely game on, sweetheart.

And this was one game he intended to win.

CHAPTER 6

A cool breeze took the bite out of the hot summer sun as it made its way across Avery's exposed skin.

Her thoughts bounced between how relaxed she felt and how incredible Garrett looked wearing nothing but a pair of swim trunks.

She'd already known the man was fit. Even fully clothed, it was obvious he stayed in excellent shape. But when he'd taken off his t-shirt earlier...

Lord have Mercy.

The man wasn't merely in good shape. He was incredibly fit and sculpted. Every muscle taut and firm. Every shadowed groove evidence of his discipline and hard work.

Even now, as she snuck a few peeks from beneath her dark lenses, Avery could make out the impressive ripples of his washboard abs.

Abs she'd had the pleasure of feeling when they'd been playing around in the water earlier.

Call it what it was, Aves. You were flirting.

It was true. She *had* been flirting. Shamelessly so. And the best part?

He'd flirted right back.

Laying in the hot sun, Avery replayed the recent moments over and over again. Him dunking her. Her splashing him. Taking every opportunity to share innocent touches as they teased and laughed in the cold blue sea.

She shivered at the thought of how his hard body had felt beneath her fingertips. Her inner muscles tightened as she thought of the impressive erection she was certain she'd felt during a particularly close encounter.

It was impossible not to imagine what it would feel like as he moved his magnificent body in and out of hers. She welcomed the erotic fantasy. Played it again and again until she felt her body begin to respond in real time.

Her heartrate spiked, and a bead of sweat trickled along her temple and into her damp hair. Her sex felt heavy and needy, and if he were to slide on over, he'd find her body ready for whatever he wanted to give.

Down girl. It was just some friendly flirting. Don't make it into more than it actually was.

Forcing the thoughts away—because this was not the time nor the place—Avery let go of the fantasy and sighed.

"That a good sigh or bad?" Garrett mumbled lazily from the chair beside hers.

"Definitely good," she answered before she could stop herself.

"Care to share?"

Crap. Crap, crap, crap!

Her mind raced to create a plausible explanation. There was no way she could tell him the truth. No. Way.

Keeping her eyes closed, Avery quickly came up with

another plausible reason for the sigh. Something *other* than the fact that she'd been fantasizing about the two of them making love.

"Just that I'm really relaxed." *Nice save.* "I spend so much of my time working, and my job can get kind of stressful at times. I guess I forgot how nice it is to just...be."

"I know what you mean."

Putting a hand over her forehead to block the blinding sun, Avery opened one eye and looked his way. "I didn't realize the insurance business was so stressful."

"You have no idea." Garrett's mouth did a funny thing before forming into a smile. "You hungry? I think they're going to start serving the food soon."

"I could eat."

"In that case"—he swung his legs around and sat up —"we'd better get in line now, before Colt beats us and takes all the food."

With a laugh, Avery started to stand but plopped back down when everything around her began to spin. "Whoa."

"You okay?" Concern laced Garrett's tone.

"Yeah." She closed her eyes and dipped her head. "I think I just stood up too quickly."

"How much water have you drank today?"

"Um...." She thought about the water bottle sitting next to her hat and purse. Garrett had bought them each one after they finished swimming, but she'd only taken a sip before laying down and losing herself in the relaxing sun.

"That's what I thought. Stay put. I'll go get you a fresh bottle."

"I'm fine." A little dizzy and a slight headache, but

those were no big deal. "Really, Garrett. You don't have to—"

Avery stopped talking when she opened her eyes and realized he was already gone. Her heart warmed at how sweet and attentive he was with her. Of course, then she wondered what was wrong with him and why he was still single.

Maybe he isn't. Have you even bothered to ask?

No. She hadn't.

She'd just assumed by his behavior toward her that he didn't have a wife or girlfriend waiting for him back home. All Avery really knew about him was his name, his occupation, and where he lived.

Better have that conversation sooner rather than later.

Avery was still going through the mental list of other things she didn't know about Garrett when he returned with two ice-cold bottles, one in each hand.

"Here." He handed her one before squatting down in front of her. "Drink it slowly but be sure to get it all down."

Feeling like a total wuss, she broke the seal on the cap and took a sip. Then she took another. And another.

God, that tastes good.

She hadn't realized how thirsty she'd gotten until that first sip. Garrett had said to go slow, but Avery's sudden need for more had her tilting her head back and chugging the rest.

"Easy," he warned. "Don't want you getting sick."

"I'm good." She swallowed the last drop. "Thanks for getting that for me."

"I actually got you two, but I'm thinking you might

want to give it a minute before starting in on this one." He held up the second bottle.

"Okay."

Garrett's focus lowered to her mouth, an odd smile spreading on his lips. Reaching up, he used his thumb to brush away some water that had dripped onto her chin.

"Thanks," Avery spoke softly.

He cupped one side of her face. "You're so beautiful."

She wanted to laugh. Men never called her beautiful. Not ones that looked like him, anyway.

Feeling as though she *was* going to laugh, Avery remembered what she needed to ask him.

"Are you married?" The blurted question was personal but necessary.

"No." Garrett dropped his hand and frowned. "Do you think I'd be acting this way with you if I was?"

"I don't know." It was an honest answer. "We don't really know each other, and when it comes to men, I haven't always been the best judge of character." One of the few things she and her sister had in common. "Okay, I'm just going to say it. I...I feel a sort of connection to you, Garrett. I know that sounds crazy, but—"

"It's not crazy."

"—Unless I'm reading things wrong, I think you feel it, too." *Please feel it, too.*

His blue eyes softened. "You're not reading anything wrong, sweetheart."

Sweetheart. The endearment sent her heart into a flutter.

"I didn't mean to insult you or your character by asking if you're already involved with someone. I just thought it would be best to ask. Because if you *were* married or have a girlfriend…"

"I'm not, and I don't." His response was unwavering and sincere. Setting the unopened bottle of water down onto the sand, he took both her hands in his. "I've never been married, nor do I have a girlfriend. And as attracted to you as I am, I wouldn't be here with you like this if I did. I'm not the kind of man who cheats, Avery."

He could be lying, of course. Most cheaters didn't come right out and announce their intentions to be unfaithful. Alex's ex sure as hell hadn't. But deep inside, Avery somehow knew this man was telling the truth.

"Okay." She offered him a smile.

With a quick lick of his lips, he said, "What other questions do you have?"

Avery thought for a moment. "Do you really sell insurance?" Because he seriously did *not* look like any insurance agent she'd ever met.

"I do." He nodded. "If you want, when we get back to the ship I can show you my license. A quick web search will give you my professional bio and all you could ever care to know about Travel Assurance. Anything else you want to know about me?"

Only everything.

"Do you have any questions for me?"

The crooked smile he wore set her insides on fire. "Sweetheart, I have about a billion things I want to ask, but there's one thing I'm dying to *do* first."

"What's that?"

"This."

Garrett leaned toward her, giving her plenty of time to

back away if she wanted...which she didn't. Closing his eyes, he brushed his lips against hers.

At first, Avery was so shocked that they were kissing, she just sat there. Stiff as a board. But when he gave her bottom lip a tiny nibble, she closed her eyes and fell into the moment.

With a groan, Garrett tilted her head and took the kiss deeper. Avery opened for him, their tongues twirling together in a soft, sensual dance.

Her insides clenched as electricity arced from his body to hers. It was just a kiss, yet somehow it felt more intimate than all the physical interactions of her past combined.

Unable to hold back, Avery released a low moan as she leaned further into the kiss.

Having forgotten everyone else around them, she put her hands on his bare shoulders. The heated skin there burning against her palms. Tingling spread throughout her lower belly...and below.

Taking her time, she savored Garrett's delicious taste as a deep, guttural sound escaped the back of his throat. Somewhere in the back of Avery's mind, she registered the thought that this was the best, most perfect first kiss she'd ever had.

With each swipe of his tongue, she wanted more. Every brush of his fingers against her cheek, or the way his bare chest pressed against her sensitive breasts...everything this man did made her want *more.*

The one thing holding her back was time.

Would it be great if he wanted to start dating after this? Absolutely. Did she expect that to happen?

Absolutely not.

Sure, they both lived in Charlotte. But it was a city of almost 900,000 people. The fact that they'd literally been across the street from each other and still hadn't met before now spoke volumes as to their chances of running into one another again once they returned home.

Which begged the question…

Did she really want to get involved with a man she'd probably be saying goodbye to in three short days?

Her sister's voice invaded her thoughts.

You're an adult, you're single…and as long as you're smart about it and take precautions, there's nothing wrong with having a casual sexual relationship.

It was true, Avery had never done the whole casual thing before. But as Garrett continued seducing her with his oral skills, she realized for the first time in her life… she wanted to.

Just this once. And only with him.

In that moment, Avery decided to forget about the future beyond the next three days. If the man was willing to offer even a small part of himself to her, she was going to take it.

No strings. No commitment. Just a whole lot of fun.

Pulling away much too soon, Garrett's chest rose and fell with heaving breaths matching her own. He stared back at her with the same wide-eyed expression Avery was certain she was wearing.

Wow.

"I'd say I'm sorry, but…" His raspy voice trailed off.

Licking his taste from her lips, Avery shook her head and whispered, "Don't you dare."

Heat filtered into his eyes as the corners of his mouth curved. When he started to lean in for another kiss, Avery tilted her chin upward to meet him, but stopped when someone cleared their throat in a loud and deliberate way.

"Sorry to interrupt, but they opened the buffet for lunch." Colt stood next to Garrett's chair with a knowing grin. "Figured you guys could use some sustenance, but it looks like you skipped straight to dessert."

"Coulter," Garrett warned his younger brother.

Heat that had nothing to do with the sun began crawling up Avery's neck.

Still crouched in front of her, Garrett gave her a smile that sent her hormones flying. "As much as I hate admitting it, Colt's right. You need to eat."

"We both do," she agreed.

Standing, Garrett held out a hand to help her up. This time, when Avery got to her feet, the world swayed for an entirely different reason.

Wrapping her towel around her waist and slipping on her shoes, she and the two men headed up the hill to where their meal was being served. Garrett placed his callused palm against her lower back, keeping it there as they walked.

Over an authentic island lunch, which included steamed shrimp, crab legs, roasted vegetables, and a mixture of fresh fruits, the three of them got to know each other even better.

"So, Avery. Garrett tells me you live in Charlotte, too. Such a small world."

"It is." She took a bite of fresh strawberry. "Do you live there, too?"

Colt shook his head. "I have an apartment in Omaha, close to where we grew up. But I'm hardly there."

"Why is that?"

"His work keeps him busy, too," Garrett finished for his brother.

"I'm in public relations. I go where my work takes me."

"That must get kind of lonely," Avery noted.

But Colt shrugged it off. "I'm around people all the time. Plus, I knew what I was getting into when I took the job, and I enjoy it. Guess that makes all the traveling worth it."

"I'll be sure to relay that sentiment to Dad next time he crawls up my ass about not hearing from you for months on end."

Garrett's sarcastic tone was impossible to miss.

"As a matter of fact"—Colt raised a defiant brow—"I called him before we left the port. Which reminds me, he wants us both to spend a weekend there after we get back." Then Colt surprised the hell out of her when he turned and said, "You should come with us. Dad would love you. And as a bonus, it would get him off G's back."

Avery blinked, the presumptuous invite to Nebraska taking her aback. She and Garrett had just shared their first kiss, and Colt was ready to introduce her to their *father?*

Relax, Aves. He's obviously kidding.

Of course, he was kidding. He had to be. Right?

Giving herself a mental slap on the head, Avery chose to bypass the comment about her accompanying them to Nebraska by asking Garrett, "Why is your dad on your back?"

After shooting his brother a *thanks a lot* glare, he looked back at her and sighed. "Our mother passed away a few years ago. I was still with the Army, and Colt had just graduated college and had started his new job. We made time for him as much as we could, and I eventually left the Army to help him on the farm. About a year later, I got hired on with Ta..uh..Travel Assurance...." Garrett paused to regroup from his near blunder. "Anyway, after that, I wasn't able to go back to visit as often as I'd like."

"What my brother is taking entirely too long to say"— Colt chimed back in—"is, our dad is lonely, and he wants grandkids. Like, yesterday."

"And since I'm the oldest..." Garrett picked up where Colt left off.

Avery smiled. "He expects you to be the first to give them to him."

"That is so cute." Colt picked up his water bottle. "You two are already finishing each other's sentences."

With a flip of the bird, Garrett began razzing Colt in retaliation for the smartass remark. Before long the two were tossing insults back and forth, the way brothers often did.

They were *still* carrying on when a Sunset Adventures staff member came around announcing the smaller boats were docked and ready to take passengers back to the Majestic.

Several minutes later, as they sat next to one another on the short ride over calm waters, Avery thought about the day's surprising turn of events.

She'd hoped to see him at the beach. Had looked for him the second she'd stepped onto the dock. It had taken her best acting skills to not act like a giddy teenager when she'd ran into Colt on the way out of the pirate-themed bar, hoping that meant Garrett had come to the island, too.

When Garrett had asked her to go swimming, Avery had considered telling him about the freezing cold water.

But then she thought better of it, wanting to see his raw reaction when he realized the island's sultry weather was deceiving.

Of course, Garrett had clearly made plans of his own... coming up behind her the way he had. She could still feel his breath teasing her ear as he'd challenged her to a race into the water.

His lips on hers as his tongue invaded her mouth in the most delectable way.

Looks like you can cross number twenty off your list a lot sooner than you thought.

Avery smiled as she imagined drawing a line through that one. There was no way her sister ever truly expected her to go through with it, but she had. Not only that, the kiss hadn't even been her idea.

Garrett had been the one to lean up and take her mouth in his. And he would've kissed her again if his brother hadn't shown up.

Yes, it had been a very, very good day. One Avery would remember for the rest of her life.

Thoughts of mind-blowing kisses had her sneaking another quick glance at the man sitting beside her. With his powerful arms stretched out along the back of the metal bench, Garrett had his hat on backward and his face tilted up toward the sun. Though she couldn't see his eyes, she knew they were closed.

God, he's beautiful.

"What do you want to do for dinner tonight?" Colt's voice rose over the boat's motor.

"I don't know." Garrett brushed her bare shoulder with his thumb. "What do you have planned?"

"I'm not sure," she answered honestly. "Tonight's the

night everyone's supposed to dress up, but I think I'll need a nap before I decide whether or not to participate."

"A nap sounds great."

Wanna come to my room and take one with me?

Avery swallowed the question down before she did something stupid like blurt it out.

They may have shared one kiss, but that didn't mean she was about to start acting like a lovesick fool. She may not have a lot of experience with men, but that didn't mean she was desperate.

"I forgot about the formal dinner being tonight," Garrett rumbled beside her. "Guess I'll have to cut my nap short so I can press my shirt and suit."

Garrett in a suit? That was something she *had* to see.

Play it cool, Aves.

Something her mom and sister had always told her.

With a casual, non-committal tone, she said, "Yeah, I should probably steam the dress I brought. In case I decide to go."

"We could...go together."

Garrett's breezy remark left her chest tightening and her heart pounding. "I don't want to impose."

He turned to her. "You're not imposing if I invited you."

"I know, but you're here with Colt. Brother bonding trip, remember? Besides, I've already monopolized enough of your day."

"Oh, no." Colt shifted in his seat. "Don't use me as an excuse. If you don't want to have dinner with my brother, just say so."

"What? No." Avery's head shook vehemently. "It's not that I don't want to go. I just feel bad getting between you two when this is supposed to be a brother bonding trip."

"Meh." Colt waved her off. "We spent yesterday together. And dressing up for some hoity toity meal isn't really my thing. Plus, we're snorkeling along the reef and playing with the stingrays tomorrow, so..."

"Stingrays?" Avery's brows arched high. "I saw that excursion on the website. The people in the pictures were actually *holding* them."

Garrett gave her a boyish grin. "Pretty cool, right?"

"Uh, no. Not cool. Suicidal, maybe, but definitely not cool."

With a low chuckle, he shook his handsome head. "Stingrays are very docile creatures. As long as you don't try to hurt them or go after them in a threatening manner, they'll swim right up to you."

The mere *thought* sent a shiver down her spine. "Well, you two have fun with that."

"We will," Colt piped up with an excited grin. "Which is why I'm saying, if you two want to have a romantic dinner tonight, go for it. 'Cause I've got this guy all day tomorrow."

Excited at the thought of an honest-to-goodness date with Garrett, Avery forced her eyes to remain on Colt's. "What about you? What are you doing tonight?"

"Probably search the ship for his first ex-wife," Garrett quipped.

Avery snickered, but Colt ignored his brother's dig and kept their conversation going.

"Don't worry about me, sweet pea. The ship is packed with places to eat and people to meet. I can handle bein' on my own. Trust me."

Several seconds passed before Garrett brushed his fingers along her shoulder once more. "What do you say? Want to have a fancy schmancy dinner with me tonight?"

Hell, yes! "I'd like that."

His lips stretched into a smile that sent her pulse racing. "Give me your phone."

"My phone?"

"I'll put my number in it. That way you can text me when you're ready."

Digging her phone from her purse, Avery handed him the device and waited. When he was done entering his contact information, he sent himself a text before returning the phone.

"There. Now we have each other's numbers." He pulled his phone from his pocket and typed something out. A half a second later, her phone dinged with an incoming text.

Glancing at the screen, Avery saw the numbers 3563. Confused, she lifted her focus back to him.

"That's my stateroom," he explained. "If the ship's WiFi gets spotty, you can come grab me, and we'll walk there together. Figured you'd be more comfortable doing it that way, rather than telling some guy you just met where your room is."

Avery studied him closely before leaning forward to look across him at Colt. "Okay, spill it."

"It?"

"The reason your brother's still single. There has to be something, because no guy I know is this good looking *and* this considerate. So what is it? Sociopathic tendencies? Bodies hidden in his basement...there has to be something."

"You're preachin' to the choir, sister." Colt smirked. "Why do you think our dad rides his ass so hard about settling down? Hell, half the family has a bet on when he's gonna come out of the closet."

"Hey!" Garrett turned to his brother. "I'm not gay." His head swiveled back toward Avery. "And I'm not a sociopath who keeps bodies in my basement."

"Not even one?" Avery teased.

"Not a one."

"So what is it? You afraid of commitment?"

Seemed like every other guy she'd dated had that same problem. They all wanted one thing, and when they realized she wasn't the type to give it up after a mediocre meal and an evening of dry conversation, they split.

"More like I don't have the time for commitment."

"Your job?"

Garrett nodded. "It's a big company with a lot of clients all over the country. I'm not gone as much as Colt, here, but my job does require me to travel. Sometimes out of the country. Most women I meet want a man who can be at their beck and call." He lifted a shoulder. "I can't promise that."

"It's the same with my job." She gave him a sad smile. "Most days, I can set my own hours. But there are times when a company with my program hits a glitch and needs me to run an emergency system check. Sometimes it happens during normal business hours. Others in the middle of the night. Not the same thing as your situation, but I get it."

And she did. Having to leave a date or time with friends or family because of work sucked. But it also came with the territory. Something she'd known when she decided to go freelance two years ago.

Sliding her phone back into her purse, she switched topics back to their evening plans. "What time should I be ready for dinner?"

Glancing at his expensive and complicated watch, Garrett moved his gaze back to hers. "Seven-thirty too late?"

"That's perfect."

It would give her enough time to shower and take a quick nap to recharge. This was the first date she'd had in months, and she wanted to be at the top of her game…just in case.

Whether this thing between them went anywhere after they got back to Charlotte was anybody's guess, and something Avery had no control over.

What she could control…what she found herself wanting more than *anything*…was to simply enjoy the here and now.

Starting with dinner.

CHAPTER 7

Garrett opened the door to find his real-life dream staring back at him.

Lord have mercy.

Dressed in black, Avery was an absolute vision. Her long hair had been clipped up into a loose mound of curls on the crown of her head. A few delicate strands fell softly around her gorgeous face.

She'd done something different with her makeup. An added layer on her eyes, cheeks, and lips.

Moving lower, Garrett couldn't help but notice the way the garment's lace-covered halter pulled her breasts together. The low neckline created a deep crevice that made his fingers itch to rip the damn thing off, just so he could catch a glimpse of what was underneath.

A wide satin banner showcased Avery's tapered waist, and the knee-length skirt flared slightly at her hips, stopping mid-thigh in the front and just above her knees in the back. Peeking out from beneath the skirt was a single layer of blood red satin that reminded him of sin.

And then there were her shoes.

Black, strappy numbers with thin leather that hugged her dainty ankles and heels that went on for days.

Garrett's mouth went dry, his heart pounding the hell out of his chest when the image of her in nothing *but* those shoes seared his mind's eye.

Everything about this woman—from the sleeveless black dress to the fuck me heels—looked exactly like the image his subconscious mind had conjured up the night before. Only better.

"Wow."

As far as compliments went, it was lame as shit. Avery must have liked it though, because her cheeks turned rosy and her ruby lips curved.

"I was about to say the same thing about you."

He would've argued that fact had her chocolate eyes not melted as they ran the length of his body.

It was a damn good thing he'd already put on his suit jacket. Otherwise, she would've gotten more of an eyeful than she'd bargained for.

Down, boy. It's just dinner, remember?

Yeah, it was just dinner. But fuck if he didn't wish it was more.

"Are you ready?" he rasped.

"Yes."

Avery's whispered answer was innocent enough, but her molten stare and rising chest held a deeper, more intimate meaning. Or maybe it was simply wishful thinking on his part.

I'm more than ready, baby. Just say the word, and I'm yours.

Stepping out into the hallway, Garrett closed the door

behind him, offering her his elbow like a gentleman should. With a shy smile, Avery accepted. Her small fingers curling around his arm in a way that made his heart swell and his zipper tighten.

Less than an hour later, with their main course only half-eaten, he was already trying to come up with a way to keep their evening together from coming to an end.

"Ohmygod." Avery took a bite of her buttery lobster tail. "This is incredible."

Garrett's steak and shrimp meal was great, too. But he was enjoying the woman sitting across from him even more.

She took another bite, releasing a moan that made his brain—and his crotch—immediately turn to sex.

"I've never tasted anything so delicious."

I bet you taste better.

Aaaand just like that, the image of Avery lying on his bed, completely naked—except for those damn shoes— flashed before him. With her hair flared out around her shoulders and her knees up and spread wide, Garrett's mouth watered as he pictured himself leaning in for that first taste of heaven.

"Garrett?"

The concern in Avery's voice brought him back to the present.

"I'm sorry, what?"

Her eyes sparkled with humor. "I asked if you were enjoying your steak."

"Oh." He shot her a quick smile. "Uh...yeah. It's great."

But not nearly as great as those sweet lips of yours.

Garrett hadn't stopped thinking about that kiss, and how it had damn near knocked him on his ass.

He'd locked lips with many a woman in his day, but holy hell. He'd *never* felt a jolt of pure electricity like the one that had zipped through him when he'd kissed Avery.

"I should stop." She tore through his scattered thoughts again. "Save room for dessert."

A drop of butter had fallen on her bottom lip, and he nearly came unglued when she caught it with her forefinger, and then wrapped her lips *around* that finger, sucking it clean.

Later, by the time dessert had come and gone, Garrett's cock was aching to the point of pain, and he was certain his zipper had already caused permanent damage.

The woman savored her food like great sex. The satisfied moans escaping her throat, and the innocent licks of her luscious lips tempting him in ways he'd never known.

Yes, Avery Webb was a temptress of the worst kind. Because she had absolutely *no* idea the effect she had on him.

"That was amazing." Her sweet voice caught his attention. "So rich and chocolatey. I can't believe I ate the whole thing."

"That good, huh?"

"Mmm hmm." She gave a solemn nod. "I'm not usually a big dessert person, but I'm going to have to learn how to make that."

The tip of her tongue met with some leftover chocolate glaze on her spoon, and Garrett clenched his fists resting on his lap. It was all he could do not to swipe the table clean and take her right there, in front of God and everyone.

"You don't like sweets?" He forced a casual tone.

Avery shook her head. "Not typically. Vanilla ice cream is my usual go-to. Chocolate chip if I'm celebrating something or drowning my sorrows." She patted her mouth with her napkin. "But that was incredible, *and* it fulfills my one new food experience quota for the day."

The odd comment left him intrigued. "You have a limit?"

"No." Avery's feminine shoulders shook with laughter. "I just have this…you know what? Never mind."

"Tell me."

A blush he was becoming familiar with filled her cheeks. "You'll think it's stupid."

"Sweetheart, I can promise you there isn't a single thing about you that I'd think was stupid."

Biting her bottom lip—Good God, the woman was killing him—Avery thought for a moment before letting him in on her little secret.

"Do you remember when I told you my sister dared me to take this trip?"

"I do."

"Well, our first day on the ship Alex texted me. Alex is my sister," she clarified. "Anyway, she told me about this list she made and how she'd snuck it into my purse when we were at the airport that morning."

Doing his best not to sound judgmental, Garrett had to ask, "Why did your sister make a list of things for you to do on *your* vacation and then sneak it into your purse?"

She rolled her pretty eyes. "To help nudge me out of my shell."

"Sounds like she and Colt could be related."

With a smile, Avery relaxed into her cushioned chair.

"Alex means well. But ever since our parents died and her fiancé cheated on her with her best friend, I've become her pet project."

Garrett's chest tightened. "I'm sorry you lost your parents. I know how hard that is."

"I meant to tell you earlier, I'm sorry about your mom."

"Thanks." He offered her a tight smile. "My dad, as you know, is still alive and kicking."

"And screaming for grandkids, apparently." Avery grinned.

"Apparently." Garrett rolled *his* eyes. "If you don't mind me asking, what happened with your parents?"

Instant sadness poured over her in waves. "Car accident. It was the middle of January, and the roads were slick with ice. There was a winter storm forecasted for the next day, so Mom and Dad decided to make a grocery run to stock up so they wouldn't have to get out in the bad weather. But the storm moved in much faster than the weather center predicted, and a group of teenagers took a curve too fast. They crossed the center line and hit Mom and Dad's car head on at a high rate of speed."

"Jesus."

Avery's throat worked as she swallowed a pain he was intimately familiar with. "Dad was driving. He died instantly, but Mom held on for about an hour and a half after the crash. At least that's what the doctor who treated her told Alex and I when we got to the hospital."

Ah, baby.

"Alex lives in Charlotte, too, and with the inclement weather, it took us a lot longer than normal to get to

Lillington. Mom was already gone by the time we got there."

Damn. Losing one parent was hard enough. He couldn't imagine losing them both in one fell swoop.

Burying his mom was the hardest thing Garrett had ever lived through. But at least he'd known what was coming. He and his dad both had time to prepare and had been blessed with the opportunity to say everything they needed to before she passed.

"I'm so sorry," he said again.

"Thanks." She rewarded him with a small smile. "Most days, I do okay. But it was really hard at first."

Several seconds passed with neither saying a word. Needing to salvage the evening and return to a more upbeat topic of conversation, Garrett finally said, "Tell me about your sister."

"Alex?" Avery barked out a laugh. "Well, let's see. She's pretty much the exact opposite of me."

"In what way?"

"Uh…every way." She reached into her purse and pulled out her phone. Scrolling through her pictures, Avery apparently found the one she wanted and held the screen up for him to see.

"That's me and Alex last Christmas."

Garrett studied the picture closely. He recognized Avery immediately; her long, dark hair flowing around her shoulders from beneath a knitted stocking cap. The attractive woman next to her shared the same, wide smile, but her hair was cut into a straight bob, her features were sharper and more defined, and her eyes were a tad smaller than Avery's.

Pretty, for sure. But as far as Garrett was concerned,

Alex didn't hold a candle to the woman sitting across from him.

"We both have my dad's dark hair and eyes," Avery explained. "But I definitely look more like our dad, and Alex took after our mom."

"You said you and your sister were opposites. How so?"

"Alex is a free spirit, and I'm more of a homebody. She's the social butterfly. Me, not so much. Alex likes going out dancing with friends on the weekends, and my idea of a fun night is to cuddle up on the couch with a good book and a glass of wine."

"Nothing wrong with that." And he meant it.

In fact, Garrett rather liked knowing Avery didn't spend her nights in bars or night clubs surrounded by a bunch of drunken, horny assholes.

Not ready for the evening to end, he rested his elbows on the table and linked his fingers together. "Tell me more about this list Alex made for you."

Avery snorted. "You don't really want to hear about that, do you?"

"Sure, I do. And who knows…maybe I can help you cross off a few things."

Garrett wasn't sure what he'd said to make her blush, but Avery's neck and cheeks turned almost crimson at his suggestion.

Now I really *want to know what's on that list.*

"It's nothing big." She seemed to read his mind. "I checked off the first three things before we'd even left the port. And, as a matter of fact, you *did* help with some of those."

"I did?"

"Yep. The first thing was to get on the damn ship." Avery giggled. "Like, literally…that's exactly how my sister wrote it." She shook her head. "But after that, there was talk to someone I didn't know, which I did when I met you and Colt. Another was to share a drink with someone I didn't know. You bought me my first drink of the trip. Let's see…" She thought for a moment. "Then there's the food. I'm supposed to try at least one thing new to eat every day."

"Shouldn't be too hard since there's food everywhere you turn around."

"Right?" Avery agreed.

Finding himself more and more interested about this list, Garrett asked, "Was there anything else I was able to help you with?"

Aaand, there it was again. That flushed, flustered look that made him think of sex.

"Um…you went swimming with me, so that sort of counts," she answered with a bit of a rush. "Number six was to swim in the ocean, so…"

"Yeah, but you'd already did that before we met up." He playfully narrowed his gaze. "Not that you bothered to tell me that…or that the water was as cold as a freaking icebox."

Biting her lip, Avery shot him an apologetic look. "Sorry."

"No, you're not," he scoffed with a smile.

"No." She shook her head and laughed harder. "I'm really not."

Staring back at her, Garrett realized the more time he spent with this woman, the more time he *wanted* to spend with her.

So he kept the conversation going.

They discussed the list further, Avery sharing more of the items she had yet to check off. Things like singing karaoke, dancing a slow dance, making a new friend, trying something scary...

With karaoke being the exception—no one in their right mind wanted to hear him sing—he had the sudden urge to help her do all those things...and more.

"Come on." Garrett stood and pushed in his chair.

Following suit, Avery did the same. "Where are we going?"

"You want to knock out that list, right?"

"Well, yeah, but—"

"No time like the present." He grinned. "What do you say? Wanna see how many we can check off in one night?"

With a smile that lit up her eyes, she nodded. "Let's do it."

And they did.

First, they hit the karaoke bar. After three drinks and a lot of prodding on Garrett's part, Avery got up the nerve to put her name on the list. And when they called her up to the small stage, she fucking nailed it.

Would she hit it big or win a Grammy? Probably not. But when she'd loosened up and let herself go, she was good. *Better* than good.

And most importantly, she'd had fun.

Grabbing the list from her purse, she'd crossed off both the karaoke line *and* the thing that terrified her. She'd told him getting on that stage had been one of the scariest things she'd ever done, so it could count as both, and he'd agreed.

After that, they went to a piano bar. It had nothing to

do with the list, but they'd enjoyed listening to the live, impromptu music anyway.

Later, as they left that bar to head to another part of the ship, they heard more music coming from up ahead.

He glanced over at Avery. "Want to check it out?"

"Sure."

Taking a chance, Garett reached for her hand. His heart sang as she looked up at him and smiled before linking her fingers with his.

They found the source of the music near one of the ship's three spiral staircases. Neon green lights glittered the entire open area, which consisted of a small bar attached to the staircase. Above that was a second-level balcony overlooking a tiled dance floor, and opposite that was a set of glass elevators that seemed to go on forever.

Right on cue, the fast-paced song that had been playing, slowed to a romantic ballad he recognized.

Without a word, Garrett led Avery onto the dance floor. Weaving in and out of the crowd, he found a spot that would give them enough room to move without making her feel as though she were suffocating.

"I like this song." She moved in closer as he put a hand around her waist.

Keeping one of her hands in his, Garrett began swaying to the music's soft, gentle beat. "Me, too."

The longer the song played, the more relaxed Avery seemed to become. She rested her head on his shoulder, pressing a hand against his lower back.

Closing his eyes, Garrett gently laid his cheek against the top of her head as he soaked in the moment...and this woman. The delicate perfume he'd been smelling all night filled his senses in the most incredible way.

Hints of vanilla and berries combined with a sweetness he could only describe as Avery. The intoxicating fragrance burning a permanent place in his memory as his new favorite scent.

Of their own accord, his arms pulled her closer to him. There was no way she could miss the hard bulge pushing against the crotch of his dress pants. But if it bothered her, she didn't show it.

It wasn't like he could control it. His body knew what it wanted, and the woman in his arms was it.

Lifting his head, Garrett looked down at her. She looked up at him. Time stopped, and everyone around them vanished as he leaned down and pressed his lips to hers.

Avery lifted on her tiptoes as they worked together to deepen the kiss. Her lower body meeting with his, igniting a spark of need that raced through every nerve ending.

They were moving fast. He knew this, yet he couldn't make himself stop.

I never want to stop.

Praying he hadn't misread the signals she'd been sending all night, Garrett pulled away just enough to ask, "You wanna get out of here?"

He held his breath as he waited for her answer.

With a tilted chin and eyes that stared into his soul, Avery parted her swollen lips and whispered, "Yes."

CHAPTER 8

"Is everything done?" Sal looked to his cousin for the answer.

Marcus nodded. "Almost. There are just a few more provisions we need to take care of, but nothing major. When that ship docks in two days, we will be ready."

We'd better be fucking ready.

Sal's ability to continue breathing depended on this job going smoothly. So did everyone else's who'd agreed to help him.

It was a crazy plan, he knew. One he still couldn't believe Emilio had agreed to. But it was all he had.

And if he wanted to stay alive, things had to go off without a hitch.

"What's the final count?"

"Twenty," Marcus relayed the number of tourists signed up for the excursion. "Eleven men, nine women."

"Any potential sales?"

"One. *Maybe* two, depending on how she looks. Both American, ages fifteen and forty."

Not bad, considering they would be bonus money.

"Good." Sal nodded. "Everyone familiar with the plan?"

Marcus groaned. "We've only gone over it a thousand times."

"And we'll keep going over it until I feel comfortable with its execution."

"Fine." The other man blew out a frustrated breath. "We ambush the buggies, force the group into the three trucks, and transport them to the warehouse."

"After that?"

"We split up the men between three cells and separate the two potential sales from the group."

"And they'll go..." Sal tested his cousin's knowledge of the plan.

"Into one of the holding cells at the far end until the ransom's been made," Marcus bit out sharply. "I know the plan, Salvador. We all do. So do us all a favor and try to relax, yeah?"

He couldn't relax. Not with so much riding on this job.

"Emilio won't give us another chance, Marcus," he reminded the other man. "We fuck this up; we're dead."

"I know." Marcus put a hand on Sal's shoulder and squeezed. "But we're not going to fuck this up. We're going to take the hostages, get their money, dispose of them, and sell the other three. And then you and I will use our cuts to finally get the hell out of here. It'll be a fresh start for both of us."

"A fresh start." Sal stared back at his cousin who seemed confident with their plan.

Maybe if he said it enough, he'd start to believe it.

AVERY'S HEART raced faster than she could ever remember as she waited for Garrett to unlock his door. With a swipe of his plastic keycard, the electronic system beeped, indicating the locks had disengaged, and they were free to enter.

Once you walk into that room, there's no going back.

Garrett opened the door and moved to the side, his eyes burning into hers as he waited for her to decide.

Avery stepped into the room.

"Sorry for the mess." His deep voice vibrated through her system as he closed the door behind them. "I wasn't planning on bringing anyone back here."

Her lips curled slightly. Knowing he hadn't assumed she'd be spending the night with him—or that any *other* woman would be coming into his private room—pleased her.

"It's fine." Avery stepped further into the room. "My room isn't much better, but we're on vacation, so I figure being a little messy is allowed. I mean, it's not like there's anyone around to hound us about our housekeeping skills, and—"

"Avery."

Her next words were caught in her throat. It wasn't the first time Garrett had said her name. But it was the first time he'd said it *that* way.

So deep and sensual. Sexually charged and filled with promises of things to come.

With her back still to him, she opened her mouth to respond, but nothing came out. Licking her suddenly dry lips, she swallowed against the ball of nerves that had worked its way from the pit of her stomach and into the base of her throat.

"Look at me."

The order was soft, almost gentle in its request.

Turning slowly, she spun on the smooth balls of her stilettos. The sound of her dress brushing against the wall broke through the quiet space, but it was her nervous heartbeat that filled her ears in an almost deafening way.

It's just sex, Aves. Fun, casual sex between two consenting adults.

Listening to her inner voice, Avery turned and faced Garrett fully. Her focus remaining glued to the black tie and pristine white shirt covering the broad chest before her.

"Sweetheart, look at me."

Her eyes lifted to meet his.

"Nothing happens that you don't want." Even in the shadows, his sincerity was clear to see. "If you're not comfortable, we can leave this room right now and find something else to do. Or we can say goodnight and go our separate ways."

Is that what she wanted? To go back to her room...alone?

"No." Avery shook her head. "I don't want to say goodnight."

Garrett's Adam's apple bobbed with an audible swallow. "You sure?"

"Yes."

The second the word fell from her lips, Avery realized it was the truth.

She felt the decision to stay deep inside her bones. This wasn't just what she wanted. It was what she *needed*.

Setting her trepidation free, Avery closed the short distance between them. The toes of her shoes met his, the palms of her hands resting on his chest.

She could feel his heart racing to the same forceful rhythm of her own. She smiled, relieved from the knowledge that this strong, gorgeous man was as affected by the moment as she was.

Garrett's warm hands fell onto her bare shoulders. His thumbs brushed along her skin, the gentle caress creating an intense current that rolled throughout her entire system, ending only when it reached the tips of her toes.

Once again, Avery was reminded of an electrical storm.

The kind that filled the night sky with sharp, jagged streaks of white. Bolts of lightning that were beautiful to watch but could be deadly if you got too close.

He won't hurt you.

Another truth Avery felt to her bones. Garrett would never intentionally hurt her.

But as his heated blue gaze remained locked with hers, she also realized that, intentional or not, this man had the power to break her.

"Avery," he whispered her name as though it were a prayer. Still, he made no move to take things further.

He's giving me the control.

And with that knowledge, she fell a little bit in love.

It was crazy and irrational, but she didn't bother to fight it. Because no matter how quickly things between them had moved, or how many times she told herself this was just a casual fling, Garrett had already marked her in ways no other man had.

With her body aching for his touch, Avery rose to her tiptoes and brought her mouth to his. Tracing his bottom lip with the tip of her tongue, she pulled the sensitive skin between her teeth and gave a gentle tug.

Garrett's fingers dug into the skin covering her shoulders and a low, rolling groan bubbled up from somewhere deep inside his throat.

He likes that. Good to know.

He moved his hands down, those same fingers gripping her hips in a way that screamed possession. The energy in the room changed, a powerful current filling the air around them.

It was the only warning she had.

Growling her name, Garrett lifted her up and crushed his mouth to hers. On reflex, Avery wrapped her legs around him. Linking her hands behind his neck, she held on tight. Never wanting to let go.

Turning, he pinned her up against the wall. Her head may have bounced a little, but she was too busy feasting on his lips and tongue to notice.

Garrett slid his hands lower. Long, calloused fingers slipped beneath her dress. Gripping the low curves of her ass as she ground her aching sex against his impressive bulge.

With a guttural moan, he thrust his pelvis forward. Closing her eyes, Avery threw her head back, the friction from his body rubbing against hers with a teasing promise of things to come, but it wasn't enough.

A raw, insatiable hunger consumed them both. Clawing

its way to the surface in search of something…*anything* to ease their overwhelming primal need.

"God, I want you." Garrett spoke between kisses. "Never wanted…anything…more."

His arousing words spurred Avery on. Sliding her hands upward, she raked her fingers through his hair. Fisting what she could grab hold of and pulling her mouth free.

"I want you, too." She kissed him wildly. "Please, Garrett. Now."

Even in the shadows, she could see his pupils expanding. The blues surrounding them becoming dark with the same blinding heat scorching the deepest parts of her soul.

Keeping his grip firm, he lifted her from the wall and walked the short distance to the bed. His mouth continued to work hers, even as he slid her down the length of his hard body and back onto her feet.

Avery wanted to take her time. To go slow and savor every breathtaking, mouthwatering second with him. But she couldn't make herself stop. Neither could he.

Already on the edge, she and Garrett began undressing each other in a frenzy. His jacket. Her hair clip. His shirt and tie. Her dress.

In less than a minute, he was shirtless, and she was standing before him in nothing but a black, lacy thong and high heels.

"Christ Almighty." Garrett's heated gaze fell onto her breasts.

Avery knew exactly what he was seeing.

Flushed skin. A heaving chest. Thick, dark hair falling past her shoulders, stopping just shy of her dusty pink nipples. Hard, aching nubs begging for his touch.

Only his touch. Only Garrett.

The pointed buds gave away the desire she felt for him. And as she released his belt and slid his pants over his narrow hips and lower, Avery rejoiced in the unmistakable proof that he wanted her just as badly.

"Need to taste you."

Garrett leaned in, cupping one of the mounds with a gentle fist while pulling the sensitive peak of the other between his lips.

She cried out, her hands flying to his biceps to keep herself from falling as he sucked and teased. Arching her back, Avery moved her hands into his hair, her nails scraping against his scalp with every incredible flick of his tongue.

"Oh, God, Garrett," she rasped.

Avery was losing control, and she didn't care. No one had ever made her feel so alive. So free.

Which seemed impossible given they'd only known each other a couple of days.

She knew nothing about his past with women, other than what he'd shared about his job keeping him too busy to date or settle down.

He may get what he wants tonight and move on to another prospect tomorrow. For some reason, however, Avery didn't believe that would be the case.

There was a lot—a *lot*—she didn't know about this man. But her gut said he wasn't the kind of guy to get his rocks off and run. Or maybe he was, and she was simply too caught up in the moment to see it.

Either way, for the first time in her life, Avery realized she didn't care. Because this...this moment *right* here... It was all that mattered.

Tonight wasn't about their pasts or their future. Or the fact that they barely knew each other. It was about the here and now and submersing themselves into the pleasure they were both about to experience.

Speaking of pleasure...

Avery reached between them, her fingertips slipping into the stretchy elastic band at the top of his boxers. She started to push them down so she could—

"Wait." Garrett covered her hand with his.

Her heart kicked against her ribs, and her mind began to race with questions.

Why was he stopping? Had he changed his mind? Was he going to tell her how this was all a big mistake and politely ask her to leave?

Oh, God. Just the idea of having to put her dress back on and walk out with her tail between her legs was mortifying, to say the least.

But if that's what was happening right now, it was better to rip the band-aid off and deal with it head-on.

Lifting her chin, Avery straightened her shoulders and braced herself for the rejection she feared was coming.

"Do you want to stop?" she asked him point blank.

"Hell no." Garrett frowned. "Do you?"

"No!" Avery blurted much too loudly. "But you—"

"Need to get a condom."

She blinked as his words sank in.

Protection. Of course. He wasn't stopping because he'd changed his mind. They needed *protection.*

"Condom," she repeated the word. "Right. Of course."

The lines on his forehead smoothed as his lips turned upward. Sliding a palm along the side of her face, Garrett brushed his thumb along the hot skin covering her cheek.

And when he looked into her eyes, Avery could've sworn he saw...everything.

"I want you, Avery," he rumbled in a sweet, reassuring way. "More than I've ever wanted anything."

Every lingering doubt she may have had vanished with that one, heart stopping confession.

"Make love to me, Garrett." She told him in no uncertain terms what *she* wanted. "Please."

"Ah, baby." He feathered his lips against hers. "There's nothing else in the world I'd rather do."

Turning, he walked over to the small bedside table and opened the top drawer. Avery tried to control her face, but he must've caught a glimpse because he started to explain.

"These aren't mine." He held up the brand-new box of condoms. "I mean, they are, but I didn't buy them."

Understanding struck. "Colt?"

Garrett nodded with a smirk. "He brought them by earlier...as a *joke*...when I was getting ready for dinner."

"Guess we got the last laugh, after all."

Smile growing, Garrett ripped the box open and pulled out a strip of foil packets. Tearing one of the squares free, he dropped the box onto the nightstand and the unopened packet onto the mattress.

And then he reached for her.

"Come here." He grabbed her hips and pulled her body flush with his.

The feel of her bare chest against his left her lungs breathless and her knees weak.

"I've wanted to do this since the moment I first laid eyes on you," he told her softly.

Avery expected him to kiss her again. Or maybe

remove her panties and shoes. Instead, he slowly began combing his fingers through her hair.

"So soft," he whispered. "So beautiful."

When he looked at her that way, Avery *felt* as though she was beautiful.

"Garrett…"

He pressed his lips to hers, taking his sweet, sweet time as he coaxed her mouth open and let himself inside. They stood like that, tasting one another at a slow, unhurried pace.

Eventually, Garrett let his hands drift lower. First stopping to caress her firm breasts before rolling their distended buds between his forefingers and thumbs.

Tiny mewling sounds escaped with heaving breaths, filling the room as he taunted and teased. Goosebumps appeared in his wake as he traced down along her sides, stopping when they reached the lacey waistband of her barely-there panties.

Avery shivered with anticipation as he slid one of his hands beneath the lace. Her breath hitched, and…*God.*

He'd barely touched her there, and already she could feel her insides quivering with her impending release. Cupping her mound, Garrett moaned with a wild hunger that Avery still couldn't believe was all for her.

She wasn't the type of woman men moaned for. They didn't pick her up and press her against a wall in a frenzy of passion and raw, wanton need.

Yet for reasons she may never understand, this man had done those things and more.

I want you.

She believed him.

Not only because he'd said them, but because she could *see* it in the way he was looking at her now. And earlier when he'd lifted her up and pressed her against the wall, his need had poured over them both in waves.

But most importantly, Avery had felt this man's desire for her when she'd placed her hand over his heart. The organ's forceful, rhythmic beating had told her everything she needed to know.

I want you.

Regardless of where this thing between them was headed, Avery knew she'd cherish those words for the rest of her life.

Garrett slid a finger along her bare slit, sending a jolt of pleasure rushing through her when he brushed against her swollen clit.

"Garrett," she moaned his name again.

He slid the finger lower, gathering her juices before rising back up to rub the tiny bundle of nerves.

Avery threw her head back, pleasure racing through her with every calculated, torturous touch. She wasn't going to last, but that didn't stop her from tilting her hips forward, her body begging him without words to give her the release it so desperately craved.

"I'm going to make you come." The statement low and filled with warning as his fingers continued playing her body in the most masterful of ways.

He slid a finger inside. First one and then another.

Avery cried out as he stretched her most intimate muscles. Muscles that had long been neglected.

"Please," she *did* beg him then.

With one hand on her hip to keep her steady, Garrett

began pumping his fingers in and out of her welcoming body at a gloriously slow pace.

In and out. In and out. In and out.

Avery's breathing picked up pace. Her heart fluttered and flipped inside her chest, and her legs shook to the point she thought she'd collapse.

And still, he didn't stop.

Garrett continued working her with his hand, changing the pace from slow to *God, yes!* And just when she thought she'd die if she didn't climax, he pulled his fingers free.

"Wha—" She started to protest.

Truth be told, she damn near *cried* from the sudden void he'd created.

But then he grabbed one side of the thin lace covering her, and yanked it with both hands. The lace snapped, and Avery gasped.

Okay, that was seriously hot.

He did the same thing with the other side, tossing the ruined panties somewhere behind him. Avery had no idea where they landed, and she didn't care.

Because Garrett had dropped to his knees in front of her.

"What are you—"

"Shh…" He wrapped his fingers around her left ankle.

"There's a little clasp on the side. I can take them off for you, if you can't get it."

Not that he was inept or incapable. But those tiny clasps could be a pain in the ass to get loose sometimes, and…

"I've dreamed about this." He began running his hand up the length of her calf. "You in nothing but these."

"Y-you have?" Avery swallowed against a sudden onslaught of nerves.

"Mmm hmm." He nodded, his eyes never leaving her exposed sex. She should be embarrassed, given that the position he was in put his face right...well...*there*.

But when he brought his gaze to hers as his hand continued moving higher, her inhibitions vanished, and she spread her legs a little wider.

Pleased by this, Garrett smiled as he stared at her most private of parts. He reached up, tracing her slit again before burying two fingers deep inside.

A tortured sound escaped her throat, and Avery reached down and fisted his hair to keep from falling. After several more mind-numbing thrusts, Garrett used his free hand to lift her right ankle, draping her leg over his shoulder and bringing himself closer.

"You don't have to—"

He put his mouth on her, and the world exploded. Crying out, Avery closed her eyes and let herself go.

Garrett's hot, wet tongue licked and lathed as his fingers moved in and out of her molten core. Sounds of her arousal filled the room, but she was too far gone to be embarrassed or even care.

Avery fisted his hair to the point she knew it had to sting. He moaned against her sex, the vibrations combined with his fingers and tongue bringing her closer and closer to that glorious edge.

"I'm close." She panted. "So...close."

Garrett's hand moved faster, his fingers pumping in and out of her at a more forceful rate. And his tongue? His talented, magnificent tongue worked her swollen clit with utter perfection.

"Oh, God," she moaned. "Don't stop. Please… don't…stop!"

He didn't stop. Instead, his hand moved harder. Faster.

Avery's inner muscles quivered with her impending climax. Garrett put her clit between his lips, and with the perfect amount of pleasure he began to suck.

A second later, Avery imploded.

CHAPTER 9

"Garrett!"

His name echoed off the surrounding walls as Avery's orgasm hit with a vengeance.

Garrett didn't immediately stop or pull away. He continued working her body, drawing out every last ounce of pleasure he could.

He wanted to make tonight so good for her she'd forget about every other man from her past. When Avery thought about pleasure, he wanted it to be his face she saw.

I don't want her to forget me.

Because he sure as hell would never forget her.

"Ohmygod." Avery panted breathlessly. "That was….I can't even…it was…"

"The most beautiful thing I've ever seen." Garrett carefully lowered her leg back down and rose to his feet.

The comment wasn't lip service—no pun intended. It was hands down, the absolute truth.

Sure, he'd had other women. But none had ever reacted to his touch the way Avery had. Like every brush

149

of his hand set her on fire, and damn. What a sight that was to see.

Reaching for his boxers, Garrett pushed them down and kicked them aside. Avery's sharp intake of air as his cock sprang free made his lips curl.

He'd always been on the larger size but had never been arrogant about it like some guys could be. His generous length and size were all God's doing, not his.

Even so, it didn't hurt to see the woman of his dreams staring at him as if he were her favorite dessert.

Speaking of desserts…

Garrett licked his lips, savoring the sweet, musky taste that was all Avery.

Tasting her had been heaven, but feeling her come unglued around him? That made him feel like the king of the fucking world.

She lifted her gaze to his, staring back at him with heavy-lidded eyes and a sated smile. Struck with a sense of peace and satisfaction he'd never experienced before, Garrett realized they could stop right now—with his cock feeling as if it would explode if it didn't get inside her— and he'd still be a lucky bastard.

Lucky for him, they didn't stop.

Avery reached for him, her delicate fingers touching him for the first time, and *fuuuck*. Garrett was lost.

His sharp breath battled with the muted sound of the ship breaking through the ocean's waves. The ship listed slightly, but not enough to knock them off balance.

What *did* damn near drop him to his knees was when Avery began moving her fist up and down, stroking him with perfection.

A throaty moan formed in his throat. Garrett closed his

eyes—or maybe they rolled in the back of his head, he wasn't sure—and let her take charge.

"You're so big," she whispered in awe. "I'm not very experienced, and I've never seen...I mean, I don't know if it's going to..."

Ah, hell.

"We'll fit, sweetheart." He cupped his hand over hers. "But you keep doing that and I won't get the chance to prove it to you."

With a chuckle, Avery's shoulders relaxed, and her eyes lifted back to his. She didn't say anything, but with that one, heart stopping look, he knew she was ready.

"Lay back on the bed."

She did as he asked. "You sure you don't want me to take my shoes off, first? They might be a little...pokey."

Pokey?

Garrett smiled and shook his head. God, he loved this woman.

Woah. Not love. It's way, way *too soon for that.*

Or was it?

He'd heard women use the term 'insta-love' before, but only when referring to sappy romance novels or chick flicks. This was real life with *real* emotions.

But the problem was he couldn't quite name what those emotions were because he'd never felt like this before. Not about anyone. And he hadn't even gotten inside her yet.

"Yet "being the operative word.

Pushing all the rest aside, Garrett looked down at the woman lying before him...and lost his ability to breathe.

Moonlight shone through his balcony window, lighting her up like an angel. With her hair splayed out around her, Avery stared up at him with heady desire.

Letting one leg fall to the side, she offered herself to him in the most precious of ways.

Garrett reached for the unopened condom, using his teeth to rip open the small, foil packet. He held back a wince as he rolled the protection over his throbbing erection, the skin there stretched to its limit by a hunger only this woman had ever created.

"I'm on the pill," Avery blurted from where she lay. "Mainly to regulate things, because I don't really date much. And it's been almost two years since I've had sex, so I know I'm clean." She swallowed hard. "I'm only telling you all this, so you'd know we're doubly protected. I mean, I know we still need to use the condom for other reasons, just to be safe. But I just thought you should know all that before we...you know."

"Have sex?" His lips twitched.

Her hair swished along the comforter as she bit her bottom lip and nodded.

She's nervous.

Her adorable rambling was a dead giveaway to that fact. As for the other...

"That's good to know." Garrett climbed onto the bed beside her. "And just so you're aware, I'm clean, and...it's been a long time for me, too."

"Really?" This seemed to shock her.

Tucking some hair behind her ear, he nodded. "Remember when I told you my work keeps me busy? It does, but that's not the only reason I haven't been with a woman in a long time."

"What's the other reason?"

"I got tired of doing the whole casual thing. Plus, this last job I went on…" *Careful, now.* "It didn't go as planned. When I finally got back home, I realized how empty my apartment felt, and how badly I wished someone had been there to welcome me home."

Garrett knew he sounded cheesy as hell, but it was the wholehearted truth.

He still didn't know what made that op so different from any others he'd been on, but *something* inside him had changed. It was the whole reason he'd agreed to go on this trip with Colt in the first place.

That first week back, all Garrett had felt was anger and confusion. But once he got here and forced himself to relax, he realized he'd been given a gift.

The gift of clarity.

Though it took him a minute, he truly understood the importance of balance in one's life.

Work. Family. Fun.

Love.

There was a place for it all if he'd open himself up to it. And the beautiful woman lying next to him made him want that…and more.

The beautiful woman next to you is waiting for you to do something other than talk.

Leaning forward, Garrett put his hand on the curve of Avery's hip and pressed his lips to hers. "I want to take my time and go slow." She deserved slow. "But this first time—"

"I don't want slow, Garrett." She reached between them and cupped his balls. "I just want you."

He was on her before he'd taken his next breath.

Bodies flush, the feel of being head-to-toe, skin on skin

sent a shot of need spiking through his veins. With his weight balanced on his forearms, he felt Avery's legs open wide.

He settled himself between them, his weeping tip positioned against her molten core.

Even through the condom's protective barrier, he could feel how fucking drenched she was. The knowledge that it was all because of him...*for* him...had Garrett's hips pushing forward before he even realized he was moving.

Avery closed her eyes, moaning as his swollen crest breached her sensitive flesh. Garret joined her, releasing a guttural sound of pleasure as he worked his way inside, inch by torturous inch.

Jesus, she was tight, and...*Holy God*...she felt so very good.

"You okay?" He somehow managed to formulate the words.

He wasn't even fully seated yet, and already being with her overshadowed all his previous sexual experiences.

Garrett waited, watching closely for her response. The last thing he wanted was to hurt her, but he was big and was going to need to stretch her body a little more to accommodate his size.

"I'm good," Avery assured him. "But I'll be even better once you start moving again."

With a chuckle, Garrett took that as the green light. In one, powerful thrust he broke through her body's resistance and pushed himself to the hilt.

Mine.

The possessive word flashed through his mind the second he took her. And when Avery tightened her grip and dug those sharp, sexy as fuck heels against his bare ass, Garrett knew that's exactly what she was.

In the span of a few days, Avery Webb had tunneled her way into his heart. And now, as their bodies moved together in perfect unison, he wanted to hold on tight and never let her go.

I'm never letting go.

Ignoring the meaning behind his silent declaration, Garrett continued thrusting his hips forward and back, moving his rock-hard shaft in and out of her hot, wet heat.

Despite his earlier admission, he started out slow. Or at least he *tried* to. But she felt so good, and he was already on the edge, his slow, steady pace didn't last long.

Jesus, he was lost. Drunk from her touch and the way her body felt as it pulled him back in.

The scent of coconuts and vanilla mixed with lust and need, and it was all Garrett could do not to say *fuck it* and just let go.

She needs to come again.

Granted, he'd already brought her to climax once, and he wasn't sure if she would be able to get there again. But he was damn sure going to try.

Reaching between them, he shifted positions, tilting her hips up at more of an angle so he'd have better access. He found her clit swollen and ready.

A strangled cry penetrated the walls, Avery's pelvis shooting off the mattress when he began rubbing it in small, tight circles.

A telltale tingling spread across his lower back. Garrett felt his balls tighten, his climax building at an unforgiving pace.

Determined to get her there a second time, he

continued giving her clit the attention it craved. He kept his thrusts steady, his body moving with purpose while forcing his mind to focus.

He wanted to remember everything about this moment.

The room. The way the ocean sounded as they traversed across the open sea.

Most importantly, Garrett wanted to remember everything about how Avery looked as he brought her to climax again.

Every. Fucking. Detail.

The way her brows pushed inward like she was focused on his every move. The tiny 'O' her ruby lips formed, allowing her accelerated breaths to move in and out of her overworked lungs.

His gaze lowered to her breasts, their rhythmic sway mesmerizing as they moved back and forth the with each new thrust.

"Please," Avery pleaded with him. Her inner muscles began rippling around him.

Ah, fuck.

"I've got you, sweetheart." He moved faster, pushing his cock in and out with more force than before.

Garrett could feel his climax racing through him. He needed to get her there...now.

"Come for me, Avery." He rubbed her clit faster. "Can't...hold...back..."

"Garrett!"

Avery's body became a vise as it clamped down on his dick. A rush of hot liquid rushed around him, her muscles contracting around him as her orgasm rolled through her.

"Oh, fuck." He gave a single, hard thrust. "Ah, God." Another thrust. "Avery!"

An explosion of pleasure erupted within him. His cock pulsed forcefully as he came harder and longer than he could ever remember.

Not wanting to bring things to an abrupt halt, Garrett continued sliding in and out of her slick heat until he felt her sated body relaxing beneath his.

Reaching between them, he gripped the condom as he reluctantly pulled himself free. Falling onto his back, Garrett closed his eyes and focused on their breathing as they gave themselves a moment to recover.

"Holy shit." His heart was still kicking the hell out of his ribs.

"I was about to say the same thing." Avery turned onto her side to face him. "I had no idea it could be like that."

The comment pissed Garrett off. Not at her, but at the bastards before him who'd clearly done a shit job at giving this woman the pleasure she deserved. But he'd be lying if he didn't say...

"Me neither."

Heavy lidded eyes lifted with her smile. "You don't have to say that on my account. I'm sure a guy like you has had a lot of women. Ones who've had a lot more experience than I have."

Garrett reached over and cupped her cheek. Praying she could see the truth in his eyes, he told her, "Our pasts don't have a place here, sweetheart. Because they're just that...the past. But for the record, that was the best, most amazing experience of my existence. And as soon as I recover, I'd love to do it again."

Tonight. Tomorrow. Next week. Next year.

Her round eyes widened slightly, and her smile grew.

Leaning toward him, Avery pressed her lips to his and whispered, "Me, too."

And they did.

After sharing a late-night pizza to renourish their depleted bodies, they'd gone back to his room for a mind blowing, toe-curling round two. Minutes later and he was here. In the tiny bathroom taking care of his second condom of the night.

Garrett caught a glimpse of himself in the mirror and blinked. Staring back at him was a man he barely recognized. One who was relaxed and...happy.

Because of her.

Back in the day, he was almost as happy and carefree as Colt. But somewhere between his time with the Army and the missions he'd done with Tac-Ops, Garrett had changed.

Killing, nearly being killed... Eventually, that shit took a toll on you.

Not that he regretted the choices he'd made. Not even a little bit. The fact was evil existed, and it needed to be stopped. And if no one signed up for the job, who knew how many innocent lives would be lost.

So no, he felt no remorse for the sacrifices he'd made up to this point. But he'd also come to realize he didn't have to keep making them. Not all of them, anyway.

The woman lying in his bed was proof of that.

So, why are you still in here when she's out there?

Tossing the used washrag onto the floor with his other dirty towel, Garrett opened the door and walked back into the room. He started to say something to Avery but stopped himself short when he saw her.

On her side with her arms tucked beneath her chin, the

gorgeous woman's eyes were closed, and her sheet-covered chest was rising and falling at a slow, even pace.

Warmth spread across his chest, and a smile formed on his face as he stepped around the foot of the bed to the other side.

Careful not to wake her, Garrett slid under the covers behind her before reaching an arm around her waist and tucking her sleeping form against him. When he kissed the top of her tousled hair, she mumbled something he couldn't understand, which made him smile even more.

"Sleep tight, sweetheart." He pressed his lips to her temple before settling down onto his own pillow.

For the next several minutes, Garrett remained awake. Lying in the silence as the room swayed back and forth with ocean's growing waves.

He felt more content than he had in...he couldn't remember how long. But still, his mind wouldn't let him rest.

Thoughts of a future he wanted so badly he could *taste* it invaded his mind, and all he could think was...

I can't lose her.

Part of him believed Avery would understand when he explained about his job and why he hadn't been completely honest about everything. After all, being a financial software designer, she had to have a sensible, logical thought process. Didn't she?

Another part of him—a part he hadn't even realized existed until now—was terrified she'd see his deception as a betrayal and decide she never wanted to see him again.

After the way her sister's ex had lied to her, Garrett couldn't help but worry Avery would lump him in the same category the second he told her the truth.

You have to tell her.

Garrett released a quiet sigh. He would tell her. Soon. But for now, he was going to relish in the fact that she was here, in his bed.

Everything else could wait.

CHAPTER 10

Two days later…

"WHAT THE HELL do you mean, you're not going?"

Avery woke to the sound of Garrett's hushed voice coming from the door.

Stretching her legs, she tested her muscles, smiling at their delicious soreness. Memories from the last two nights flashed through her sleepy mind, and Avery closed her eyes as she replayed every amazing, tantalizing frame.

Garrett wasn't just a sweet, caring man who put her needs before his own. He was a sexual god. One who, in two short days, knew more about her body than she did.

"Dude, these waves are kicking my ass." Colt's low voice joined Garrett's. "I haven't felt this sick since that time in the eighth grade when everybody in my class got the flu."

Her intention wasn't to eavesdrop, but the room was small, and she was *right* there. It wasn't like she could really help it. But rather than make the situation awkward for all involved, she remained where she was, deciding she needed a few more minutes before becoming vertical.

"You don't have the flu," Garrett responded. "You're seasick."

Though she couldn't see the two men from where she lay, Avery didn't miss the humorous lift in Garrett's voice. Neither did Colt.

"Glad you think this is funny, asshole," he growled. "I was hugging the damn toilet the entire damn night."

"I'm sorry. You're right. It's not funny." Garrett was clearly trying not to laugh. "You try that patch they gave you down in medical yesterday?"

The ship had hit rough waters the night before last, and they grew even rougher yesterday afternoon. When Garrett and Colt returned from their snorkeling and stingray excursion, they'd invited her to join them for dinner. Avery had noticed then that Colt wasn't a fan of the rough waters.

Lucky for her, motion sickness had never been an issue. As long as she walked with the tilt of the ship, rather than fighting it, she was fine. For Colt, however, this clearly hadn't helped.

"I tried the patch, tilting my head with the movement like I read online...I even forced myself to go up to the main deck to try to talk one of the pizza guys into finding me some fresh ginger. Nothing's working."

"We'll be docking soon." Garrett spoke up again. "Once you get back on dry land, I'm sure everything will even itself out."

"Even if that's true, my ass is beat. Seriously, G. I got like *maybe* two full hours of sleep. There's no way I'm up for a forty-minute hike, half a day in a river, and then a two-hour ride on a fucking rough as shit dune buggy. I'm sorry, man. My ass is staying in bed."

"I understand. Get some rest. Weather reports are showing smooth sailing for the remainder of the trip, so hopefully you'll start feeling better soon."

"Thanks," Colt muttered. "Sorry to ditch you like this. Hey, maybe Avery can take my ticket and go with you. I'm sure if you explain the situation, they'll let her take my spot."

"Yeah, maybe. I'll see if she's interested."

Excitement filtered through Avery's lazy bones. They were talking about the excursion she'd read about the night she booked the cruise. The one with the waterfalls.

Heck yeah, I'm interested!

When she'd first read about the adrenaline adventure, Avery didn't believe she was up for something so daring. But now, she was bursting with excitement over the possibility.

Things had definitely changed these past few days. As much as she hated to admit it, Avery knew her sister had been right.

Since boarding the ship, she hadn't merely come out of her shell…she'd practically shattered the damn thing.

And it wasn't all because of Garrett, either. Though he certainly helped. The list Alex had snuck into her purse—that was almost completely crossed off—helped, too.

Stepping out of her comfort zone and experiencing new things was still a bit scary, but also invigorating. And somewhere within the last few days, Avery had gone from being the type of person to shy away from change and spontaneity to a woman who chased it.

Yesterday, while Garrett and Coop hung out with the

stingrays—*yikes*—Avery had taken her time exploring the island of Grand Turk. She'd picked up a souvenir globe for Alex, a new hat and t-shirt for herself, and even visited with one of the locals for a few minutes.

But as enjoyable as the day had been, she'd often found herself wishing Garrett was with her. Things were just... *better* when he was there.

"Probably best if she goes with you, anyway." Colt's odd comment caught her attention once more.

"Why do you say that?"

"Dude, I saw how distracted you were while we were out and about yesterday."

He hadn't been distracted. Had he?

Avery's ears perked up as Garrett scoffed. "I wasn't distracted."

"The fuck you weren't." There was no heat in Colt's accusation. "It's all good, though. I get it."

There was a slight pause before Garrett relented. "Sorry, man. I really did have fun hanging out with you."

"I know you did, bro. And there's nothing to be sorry for. I like Avery. She's good for you. Seriously. I haven't seen you this happy since...I don't know when."

A smile spread across Avery's sleepy face and warmth filled her chest.

"I like her, too," Garrett confessed. "A lot."

Her heart did a little flip. Garrett's sweet, attentive demeanor and insatiable appetite these last two days had been a dead giveaway to his interest in her, but it was still nice to hear him say the words aloud.

"Think you'll keep seeing her after we get home?"

Beneath the crisp sheets, Avery's heart thumped wildly as she waited to hear his answer.

"We'll have to work some things out as far as my schedule and all that. But I hope so."

Yes!

Her inner girlie girl did a little happy dance. After their second round of sex last night, Avery had been wondering the same thing—whether or not this thing between them would continue on past their disembarking in a couple of days.

She'd wanted to bring it up but chickened out. Hope bloomed inside her hearing Garrett confirm his intentions for the two of them.

"Glad to hear it." Colt clearly approved. "Now if you'll excuse me, I'm pretty sure I need to throw up again. Have fun today. And try not to wreck the buggy."

"No promises," Garret teased his brother. "I don't know what the service will be like, but you need anything, call the excursion company. Number's in the email they sent. I'm sure they'll be able to track me down."

"I'll be fine. Nothing a little sleep and a solid, stable bed won't cure."

Avery heard Garrett's sexy rumble of laughter before, "We'll check on you when we get back."

"Sounds good, man. See ya later."

The door clicked shut, and she couldn't bring herself to close her eyes and pretend she was still asleep.

When Garrett appeared from the room's small entry-way, he caught sight of her stare almost immediately.

"Morning." His oh-so-talented lips curved.

"Morning." She held the sheet to her chest and shifted into a sitting position.

Walking over to her, Garrett leaned down, brushed

some wayward hair from her face, and kissed her softly. "Sleep well?"

"I did." She kissed him back. "Better than Colt, apparently."

"You heard?"

Avery nodded. "Poor guy."

"Yeah. He looked pretty green." Sitting on the mattress beside her, Garrett trapped her with an arm across her blanketed legs. Keeping his weight propped up with one hand, he raised his other to her face, brushing the back of his knuckles across her cheek. "You're so beautiful in the morning."

An unladylike snort before she could stop it. "You're delusional."

"I'm serious." He stared back at her in a way that made her believe him.

As ridiculous as it was, given the things they'd done to each other the past two nights, Avery felt herself start to blush. "Thank you."

Garrett's gaze held hers a moment longer before he asked, "So, what do you say? Feel like taking a forty-minute hike, spending half the day in a river, and then trekking through the countryside on a bumpy as shit ride?"

Laughing at the way he'd repeated Colt's description almost verbatim, Avery said, "Actually, I'd love to."

"Yeah?"

She nodded. "Believe it or not, I looked at that exact same excursion on the cruise line's website the night I bought my ticket. I thought it looked amazing, but I wasn't sure how the cruise was going to go, let alone an adventure like that. So, I decided not to book it."

"And how do you think the cruise is going so far?"

In a bold move, Avery let the sheet fall to her waist as she reached her arms around him and grinned. "So far, so good. What about you?"

Garrett's pupils grew with heat. He started to reach for her exposed breasts, his lips parting to speak, when a blaring announcement interrupted the moment.

"Attention passengers! Martin here!" Their jubilant cruise director came through the room's speakers. "We have arrived at Amber Cove, the Caribbean's newest port of call. Whether it be shopping, swimming, enjoying authentic Dominican cuisine, or more, the village offers plenty to do for all. If you have purchased one of the port's excursion packages, we suggest you depart the ship within the hour, so you don't miss out on the opportunity of a lifetime."

Groaning dramatically, Garrett dropped his hand and planted a chaste kiss on her forehead. "Guess that's us." He rose to his feet. "If you're sure you want to, that is. If not, we can skip it and find something else to do."

As much as Avery loved the fact that he was willing to change his plans for her, she also didn't want him making everything all about her.

"Oh, no. We're going on that adventure." She threw the sheet off and started getting dressed. With the clothes from last night back in place, Avery rose to her tiptoes and kissed him on the lips. "Give me twenty minutes to take a quick shower and change, and then I'll be ready to go."

"Yes, ma'am," Garrett drawled. "I'll meet you at your room."

Waiving over her shoulder, she opened the door and hollered, "See you in a few!"

Forty-five minutes later, excitement swirled in her

belly as she and Garrett boarded the bus that would take them to their excursion sight.

At first, their view looked much like the previous islands they'd visited. Palm trees blowing with the morning breeze. People bustling around. Small shops that weren't commercial, but rather authentic.

But as the bus made its way past the main tourist area and deeper into the tropical jungle of the Dominican Puerto Plata—the province where Amber Cove was located—Avery was struck with a sudden sense of sadness.

Watching the scenery pass them by, there was a noticeable change in the community vibe.

Trash littered the sides of the road. Cattle with visible ribs grazed on the sparse vegetation in the unimpressive fields. And houses that were little more than shacks stood side by side in yards made of little more than dirt.

Seeing this way of life made Avery realize just how much she took for granted in her own.

A handful of miles later, the bus turned onto a gravel road that dropped down in a steep decline. After breaking through a clearing of trees, they finally arrived at their destination.

"You ready?" Garrett gave her hand a light squeeze.

Avery turned to him and smiled. "Ready."

The hiking came first. Forty minutes—*all* uphill—turned into an hour and fifteen with two short breaks in between. Dressed in a one-piece swimsuit and water shoes, she—like everyone else in the group—carried a lifejacket and helmet for the water portion of the trip.

Thanks to the treadmill in her apartment, Avery kept herself in relatively decent shape. But the steep incline and uneven dirt path—not to mention the thick, humid air—made the long walk a bit challenging.

For her, anyway. Garrett, on the other hand, barely broke a freaking sweat.

With his breaths even and relaxed, the frustratingly sexy man looked as though he was out for a Sunday stroll rather than a grueling trek through a tropical jungle.

Showoff.

What felt like an eternity later, they finally made it to the river's entry spot. Avery blew out a breath, more than a little relieved...until she saw the bridge.

Made of wood that looked like it had seen better days, the bridge spanned fifteen feet across and twenty feet high. At least.

The portion of the small river running below it ran at a slow, calming pace. Avery had never been afraid of the water, but the ladder their guide was telling the group to climb down was utterly terrifying.

"Is there another way in?" She immediately began scanning the area for someplace closer to the water's edge. A nice sandy bank where she could just ease herself in.

Picking up on her fear, Garrett cursed beneath his breath and blocked her view of the bridge. With his hands resting gently on her shoulders, he tipped her chin upward, so she'd look only at him.

"You're going to be fine. I'll be with you the whole time."

But Avery was already shaking her head. "Garrett, I can't—"

"Yes, you can." His tone was confident and unwavering.

"No, I *really* don't think I can."

He was quiet for several seconds before asking, "Did you ever think you could take a cruise by yourself? Or sing karaoke on stage in front of a room full of strangers?"

"No, but that's not the same thing."

"Except it is." He stepped a bit closer. With his life-jacket and helmet dangling from one hand, he used the other to palm the side of her face in a loving caress. "You're stronger and more daring than you give yourself credit for. And if you need proof of that, all you have to do is look at us."

"Us?"

His blue gaze softened, his voice lowering so only she could hear. "You ever think you'd spend two incredible nights letting some strange man make you scream?"

Garrett's words sent a rush of heat crawling up her neck.

"You're not all that strange." A lame attempt to add humor to the situation.

One side of his kissable mouth curved. "Avery, you can do this." He spoke with a confidence she didn't feel.

She glanced over at the ladder and back to him. Opening her mouth—to say what, she wasn't sure—she closed it, saying nothing.

"Tell you what," Garrett spoke again. "If you truly don't want to do this, we'll turn around, and walk back the way we came. We'll just meet up with the group down at the dune buggies."

The offer made Avery's heart swell. "You'd do that?"

"As opposed to forcing you to do something you don't want to do?" He shot her an incredulous look. "Hell, yes."

His answer was instant and sincere. And it made her realize what she had to do.

"No." Straightening her spine, Avery took a step back and slid her lifejacket on. "I can do this." She buckled the preserver in place and secured the helmet to her head with its chin strap.

"Are you sure?" Garrett frowned. "I seriously don't mind if we—"

"I'm good." She looked up at him. "Besides, you said you'd be right there with me, right?"

He tipped his chin in a single nod. "I'll go down the ladder first. Be right behind you the entire way."

"Okay, then." Avery blew out a breath. "Let's do this."

With one final glance from those crystal blue eyes, he promised, "I won't let you fall."

And he didn't.

Having the patience of a saint, Garrett moved down the ladder slowly, keeping the pace she'd set for herself.

Rung by terrifying rung.

Sweat covered her palms and Avery's knees shook with the magnitude of a category five earthquake. But she didn't stop.

Finally reaching the bottom rung, she stepped down to join Garrett on the small wooden platform overlooking the river. Together, with her hand in his, they jumped the remaining five feet into the water.

Avery beamed as she bobbed up and down with the lifejacket's support. "I did it!"

"Yes, you did." Garrett pulled her close. In front of the others, he kissed her gently and said, "I'm proud of you."

She smiled wide. "I'm proud of me, too."

For most, that one, small feat wouldn't even register as a blip on their accomplishment scale. But for Avery, it almost felt like a defining moment.

The river was freezing, but she was having too much fun to care. Over the next hour and a half, she and Garrett —along with the others in the group—followed their guides as they made their way through the water to seven natural waterfalls on their way back to the base of the mountain.

As it turned out, the waterfalls were really natural water*slides*. Decades of the river's constant flow had smoothed and shaped the rocks, making it possible for a person to slide down them with ease, and then continue on with the river's path.

Every slide they came to, Garrett would go down first and wait below to catch her. And each time she came up for air, he'd give her a sweet kiss and a smile.

After braving the final fall, the hike's remaining thirty minutes was spent walking in ankle-deep water down the middle of the riverbed. She and Garrett held hands the entire way, him helping to keep her steady as they traveled over the small, uneven rocks.

Back at the business's main building, the group was instructed to turn in their lifejackets and helmets before walking a few yards across the lot to where their dune buggies awaited. With a quick restroom and drink break behind them, Avery went with Garrett and the others to their designated spot.

Two guides with heavy accents ran through their standard safety spiel before showing each pair which buggy was theirs.

"You want to drive?" Garrett asked with a smirk.

Avery barked out a laugh. "Uh...definitely not."

She may have discovered a new, braver side of herself,

but death by dune buggy wasn't something she cared to experience.

Giving her a wide, ornery grin, he nodded to the passenger seat's harness and said, "Better buckle up."

Something in his tone kicked her nerves into high gear. But this man had kept her safe in the river, and she had no doubt he'd do the same now.

Buckled in and ready to go, Garrett flashed her a panty-melting smile before sliding his black helmet over his head and firing up the buggy's ignition. Determined to live in the moment, Avery donned her second helmet of the day—this one covering her entire head—and settled back into her seat.

Positioned second to last in a trail of ten vehicles, they waited their turn before taking off. With one guide leading the group in the front and the other picking up the back, they began riding along a dirt road in the opposite direction from which they came.

"Woohoo!" Garrett hollered over the sound of the engine. Avery laughed, loving how much fun he was having.

And it's only just begun.

Letting the buggy in front of them gain a good distance from where they were, the daring man behind the wheel waited for the exact right moment and then pressed the gas pedal down as far as it would go.

Avery let out her own loud *whoop* and grabbed the safety bar in front of her as they began to fly.

The first part of the ride took them through the beautiful Dominican countryside. The narrow road snaked around a flat section of land with a gorgeous, peaceful creek running straight through the middle.

She watched from behind her helmet's tinted shield as the vehicles in front of them took the small dip into the water. Once they were safely across, each one picked up speed, taking off down the road before disappearing around a sharp bend.

Garrett didn't take the dip nice and easy. Instead, he exposed his adrenaline junky side and gunned the engine. They splashed through the cool water with such force it rained down on them in sheets.

"Ah!" Avery screamed and laughed as the entire vehicle became drenched.

Lifting the tinted shield on his helmet, Garrett slowed their buggy and turned his head toward her. "You doin' okay?"

"This is so much fun!" she hollered over the engine's rumble.

"It's not too rough?"

Another dune buggy passed them by right as he spoke, and Avery waited for the noise to die down again before yelling, "What?"

Lifting his helmet off his head, he asked, "Am I going too fast or too rough for you?"

She shook her head vehemently. "This is great! Keep going!"

Garrett's face lit up with a youthful grin and he leaned over to give her a chaste kiss. "Hold on tight, sweetheart. I'm gonna open her up and see what she can do."

With a chuckle, Avery repositioned the helmet, and as instructed, she held on tight.

Over the road and around the bend, they became immersed in the long stretch of scenic beauty.

As they traversed the unfamiliar territory, Avery

committed their surroundings to memory. She had the fleeting thought that she'd never had so much fun...or felt so free.

Looking at the road in front of them, she noticed the line was slowing down, and there was a row of buildings up ahead.

It's a town!

Giddy excitement had her stretching her neck to see. As they drew closer, Avery realized 'town' was a bit of a stretch for the small community. It was more like a village, and from the looks of things, this one was littered with poverty.

Small storefronts lined both sides of the crudely paved road. The few cars that were parked along the street were older, most with rust or dents marking their bodies.

A few locals stood on one corner, one bartering with the other two over a cart filled with fresh melons and what looked like papaya. And as they approached a small four-way intersection, they saw an old farm truck approach, it's back filled with the biggest heap of fresh bananas Avery had ever seen.

Children stood on the broken sidewalks with their parents, waving at each buggy as it drove past. Their little faces lit up, smiling back at them as if the caravan was taking part in some sort of makeshift dune buggy parade.

To those children, Avery realized that's probably exactly what she and the others looked like. A parade of tourists catching a glimpse of how these people lived.

Filled with a sympathy for a community she didn't know, Avery wished she could do more than wave and move past. Give them money or food or clothes. *Something* that would make their lives a bit easier.

Then she almost immediately felt ashamed. Despite her good intentions, those thoughts would probably be considered offensive if she were to ever verbalize them.

Though they couldn't see her face, Avery pushed past the heart wrenching scene and smiled and waved as they came upon another group of young children.

From the corner of her eye, she caught sight of something else waving in the air. A flag flying high on one of the villages few electrical poles. She could tell from its design that it was political in nature.

Having taken Spanish in high school, Avery still remembered some of the words. One she recognized immediately was *presedente*, or president.

It's a presidential candidate's flag.

Looking around, she realized there were several more just like it posted around the remaining buildings. Some taped on doors or windows. Some flying from light poles or makeshift posts.

Emilio Garcia was the candidate's name. And from the looks of things, he had the support of this entire village.

Suddenly curious about this country and its current political status, Avery made a mental note to research their upcoming election—and Emilio Garcia—when she got back home.

Reaching over to give her bare leg a playful tap, Garrett pressed down on the accelerator as the trail of buggies left the south end of the village and headed out into the countryside once again.

Several minutes later, they pulled onto another narrow street. A neighborhood of sorts, there were a handful of houses on one side of the road and a small, shelter-type structure on the other.

Falling in line, Garrett parked on the side of the road and cut the engine. Unbuckling, Avery removed her helmet and set it in the seat when she got out.

"This is incredible." She looked around at the goings on as she moved over to where he stood.

A small group of older men sat in chairs under the shelter's roof. Using the instruments in their hands, they began playing upbeat merengue music that made Avery smile.

"Come on." Garrett took her hand in his. "I don't know about you, but I could use something cold to drink."

Same.

Walking up the hill to the shelter, they went straight to the small concession area located inside. Speaking fluent Spanish—which was both impressive and arousing—Garrett ordered for them both. The young man behind the partition exchanged two tall, canned beers for cash.

Looking closely at the label, Avery realized it wasn't any she'd ever heard of.

"It's local," Garrett informed her. "And it's good."

"You've had this before?"

He nodded. "Told you, my job requires me to travel."

"Here?"

"Not this place, specifically. But this isn't my first time in the Dominican."

Wow. He really *did* go far for his job.

Popping the top, Avery took a long, smooth draw of the ice-cold beverage. "Wow." She took another sip. "That really is good."

"Told ya." Garrett winked. "Let's see what they have over there."

Turning, Avery saw three stands like the kind she'd

seen at a farmer's market. One selling hand-made beaded jewelry, another shelved with small, souvenir-type trinkets, and the third was filled with the most beautiful wooden carvings she'd ever seen.

"Wow." She went to the jewelry booth first. "These are incredible."

"Gracias." The middle-aged man running it gave her a nod.

"See anything you like?"

Shivers raced down Avery's spine as Garrett's lips brushed her ear from behind.

In the past two days, his talented fingers, tongue, and cock had brought her to orgasm more times than she ever thought possible. And still, the simplest of touches left her body primed and aching for more.

He's doing that on purpose.

She smiled, loving the fact that her inner voice was right.

With a cleared throat, she zeroed in on one of the other man's multi-colored bracelets. "How much for that one?" She pointed to the wide, stretchy piece of handcrafted jewelry.

"Ten."

"Ten dollars?" She clarified.

"Si." The man nodded.

Bending down, Avery started to pull the small roll of cash she'd tucked safely into her shoe, next to her ID. But a warm, recognizable hand on her lower back stopped her.

"Here."

Avery stood to see Garrett handing the man a ten-dollar bill.

"You didn't have to buy that for me."

"I know." He grinned, handing her the newly purchased gift. "I wanted to."

Stretching the bracelet's elastic over her hand, Avery held out her wrist to admire the bright beads. "I love it. Thank you." She planted a kiss on his lips.

"You're welcome."

The group stayed in that location long enough to enjoy their drinks, a sample of locally grown fruit, and live music before saying their goodbyes and heading back to their buggies.

Following their guide, the train of vehicles drove through a more desolate area of the country filled with peaceful fields and trees, as well as the occasional run-down farmhouse.

With her head leaned back as she relaxed in the afternoon sun, Avery gasped and shot straight up when Garrett slammed on his breaks and brought them to a sudden, jolting halt.

Removing her helmet, she brushed some hair from her face and asked, "What's wrong?"

He slipped the helmet from his head and shook his head. "I don't know."

Avery could almost *feel* the change in his demeanor. The relaxed, fun-loving man was gone, replaced by a focused, intense warrior.

Straightening her spine, she tried to look over the buggy's windshield to figure out why the entire group had suddenly stopped. But she was still too short.

"Looks like there are some trucks blocking the road," Garrett explained.

"Are they stranded?" She looked in vain again. "Do they need help?"

Before he could answer, the group's rear guide walked past in a rush. Speaking into his handheld radio, he spat off something in rapid Spanish, assumably to the other guide at the front of the line.

When the other man's response came through the small speaker—also in Spanish—Garrett's entire body locked down.

"What is it?" she asked, knowing he spoke the language and had understood the conversation. "What did he say?"

The sound of men yelling rose over their idling motors.

"Sweetheart, I need you to listen very carefully." Garrett unbuckled his shoulder harness and reached for something behind his back. "There's a group of men up ahead. They have guns."

"*Guns?*" Her voice rose two octaves. Heart slamming against her chest, her mind whirled to accept what he'd just told her. "W-what do they want?"

"I don't know." He pulled his hand—and a *pistol* —free.

He had a gun, too?

What is happening?

Avery swallowed against her suddenly dry throat. With her pulse racing and fear zipping through her veins, she searched his eyes for answers.

"What's going on?"

His lips parted to answer as tires squealed from behind. Jumping from the unexpected sounds, Avery turned her head just in time to see two men with really big guns climbing out of another truck and heading their way.

"Garrett..."

He slid the weapon she hadn't even realized he had

beneath his right thigh and reached for her hand. "I need you to stay calm."

"Calm?" she spoke with a not-so-quiet whisper. "We're being ambushed, and you want me to be calm?"

"Yes." Garrett locked eyes with her. "Look, they're probably just looking for money and jewelry. Just follow my lead and listen to what I say. No arguments."

"O-okay." Avery swallowed again.

Hell yes, she was going to listen to him. It wasn't like she had a death wish.

Doing her best to keep her breaths steady, she sat and waited for whatever was about to come next.

The men coming from the rear waited until they were only a few feet away to begin shouting their orders.

"Get out!" one demanded.

Dressed head-to-toe in black—including some sort of thin, mesh masks that covered their faces—the men held their weapons in front of them. Their long barrels pointed directly at Avery and Garrett.

Oh, god!

"Do as they say, sweetheart."

The quiet words were a calm in the midst of a terrifying storm.

Following orders, Avery fumbled to open the door, nearly stumbling as she rushed to get out. Her gut churned and legs wobbled to the point she thought she'd collapse.

Never, not once in all her twenty-eight years, had she ever felt such pure and utter terror.

Glancing down at Garrett's empty seat, she looked to his hand, expecting it to be filled with the gun she'd seen seconds before. But he held nothing.

Where did it go?

She didn't have time to figure it out because the two men holding them at gunpoint motioned for her to walk around to the other side, where Garrett stood.

Keeping her eyes on those guns, Avery focused on every step she took. When she got close enough for him to reach her, Garrett grabbed her hand and pulled her to his side before shifting his body to block hers with his own.

"Give me your wallets and phones," one of the two goons ordered sharply.

Okay, so Garrett was right. All they had to do was give these men their cash, and then they'd be set free.

Pulling his wallet from his pocket, Garrett handed it over to the man. Following his lead, Avery bent at the waist, her trembling fingers struggling to dig into her damp shoe.

She started to pull the small wad of cash out when the second man rushed toward her and jabbed her in the ribs with his gun.

"Hey!" He pushed her to the ground.

Landing chest first, the air from Avery's lungs was forced out in a rough *woosh*.

Panic thundered through her body, her blood turning to ice when the man shoved the weapon's barrel against the back of her head. Avery cried out in pain.

No! He's going to kill me!

"Don't touch her!" Garrett growled.

From the corner of her eye, she could see him starting to advance on the man who'd assaulted her. But he was stopped short when the *other* man in black rammed the butt of the long rifle against the back of Garrett's head.

He dropped to the ground next to her, groaning and fighting to stay conscious.

"Garrett!" she hollered for him, but his only response was another raspy moan.

Oh, God. This can't be happening.

"He has a gun!" the asshole holding her at gun point yelled. "Back waistband."

The man who'd struck Garrett bent down and yanked the pistol she'd seen earlier from his shorts. How he'd slipped it back beneath his shirt without her seeing was baffling. It was also irrelevant.

"You planning to shoot me, estúpido?" Asshole number two checked the chamber of the gun before pointing it at Garrett's head.

"No!"

Before she even realized she was moving, Avery pushed herself onto her knees and flew to the side to cover Garrett's prone body with her own.

"He wasn't going to shoot anyone!" she spoke with in a terrified rush. "And I was just getting my money from my shoe! M-my phone's in the buggy. Please. We'll do what you say, just...*please*. Don't shoot him!"

Half expecting the bastard to turn the gun on her and kill them both right then, Avery was shocked when the man started to laugh.

"Aren't you a brave little puta? Jumping over your man like that. But what kind of man is he, really, letting his woman risk her life for his?"

The kind of man who will kill you the second he has the chance.

Avery had no idea where the thought came from, but in her gut, she knew it was the truth.

"Take her shoes," he instructed his partner.

Less than a second later, she felt her water shoes being

ripped from her feet. Her money and driver's license were taken, the shoes tossed aside.

"Avery Webb," the man who'd given the order stared at her I.D. "A simple name for such a beautiful woman."

Fear raced down Avery's spine and her gut churned. She hated the way that man had said her name. She also didn't like the way he was looking at her from behind his mesh mask.

Even from behind the mask, she could see his heated eyes and sick, twisted smile.

"Get them up."

Grabbing her arm in a bruising grip, asshole number two yanked her to her bare feet with such force, she was sure he'd pull her shoulder out of its socket.

Garrett was next, the man struggling a bit more to get him up. Thankfully, he was conscious and mostly alert.

And really, *really* pissed.

Sounding strained, as if he were in pain, Garrett locked his angry gaze onto hers and asked, "You okay?"

Not even close. "Yes." Avery nodded. "You?"

"Enough!" Garrett was shoved from behind. "Let's go."

"Go?" She swung her head around. "Go where? Y-you have our money and our phones."

"Avery." The low warning came from Garrett.

More terrified than she'd ever been in her life, Avery continued with her efforts to talk them out of the situation. "Please. You got what you came for, so just—"

She stopped abruptly when the man who'd been giving the orders put himself directly in her path. Standing close enough she could feel his hot breath, he traced a finger down the side of her face. Moving lightning fast, he reached his hand around and grabbed the back of her hair.

Spikes of pain shot through her scalp, causing her to whimper.

"Get away from her," Garrett's voice sounded stronger. Deadly.

But the man standing before her ignored him.

Moving his mouth so close she thought he might try to kiss her, the jerk spoke with an eerie calm as he said, "You're right, beautiful Avery. We have *exactly* what we came for."

CHAPTER 11

Tactical Operations Headquarters—Charlotte, N.C.

"WHAT THE FUCK do you mean, Falcon's missing?" Ethan "Apollo" McAllister demanded to know.

Rafe Owens, owner of Tactical Operations, looked at the three men standing in his office before addressing Apollo directly.

Apollo wasn't his real name. Just like Bones, Digger, and Falcon weren't the legal names given to the other men of Tac-Ops One. But when they were in operative mode, those nicknames represented not only who these men were, but what they were capable of.

And right now, Apollo was staring back at him with eyes so dark they almost matched his black hair. Looking ready to beat the hell out of someone, just as the former SEAL's nickname suggested.

"Let me rephrase," Rafe corrected himself. "We know where Falcon is. Or rather, we know where his *tracker* is. But our efforts to reach him have been unsuccessful."

"Back up." The man they all called Bones raised a hand.

Not only was Beckett "Bones" Stone their team medic —which required extensive knowledge of the human anatomy—but the former Marine had also broken damn near every bone in his body at one point or another throughout his thirty-two years.

Hence, the nickname.

"I thought you cut our vacation short because we had another op," Bones pointed out.

"I did." Rafe tipped his chin.

"So…what are you saying, Boss?" Apollo spoke up again. "That *Falcon's* the job?"

"Affirmative."

As expected, the room filled with several expletives and demands to know what the hell was going on with their teammate. Raising a hand, Rafe waited for them to grow silent before speaking again. When the men quieted, he brought them up to speed.

"THIS IS WHAT WE KNOW. Two hours ago, Shadow received an emergency transmission from Falcon's watch. She immediately began trying to contact him, but when she couldn't get ahold of him, I tried tracking him down as well."

"Two hours?" Bones' voice rose an octave. "Why the hell are we just finding out about this now?"

"This isn't your first rodeo, so you should know the answer to that," Rafe reminded the other man. "First, we exhaust all capabilities to make contact, then we verify with every source we can that there is, in fact, a hostage situation. Once we have a location, we can start planning."

"This is different, Boss." Bones shook his head. "Falcon's one of us."

"I'm aware." The back of Rafe's teeth ground together. "I'm also aware of the fact that just because Falcon's watch and phone are pinging from one location, that doesn't necessarily mean he's there, too. You know how this works, Bones. The minute we start assuming things, shit goes sideways."

Rafe may be former British Intelligence, but he wasn't a heartless bastard. During his twenty years at MI6, he'd lost more friends and co-workers to the job than he cared to remember. Those ghosts still kept him up at night, so the last thing he wanted was to lose a member of Tac-Ops, too.

It was *because* Falcon was one of them that they had to do things the right way...in the right order.

"You try calling his brother?" Digger—A.K.A. Slade Garrison—chimed in. "Last time I talked to Falcon, he said he was taking a trip with Colt."

As usual, the former SEAL's dark gray eyes held little emotion. The man held things close to the vest and could compartmentalize like a motherfucker.

One of the many reasons Rafe had chosen him to lead Tac-Ops One.

"I spoke with Falcon's brother less than an hour ago," Rafe answered Digger's question. "The cruise ship they were on docked at Amber Cove early this morning, and Falcon left shortly after to go on a pre-paid excursion."

"What kind of excursion?"

"All-day river hike and dune buggy ride through the province's countryside."

"Why didn't Falcon's brother go, too? Doesn't make sense that our boy would go on something like that alone."

Something Rafe had wondered, too, when he'd first heard the news that one of his men was missing.

"According to Coulter Morgan, he'd come down with a bad case of sea sickness the night before. He opted to stay aboard the cruise ship to rest while Falcon and a woman named Avery Webb went on the river and dune buggy trip together."

"Avery Webb?" Bones looked to the others and then back to him for the answer. "Who the hell is Avery Webb?"

"A woman Falcon and his brother met on the ship the first day. From what Coulter shared, the three of them hit it off from the start, but the Webb woman and Falcon had become quite...close.

Normally, this is where Bones or one of the others would make some crude, smart ass comment about their teammate and the woman. But no one, not even Bones, was in a joking mood.

"Falcon hooks up with some strange woman and now he's missing?" Digger's expression was unreadable. "Do we think she's involved?"

With their line of work, enemies looking for revenge was always a possibility. But in this particular instance, Rafe didn't believe that was the case.

"Shadow ran a preliminary background on Miss Webb." He went on with what he knew. "She's a financial and accounting software designer who also happens to live here, in Charlotte. From what Shadow told me, the Webb woman is clean. As in squeaky. She's single, lives alone, is successful at what she does... And there's not so much as a parking ticket on her record."

"What else do we know?" Bones sounded anxious. Unlike Digger, the man's brown eyes gave away damn near every emotion he felt the second he felt it.

And right now, he was itching to get the hell out of here and go after their man.

"I was already putting together a plan to locate and extract when Shadow phoned me again," Rafe answered the other man. "Forty minutes after she got Falcon's alert, authorities within the San Francisco area were made aware of a ransom demand made by unknown individuals to one of the cruise passenger's sisters."

"Ah, shit." Bones fell back into his chair. "Let me guess. They were on the same excursion as Falcon."

Rafe's nod was his answer. "The hostage takers demanded one million dollars be transferred to an offshore account in the Cayman's. They left account numbers with instructions not to involve the authorities, but the sister was so distraught, she called nine-one-one as soon as the HTs ended the call."

"Wait," Bones spoke up again. "So, it's not just Falcon and another passenger who's missing, but the *entire* excursion group?"

"Plus, their two guides. That's correct."

There were several low curses.

"When I spoke to Falcon's brother, he told me he'd received a ransom demand, as well. Shadow confirmed the same type of call was made to a family member of each of the other missing passengers. Each time the caller demanded a million-dollar transfer."

"What's our deadline?" Digger inquired.

"Forty-eight hours." Which meant they had two days to get Falcon and the others the hell out of there.

Shoving his hands into his jeans pockets, Bones asked, "Did Colt inform authorities when he got the call?"

"He did," Rafe decided to share that fact with the group.

What he didn't share was *which* authorities Coulter Morgan had contacted. Authorities who'd immediately called Rafe to apprise him of the situation.

Another story for another day.

"Do we have an LKL?" This came from Digger.

"We do." Rafe spun his computer monitor around to reveal a satellite image of the group's last known location. "Their last known location was here. The route is supposed to take them up over this hill, around this bend for a U-turn, and then back to the business's location, where they started. We know the group made it to this spot"—he pointed to the screen—"because that's where a local farmer discovered the twelve abandoned dune buggies."

Apollo studied the screen closely. "Anything else left behind?"

"Only their helmets and a pair of water shoes. Small, so we're assuming they belonged to one of the women."

"Anyone claim responsibility?" Digger looked up from the screen. "A militia group using the hostages for a political statement? Or do we think this is all about the cash?"

"So far, the evidence points to money."

"How are we playing this thing out, Boss?" Bones stared back at him. "Are the locals going to let us come and set up camp, or do we do this thing under the wire?"

"Local authorities can't be trusted. Too many have connections to Emilio Garcia."

"Garcia..." Apollo let the name roll off his tongue. "That the guy that's been in the news lately? The presidential candidate who's promising to bring change to the DR?"

"The very same."

"Any particular reason we shouldn't trust him?"

One giant one. "Garcia is a career politician," Rafe informed them. "He's also believed to be the head of the El Sur Cartel."

His office erupted in *what-the-fucks.*

"Let me guess..." Apollo gritted his teeth. "We can't get any evidence to prove it, and the people there are too afraid to go against him."

Rafe gave the man a nod. "Got it in one."

"Why isn't that part on the news?" Digger grumbled.

Bones answered with a quipped, "Fucker probably owns the news stations, too." Then, with a loud exhale, the former Marine let his frustration fly. "Enough of this bullshit. We know where Falcon and the others were last seen and when, and you have a bead on his tracker. So what the hell are we waiting for?"

Right on cue, Rafe's secured line began to ring.

Answering, he listened as the man on the line informed him, "Sir, the jet is fueled and ready."

"Thank you." He ended the call and looked at Bones and the others. Grabbing his keys, phone, and jacket from the back of his chair, he said, "We're not waiting on a damn thing. Grab your weapons and gear, gentlemen. We're going to get our boy back."

~

"I CAN'T BELIEVE this is happening." Avery pulled away enough to turn her watery eyes up to meet his.

Neither could Garrett.

Holding her trembling body closer to his, they swayed as the cargo truck they were in hit a bump. With his back against the vehicle's hard, inner wall, he'd kept her cradled in his arms since they were forced at gunpoint to climb inside with a handful of others.

There had been three trucks in total, and the group of tourists plus the two guides had been split up between them. Keeping track with his watch, Garrett made a mental note that they'd been on the road for nearly two hours.

With everyone else lost in their own fear and conversations, he kissed the top of her head and rested his cheek there. "We're going to be okay."

As long as his team got to them in time, that is.

Earlier, while he'd been lying on the ground, still dazed from the hit he'd taken, Garrett had pressed the button on the side of his watch three consecutive times.

The clicks were designed to activate his emergency tracker signal. The second he'd pushed the button that third time, an alert was sent straight to Shadow's system.

At least that's how it was supposed to work. Neither he nor any of the other guys on the team had ever had to use theirs before now.

Please let it have worked.

Avery choked out a half-laugh, half-cry. "That man almost shot you!"

"But he didn't," he reminded her.

The fucker *would* have if Avery hadn't thrown her

body over his. Christ Almighty, he'd never forget the way she'd risked herself trying to protect him. Or the terror he'd felt thinking she may die because of it.

He'd never been so goddamn scared in his life.

Before that, when he'd seen the men at the front of their trail, Garrett had made the decision to bring his Glock 26 out from behind his back.

He'd known Avery would see it—there was no way for her *not* to see it. And there would be questions he'd have to answer. Ones that could end up ruining what they'd only just started to build.

But in that moment, when he'd realized something was about to go down, his need to protect her had risen above everything else.

It had been a rookie mistake, missing the two bastards coming up from behind. When he finally *did* see them, he'd had no choice but to conceal the weapon once more.

If he'd been alone, there would've been zero hesitation on his part. He would've opened fire and taken them both out.

But he hadn't been alone. Avery had been standing right beside him with that bastard's gun pointed at her head. And she was something he would never, ever risk.

She risked herself for you, though.

Yes, she had. The crazy, incredible woman had literally put herself between him and a fucking M13.

Never again, baby. Never. Fucking. Again.

Garrett gently guided her head back to his chest and drove that point home.

"I need you to promise me something," he spoke with a soft, calming voice.

"What?"

"No matter what happens, you won't put yourself into harm's way for me like you did earlier. Not ever." When she didn't respond, he gave her a little shake. "Avery? Did you hear what I said?"

"I heard you." Her voice sounded small.

"Promise me."

She waited a beat before looking back up at him again. Shaking her head she said, "I can't promise that."

"Avery—"

"No, Garrett." She sat up straighter. "I know I'm not strong enough to fight these men off by myself, but I also can't stand back and watch them hurt you without at least *trying* to help." A tear fell down her cheek, leaving a silver streak through the dust on her skin. "I know this thing between us is new, but I...I care about you, Garrett. More than I ever thought possible. So, no." She swiped at another falling tear. "I'm sorry, but I won't promise you that."

Ah, baby.

Her words made his heart swell to the brim and shattered, all at the same time. Waves of unprecedented feelings brewed from somewhere deep inside. A perfect emotional storm created by both the love he felt for this woman, and the fear of what may come.

Holy fuck. You love her.

If he wasn't already sitting down, Garrett would've fallen to his knees.

It was too soon for that. Way, way too soon.

Except...somehow, it wasn't.

In that one, horrific moment when he'd thought she was about to be killed and he was too out of it to stop it, Garrett's entire world had shattered in an instant.

A world he couldn't imagine living in without her.

I never want to be without her.

Things had happened so fast he hadn't had time to stop and analyze his thoughts or feelings. But now that he had, Garrett knew with utter certainty that his feelings for Avery weren't just real...they were everything.

Cupping one side of her face, he brushed his thumb across her smooth cheek and whispered, "I don't deserve you."

"Don't say that." Her chocolate eyes softened.

"It's true."

He blinked at the sudden stinging in his eyes. Nausea churned in his gut at what he was about to reveal, but he couldn't avoid it any longer. She deserved to know the *whole* truth.

Starting with what his job really entailed.

Bolstering up the courage, he drew in a breath and said, "Sweetheart, there's something I need to tell you."

"Does it have to do with why you brought a gun on a cruise?" Avery frowned. "How did you even get it onto the ship in the first place? And where was it when we were in the water earlier?"

All valid questions that could be answered with one simple statement.

I'm a covert agent working for a highly classified black ops group owned by a former MI6 operative who answers directly to the President of the United States.

Simple, his ass.

With his heart kicking the shit out of his chest, Garrett swallowed his nerves and said, "Avery, I—"

The truck jolted to a sudden stop, the force damn near throwing them onto their sides.

"We stopped." Her wide eyes found his again. "Why did we stop?"

"I don't know." He looked toward the truck's back door. "My guess is, we've made it to wherever these assholes plan to keep us until our ransom is paid."

He'd overheard the two men who'd approached them discussing their plans for a big payout. A million each. That's what they expected his and the others' family members to pay in exchange for their freedom.

Hoping it would ease Avery's worry—as well as the other hostages who'd been placed in the same truck as them—he'd waited for the doors to close and the truck to take off before sharing that information with them.

Some found it a relief, while others—like Avery—felt as though it was a death sentence.

A million dollars. Not many people could come up with that kind of money. Certainly not Alex, Avery's sister. At least, that's what Avery had told him.

After that plan to comfort her had backfired, he'd held her while she silently cried. Garrett assured her Colt could get enough money for them *both* but had held off telling her about his team for fear the signal hadn't worked.

"Let's go," the man who'd just opened the door ordered gruffly.

One by one, the small group was led out of the truck and toward a large, cinderblock building in the middle of nowhere. Garrett surveyed the area and hostage takers with an operative's eye, gathering as much intel as he could about who and what they were up against.

The land immediately surrounding the rundown building was barren. Closed off from the long dirt road leading up to it by a concrete wall that ran the property's perimeter. A big, wooden gate was the only way in, but off to the south, west, and north was a forest that spanned miles.

If he could find a way for them to escape, he and Avery could head for the trees and lose themselves in their cover.

Then he'd find someone willing to help him contact his boss and the others. And Colt.

Garrett's heart sank as he thought of his brother and how all this would affect both him and their dad.

They'd suffered through the loss of their mom. He hated knowing the news of his capture would cause them even more pain.

With another reason to hate these sonsofbitches, Garrett held onto his renewed rage, locking it away for safe keeping. Because the second he saw an opportunity, he was damn sure going to use it.

"You." The man who'd hit him earlier walked over to Avery and grabbed her arm. "Come with me."

"What?" Avery's eyes flew to his. "Garrett?"

His fists became two balls of tight, white knuckles. "Let her go."

"You want me to hit you again, tough guy?" The asshole mocked him with his heavy accent and humorous glare. Then the bastard tightened his grip on Avery's arm and ripped her from Garrett's grasp.

"No!" she screamed, the sound shredding him. Struggling against the man's strong hold, she did everything she could to get herself free. "Let me go!"

At the same time, another scream filled the hot, humid air. This one from a teenage girl who'd been at the front of the line.

"Daddy!" The blonde who couldn't be more than

sixteen reached in vain for her father as one of the HTs pulled her from the distraught man's arms.

Others around him began crying or yelling at the men to stop, but Garrett was focused on the fact that both the girl and Avery were being led away from the group. Toward the north end of the building.

Fuck this.

"Get your hands off her!" He went after the prick manhandling Avery. Giving the bastard a hard shove, Garrett wrapped his hands around her tiny wrists and pulled her back toward him.

He almost had her free when...

"Look out!"

Avery's eyes grew wide as saucers as she stared at something over his shoulder. Spinning toward the source of her terror, Garrett saw the butt of a gun half a second before it slammed against his temple.

He dropped to the ground, and no matter how hard he fought against it, the darkness pulled him under. The trickle of warm blood—his blood—followed a path from his hairline to just beneath his eye, dripping down to the dirt below.

The last thing he heard before losing consciousness was Avery screaming his name.

CHAPTER 12

There's something I need to tell you.

Avery had been replaying Garrett's words ever since she and Jessica—the young girl who'd also been separated from the others—had been left in this tiny room like a couple of caged animals. With nothing else to do but sit, she had all the time in the world to just...think.

About Garrett. Alex. Her deceased parents. Even Colt.

She tried so hard to focus on their faces and memories she'd made with them along the way. Because if she allowed other things to seep in, if she stopped to think about how indescribably *terrified* she was, Avery feared she'd go mad.

So instead, she passed the time by thinking of anything *but* the fear slowly eating away at her from the inside out.

As thoughts and memories filtered in and out of her cluttered brain, her mind also began formulating questions. So, so many, each unwinding endlessly through her mind like an endless ball of yarn.

Questions like, was Garrett okay? Her heart ached as

she pictured him lying so still on the ground, his head bleeding from where that man had hit him.

In the truck, he'd been so adamant about her promising not to put herself at risk for him. But he'd done that exact same thing for her...and because of that, he'd been hurt. Again.

Avery rubbed her chest, hoping to ease the ache she felt in her heart. The fear she felt for him worse than any physical pain she'd ever experienced.

Because you love him.

No, that couldn't be right. True love didn't happen that quickly. In her favorite books, sure. But not real life.

Yet, Avery had never felt this way for any man...no matter how long she'd known or dated him. So maybe... maybe the whole insta-love thing *was* real, after all.

Great. I finally find a man who checks all my boxes and then some, and then this happens.

Damn, fate had a seriously sick and twisted sense of humor.

As the minutes dragged on, Avery's mind eventually wandered to her sister. More questions formed, like did Alex know she'd been taken? Had she gotten the call asking for money in exchange for Avery's life?

She still couldn't believe it when Garrett had told her what he'd overheard. A million dollars? Who had that kind of money just lying around?

She sure as hell didn't. Neither did her sister.

Which opened up a whole new can of questions. The main one being...what would these men do to those in the group whose families couldn't pay?

Would they be executed? Raped or tortured? Both?

Oh, God. Please let someone find us.

"Maybe someone from the ship contacted the local police." Jessica's small, scared voice reached her from the far corner of the room. The poor girl was curled up with her back to the wall and her knees pulled protectively against her chest. "Maybe...maybe there's a giant search party out there right now, looking for us." Her hopeful blue eyes slid to Avery's. "Do you think that's possible?"

About as possible as Santa Clause coming through that broken window we can't reach and handing us an Uzi so we can blast our way out of here.

Her voice of reason—the snarky bitch—was right. The ship had probably taken off without them. Avery had read horror stories of that happening to passengers who missed the cutoff to reboard. Not that she would ever say that to a petrified child.

Instead, she limited her response to a quiet and simple. "Maybe. I don't know."

The only thing they *did* know was that they'd been locked in this ten-by-ten shack of a room for over an hour...and there was no way to escape.

The walls were made of old, decrepit cinder blocks, but even though most were cracked or chipped, they were still surprisingly sturdy.

A single window was the room's only source of light, but even with Jessica standing on Avery's shoulders, their bodies still weren't tall enough for her to reach it and break free. They knew this because they'd tried...and failed.

Many, *many* times.

They were scared, tired, thirsty, hungry...and both she and Jessica just wanted to go home.

A sound like keys jingling came from the other side of

the door. Avery pushed herself to her feet, but Jessica only pulled her knees in further with a whimper.

"It's okay," Avery tried reassuring her. "They're probably just bringing us some water or something."

Praying she hadn't just lied to the poor girl, Avery moved herself over so she was standing in front of Jessica. Working to control her fear, she forced her spine to remain straight.

She'd read about guys like these. How a woman's fear turned them on.

Well, she may be scared out of her wits, but Avery was determined to stay strong. For herself, for Jessica...and for Garrett.

You're stronger and more daring than you give yourself credit for.

He'd told her that back at the river. She hadn't believed him at first. But now, more than ever, she needed it to be true.

The door opened, and the man from earlier stepped inside. Still wearing the mesh mask, he pointed to Avery. "You. Come with me."

"Where are we going?" Her words came out surprisingly strong.

"Wherever I tell you to." He pulled a gun from his back waistband and pointed it at her chest. "Let's go."

"Avery?" Jessica's horror-stricken eyes shot to hers.

"It's okay, Jess," she lied. "Everything's going to be fine. They're not going to kill us."

The man with the gun snorted. "How can you be so sure?"

Avery looked him square in the eye. "You kill us, you get nothing." When the muscle under his eye twitched, she gave him a smirk of her own. "That's right. We know about the ransom. So that's how I know you won't kill me or Jessica, or anyone else. Because if you do, you won't get a penny of our money."

"You're right." He put the gun away and went to her. "I won't kill you. Not yet anyway." The man's hand shot out and grabbed her by the chin. Squeezing her with enough force to damn near break her jaw, he said, "But sometimes there are worse things than death."

With a hard shove, he released her before yanking her arms behind her back and securing her wrists with plastic ties. Grabbing the top of her arm that was already bruised from before, he forced her out of the room and down a long hallway.

Oh, God! Oh, God! Oh, God!

The sound of her own pulse filled Avery's ears as her heart pounded so hard she thought it would explode.

"W-where are you taking me?"

Damn, Avery. Stay. Strong!

"To see the boss."

Boss? So, these guys weren't the ones in charge?

Good God, how many of these assholes were there?

Passing by several other doors—some open, some closed—Avery thought she heard muffled voices behind them. Was Garrett in one of those rooms?

She thought about his head injury, again. It was the second one in such a short period of time, she couldn't help but worry for his well-being.

Screaming for help entered her mind, but that was how he'd gotten hurt to begin with, wasn't it? That man had grabbed her, and she'd panicked. Had reached for him and screamed his name.

And when he'd tried to help her, he'd been smacked in the head with a gun.

"Here she is." She was shoved from behind into another, larger room.

An old, metal desk and two folding chairs were the only furniture adorning the hot, dusty space. Standing in the center was a man she hadn't seen before. And he wasn't wearing a stocking cap like the others.

Dark hair, olive complexion, a straight, narrow nose, and coal black eyes that met her stare.

He's letting me see his face.

From the books she'd read, to the shows and movies she'd watched, Avery had come to believe seeing a criminal's face was never a good thing.

"Shut the door on your way out," this newest man ordered the one who'd brought her here.

As instructed, the other man left the room, leaving her alone with the supposed boss.

"My, my." He sauntered toward her, undressing her with his dark, beady eyes. "Aren't you a pleasant surprise?"

The comment confused her. "Surprise?"

"I was led to believe there would only be nine females in your group. And only one under the age of thirty. But you..." he got close enough to brush some hair from her face. "You're an unexpected gift from the gods."

There's only one God, asshole. And He's going to send you straight to Hell.

"I know you're waiting to get a ransom for each of us," she informed him. "So if you kill me..."

"Oh, I'm not going to kill you, Avery Webb." He exaggerated the Bs in her last name. "And while it's true, my cousin and I have contacted your family to demand a hefty payment, you and the little blond bitch are going to bring in much, much more."

What?

Avery's swimsuit-clad chest rose and fell with heavy breaths. "What do you mean?"

"I mean…" He traced an invisible line down her arm as he walked behind her. "We have customers willing to pay handsomely for a beautiful American woman such as yourself. And the girl"—he chuckled—"well, the younger the product, the more money they're worth."

He's talking about sex trafficking.

Avery thought she was going to be sick. "You're going to sell us?"

"That's my cousin's plan. He ordered us not to touch the merchandise, but for me…well, I know he'll make an exception."

"Your cousin…" She swallowed the bile threatening to break loose. "He's the one in charge?"

"Of this little operation, yes. But he's not *the* boss. That man is the reason you are all here."

Avery's head swam with confusion, but she did her best to lock away everything this man was telling her. If by some miracle she was able to get free, she wanted to be able to tell the authorities everything she could about who had abducted her and why.

"Your breasts are so perky." He reached around and cupped her right one from behind. "So firm."

A tear fell from the corner of her eye, but she kept her chin up and her shoulders back. As much as she wanted to fight him, she had a feeling things would only get worse for her if she did.

With a rough squeeze, the man released her breast before sliding his palm to her ass. Giving it the same, disgusting attention, Avery worked to control the tremor in her bare legs.

She wanted to kick herself for not packing a change of clothes for the dune buggy ride. Not that it would matter much with this asshole.

He moved around to her front once more, his hand sliding down her body toward the apex of her thighs. Another tear fell down her cheek. And another.

Squeezing her eyes shut, Avery's bottom lip quivered as she pictured Garrett's face. She thought of *his* hands on her body, instead of this monster's.

She was about to give into her fear and pull away when the door to the room swung open.

"Marcus!" A man she hadn't seen before stormed into the room. "What the fuck are you doing?"

"Sampling the merchandise." The man she now knew as Marcus smirked. "What the fuck does it look like?"

"I told you before, she and the girl are off limits."

Like Marcus, this man had also left his face unconcealed. Both men shared a remarkable resemblance, and she understood why with Marcus's next spoken words.

"You told the others. But this is me, Cuz. I think I've earned a little bonus, don't you?"

So Marcus and this guy are cousins.

"No, I fucking don't."

"Why not? You said it yourself, as soon as we are paid, we ship her and the girl off and get rid of the others. Then you and I---"

"Shut the fuck up!" Salvador got into Marcus's face. "Have you lost your mind? Boss will be here any second.

207

If he catches you in here with her, he'll put a bullet in that pea-sized brain of yours without so much as a blink."

"Relax, Salvador." Marcus rolled his eyes. "It's not like the bitch is going to be able to tell anyone."

"I don't care. I told you before there is to be no deviation from the plan. Period. That includes getting your fill of the product."

Product. Merchandise. These guys really were soulless bastards.

"Fine." Marcus blew out a breath. "I'll take her back to the room."

"You do that. And keep your goddamn hands off her."

With a grumble, Marcus dug his fingers into her arm once more. Pushing her through the door, Avery turned her head to the right when she heard another man's voice.

Though they were several feet away, Avery caught a glimpse of two additional men entering the building from a second entrance further down. One was tall—really tall. And he had dark hair, dark glasses, and a jaw that looked as if it were made of stone.

The man walking next to him was dressed in a dark blue suit, white button-up, and red tie. Looking as though he were attending a business meeting, rather than being in a rundown warehouse in the middle of nowhere, the man turned in her direction, his dark eyes meeting hers in a split-second exchange.

He looks familiar.

Avery was still trying to place where she'd seen the man before when a look of rage blanketed his face. Spinning on his expensive heels, the man turned his back to her before talking to the giant next to him.

"That your boss?" She shot Marcus a look.

Marcus swung his head behind them. Eyes wide, he cursed beneath his breath and shoved her forward, picking up speed as they went.

Guess she had her answer.

Unlocking the door to the room he'd taken her from, the jerk pushed her back inside.

"Avery!" Jessica stood and ran to her. "Are you okay?"

"I'm fine." She gave the young girl a small smile. Turning back around, she sent Marcus a smirk. "Your boss looked pretty mad. Sure hope you don't get into trouble."

Avery wasn't sure where the sudden cockiness had come from, but the smartass comment was something she quickly regretted.

Moving lightning fast, Marcus punched her in the jaw with the force of a two-by-four. Her head snapped to the side, and with her hands still tied behind her back, Avery was unable to break her fall.

Landing with a thud on the building's dirt floor, she heard Jessica's sharp cry of denial just before the door slammed shut. As cloud of darkness swallowed her whole, a tear fell from her eye to the dirt below as she pictured Garrett's handsome face.

CHAPTER 13

"Avery!" Garrett's eyes flew open. He shot to his feet...
and then promptly fell back on his ass.

"She's not here."

Garrett turned his throbbing head toward the unfamiliar voice. A man was sitting against the opposite
wall, his knees up, hands hanging loosely between
them.

Clean-cut in a pair of khakis and a Hawaiian shirt, he
appeared to be in his mid-to late forties. But what struck
Garrett the most was the way the man was staring straight
ahead, almost as if he was in a trance.

"Where is she?"

"They took her. Her and my daughter."

A flash of a memory struck, and Garrett realized who
the man was.

They'd been in line. The HTs were leading them into
an old warehouse of some sort. One had taken Avery away
from him. She'd been screaming. So had this man's
daughter.

"Where did they take them?" He grimaced at the gnawing headache filling his skull.

"No idea. One minute she was beside me, and the next that bastard was ripping her from my arms."

Ah, Christ.

Nausea churned in his gut to the point he thought he would puke.

"Dude, are you okay?"

Garrett's head snapped up to another voice. Younger but still male.

Sitting in the corner to his right, a twenty-something man with chin-length hair and dazed, bloodshot eyes drew circles in the dirt next to his leg.

"What?"

"I asked if you were okay. You look like you're about to hurl."

The guy talked like a surfer who'd smoked enough weed to last him a week.

"I'm good." Garrett—slowly—got to his feet again. Once he was sure he wouldn't face-plant, he walked to the door and began assessing the knob.

"It's no use," the girl's dad mumbled. "The lock and hinges are both on the outside."

The man was right. The building might be old, but the door wasn't. It was metal and sturdy...and there was no way he'd be able to break it down without an entry ram.

Fuck.

Swinging his gaze to the right, he squeezed his eyes shut and waited for the spinning to stop. Damn, he'd have to watch that.

Carefully, Garrett opened his eyes again and studied the rest of the room.

Small, probably twelve-by-twelve. Cinder block walls, dirt floor, and a tiny as fuck window that he could probably pull himself up to, but no way would he or the other two men fit through it.

Goddamnit. "We need to get out of here."

The father shook his head. "Already told you, there's no way out."

Not good enough.

"So we *find* a way."

"You think I haven't tried?" The distraught man stood. "What, you think I don't want to get out of here? To find my daughter...my fifteen-year-old daughter who's going through God knows what?"

"Then help me think of a way out!" Garrett seethed.

He knew he was losing his shit, but damn it...this was Avery. Sweet, caring Avery who'd risked getting shot to save his ass.

No way in hell would he just sit back and let these assholes decide their fate.

Sure, they'd demand a ransom in exchange for their safe return. Probably already had. But Garrett knew better. He'd seen it in their soulless eyes.

The men who'd taken them had no intentions of ever setting them free.

"He already told you, man," the stoner chimed in. "There's no way out. We just need to sit back, relax, and let the cards fall where they may."

"Yeah well, you do that," Garrett bit out harshly. "In the meantime, I'm getting the fuck out of here."

"You're just going to make things worse."

He turned back to the father. "No, I won't. Trust me."

"Trust you? Man, I don't even know you!" Spit flew

from the guy's mouth as he seethed. "And those men… those monsters took my daughter! What if we do something to piss them off, and they hurt her in retaliation?"

"I understand you're scared, but—"

"You understand?" The angry man's face twisted with painful emotions. "How can you possibly understand? They didn't take *your* daughter!"

"No, but they took the woman I love!"

Garrett's declaration echoed off the room's cement walls. *Shit.* He hadn't meant to say that out loud. Not to this man, and certainly not before he'd had the chance to tell Avery how he felt.

Must be the concussion.

No matter the reason, it was out there now, and he couldn't take it back. Funny, he didn't even want to.

"Then don't you care about what's happening to her?" The guy challenged. "To both of them? For Christ's sake, Jess is only fifteen." His voice cracked. "Who knows what they're doing to my baby girl."

Tears filled the poor man's eyes, and Garrett's chest tightened with sympathy. "Look, man. I get it. And I can promise you, I care very much about what happens to both your daughter and Avery. But sitting on our asses won't do either of them any good."

"Neither will getting ourselves killed." The man began pacing the small space.

He was right. Now wasn't the time for emotions.

If he had any chance of getting to Avery in time, he needed to start thinking like the operator he was, and not some heartsick boyfriend ready to tear down the walls to find his woman.

Think, damn it. Think!

213

"How long was I out?" Garrett began gathering as much information as he could.

The dad stopped and looked at him. "I don't know. Couple hours, maybe? They took our watches and jewelry before they split us into these rooms."

Glancing at his wrist, he realized the man was right.

He had no idea if his alert went through. And since the son of a bitch who'd struck him had stolen his watch, he couldn't try to send it again.

Come on, Shadow. Tell me you got the signal.

Moving on, he went back to the timeline, again. If the father was right, they'd been here two hours. Add that to the two hours it had taken them to drive here, and four hours had passed in all since the group had first been ambushed, and he'd sent the alert.

From past experience, Garrett knew a flight from Charlotte to the DR took approximately three hours. Shadow and his boss would've needed an hour or more to gather intel, wrangle the rest of the team together, and put a plan into place before heading this way.

So, if his math was correct, his team should be on sight within the hour. Maybe less.

But that was only *if* his alert had gone through. And he couldn't—he *wouldn't*—risk Avery's life on an if.

"You said rooms." Garrett addressed the middle-aged man again. "As in plural?"

The man nodded.

"How many?"

"Six. Maybe eight." The guy shrugged. "I didn't have a lot of time to count. Those jerks just grabbed people and pushed them inside as they came to each door. A few here, a few there. Didn't seem to be any specific rhyme or reason to who they put where, either."

Ignoring the skull-splitting headache still pounding away inside his brain, Garrett turned in a slow circle, studying the dark, dank room again.

They were in an old warehouse of sorts. From what he'd seen when they first arrived, it was one level, about six thousand square feet, and surrounded by that huge ass concrete wall.

As far as schematics went, it wasn't nearly as detailed as he would've liked. But it was enough to maneuver his way around.

These HTs, however...those bastards were a different story.

Before every op, he and his teammates gathered as much intel on the hostage takers as they could, so they knew exactly who they were dealing with.

All Garrett knew about the assholes who'd ambushed them was that they were local, and they were ruthless. And, just like every other HT, they believed they were owed something.

On top of all the unknowns, this op was different than most on multiple levels.

Not only was *he* one of the hostages—a fact that burned his ass on principle, alone—but the woman he'd come to love was also being held against her will.

If they've hurt her, so help me God...

They had no idea where Avery and the girl had been taken, nor did they know what these bastards were putting them through.

God, please let her be okay.

A renewed sense of purpose filled the cells of his body.

The rage he'd tampered down before came out in full force.

But rather than act out with useless words or fists to a wall, Garrett used it as fuel for the hell he was about to rain down upon his enemies.

Because Avery was out there somewhere. She needed him. And in this moment, in every moment going forward, *she* was all that mattered.

Running a hand over the stubble on his jaw, he looked at the father and asked, "What's your name?"

"Brett." The man stopped moving and faced him. "Brett Caldwell."

"Nice to meet you, Brett," Garrett spoke with his calm and steady hostage negotiator tone. "I'm Garrett. And you..." He turned to the kid who didn't act concerned in the least. "What's your name?"

"Danny."

"Hey, Danny." He tipped his head. "Okay, here's what we're going to do. I'm going to do my best to get us out of here so we can go find Jessica, Avery, and the others. But first, I need you two to promise you'll do what I say, when I say it. Can you do that?"

"Hell, yeah," Danny agreed instantly.

Brett was expectedly hesitant. "I want to find my little girl more than anything, but—"

"I know you do." Garrett didn't give him a chance to opt out. "And I have an idea I think will work, but only if you trust me."

The other man's skepticism shone through his worried gaze. "You're talking about risking Jess's life. Give me one good reason why I should listen to anything you have to say?"

"How about I give you two?" Garrett offered. "One, you were right. We won't do our girls any good if we're dead. And if we stay here and do nothing, that's exactly what's going to happen."

"How do you know that?"

"Reason number two." He drew in a deep breath before revealing, "I'm a hostage rescue specialist."

He felt shitty telling these guys the truth about his job before sharing that bit of information with Avery. But he'd done so because he needed them to trust him. Otherwise, they were all fucked.

"Cool." Danny let the word drag as he grinned. Almost as quickly, he dropped his brows in confusion and asked, "What's that mean?"

Lord save me from pot-smoking millennials.

Resisting an eye roll, Garrett explained, "That means my job is to locate and rescue people who are being held captive."

"Like us!" the kid responded with pride.

"Yes, Danny." He spoke with patience he was about to lose. "Like us."

"Is that true?" Brett stared back at him with clear eyes. "You really do this sort of thing for a living."

"It's true." Garrett nodded. Then, with a smirk to help put the man at ease, he jokingly said, "Of course, I'm usually on the outside looking in, but it can't be all that different, right?"

Brett's thin lips twitched, and Garrett took it as a win.

"Okay, listen. Since coming to, I've heard the occasional movement coming from the other side of the door."

"Like feet padding across the dirt."

"Exactly." Garrett nodded. "That means at least one of

the HTs, er…hostage takers…are still here. Now, I have a way to get them in the room so we can overpower him. But the only way this happens is if we work together as a team. Can you guys do that?"

"Whatever you need, bruh." Danny stumbled to his feet.

Brett, however, was still hesitant to agree. "How solid is this plan of yours?"

"It's our best shot of getting out of here and finding your daughter."

The other man thought for a second longer before nodding. "Okay, then. Tell me what I need to do."

CHAPTER 14

"She saw my face." Emilio Garcia glared daggers at the man he used to trust with his life.

Used to being the operative term.

"From ten yards away," Sal rebutted. "And it was only for a second, plus the lighting in here is horrible."

Dabbing his handkerchief across the back of his neck, Emilio blotted at the sweat beading on his skin as he stood at the edge of the lot near the warehouse.

The concrete had kept the inside cooler, but this part of the job was messy and better suited for the birds than a broom.

"A second is all it takes, you idiot," Felix—a man Emilio *did* trust with his life—pointed out.

"Felix is right." He stared back at Sal. "A single, solitary second can change everything. Including destroying the life I have worked years to build. For me. For my family. Even for your ungrateful ass."

"I'm not ungrateful, Emilio. I appreciate everything you've ever done for me. But I'm telling you, even if the

Webb woman *did* see your face, she's an American tourist who's scared out of her mind. She has no idea who you are, and probably won't even remember you ever being here."

"I can't run that risk, Salvador." Emilio shook his head. "I won't."

Fear filled the other man's dark eyes, for he knew what was at stake.

"W-what do you propose we do?" the imbecile asked nervously. "The transfer of money has not gone through yet. We gave the hostage's families forty-eight hours, as we'd planned."

"Thanks to your idiot cousin, the *plan* is no longer valid." Another good point made by Felix.

Sal's swallow was audible. "So what are you saying?"

"I'm saying"—Emilio made himself perfectly clear—"I want the Webb woman and the girl taken out of here. Now."

"Now?" Sal's brows shot up with surprise. "Where am I supposed to take them?"

"There's an abandoned farmhouse forty miles north of here. I want you to personally escort them there and stay with them until the transfers are complete. Use one of the trucks so they can't be seen. If the family demands proof of life, you can give it to them. With only two women to watch, you'll have less responsibility. This means there's less of a chance you'll fuck up again."

"My men and I *have* been watching them, Emilio," Sal assured him. "Nothing has happened that puts our plan at risk."

"I disagree. And since I am the one in charge…"

"Fine. I'll have Marcus help me, and—"

"No." Emilio cut him off. "Marcus stays here."

"But Marcus is—"

"The reason we're having this discussion in the first place." Emilio turned to Felix. "Bring him to me."

"Emilio, please," Sal pleaded for his cousin.

This time, his pleas fell on deaf ears.

"Go," Emilio told his trusted confidant.

A minute later, Felix returned with Marcus in tow.

"You wanted to see me, Boss?"

Sal's face turned green, and the poor bastard looked as though he would pass out any second. "Please don't do this," he begged. "It won't happen again. I-I'll make sure of it."

Emilio shared a look with Felix. The other man nodded, signaling he understood the silent order.

Standing behind Marcus, Felix silently pulled his weapon free of its holster.

"What's wrong?" Confused, Marcus turned to his cousin. "What's going on?"

"*Please,* Emilio," Sal continued to beg.

But Emilio was focused on Marcus. "What's going on is a lesson in following orders. Hopefully one your cousin will take to heart."

With a final glance at Felix and a slight tip of his head, Emilio gave the order.

Still clueless, Marcus shook his head. "Sal, what's he talking abou—"

Felix fired his weapon, the deafening sound echoing through the early evening sky. The bullet entered the back of Marcus's skull before the ill-fated man ever knew what hit him.

He dropped to the ground near his cousin's feet.

"*No!*" Sal fell to his knees, the look of sorrow and loss on his face almost enough to make Emilio feel badly about his decision.

Almost.

"I will give you a brief moment to mourn, and then I expect my order to be followed to the letter. Is that understood?"

Silent sobs wracked Sal's pathetic body as he gave a jerky nod, his eyes never leaving his fallen cousin.

THE PLAN WAS A GO.

Brett...and God help them, even Danny...knew their roles and were getting into position.

In the back of Garrett's mind was the gunshot they'd heard several minutes before. One coming from somewhere in the distance.

Garrett's immediate thought had been of Avery, but then he'd reminded himself that these men needed them alive if they were to get the payday they were expecting.

His next thought was of his team.

But they were trained better than that. The men he trusted with his life wouldn't start shooting from that far out before first securing entry into the building where the hostages were located.

And if by some chance they'd had no choice, his guys would've used a suppressor to lessen the noise.

No, his gut was telling him the shot they'd heard had nothing to do with Avery or his team. Which left two other possibilities he could think of...

Either someone had screwed up and paid the ultimate price, or the HTs were starting to turn on each other.

Either way, that meant one less asshole to have to worry about.

"Who do you think got shot?" Danny looked worried for the first time since they'd been locked away.

Garrett shook his head. "Doesn't matter. Sooner we do this, the sooner we can get the hell out of here. Now, I'm not going to be able to move until the exact right time. I'm trusting you both to follow the plan exactly as we discussed."

Danny slapped him on the shoulder. "No worries, man. We've got your back."

"He's right, Garrett." Brett gave him a nod. "We can do this. We *have* to. For Jess."

Garrett's chest tightened. "For Avery."

The two men shared a solemn look before Garrett laid in the middle of the room and closed his eyes. Positioned on his back, he had his head tilted away from the door, his arms flung to the side as if he'd simply collapsed into an unconscious state.

Brett positioned himself so he'd be hidden behind the door when it opened, and Danny drew in two long breaths before pounding his fist against the metal and yelling for help.

"Help! Somebody, please help!" The young man sounded surprisingly convincing. "Please! Something's wrong! He won't wake up! Please!"

Danny continued pounding and screaming as if his life depended on it. Which it did.

"Come on, man. He's hurt!" Danny tried again. "If he dies, you won't get jack shit!"

Someone yelled at him to shut up seconds before the sound of keys against the lock reached their ears.

"Someone's coming!" Danny whispered.

Garrett's heart thumped against his ribs. If this backfired, they may all end up dead. And Avery would be left to a fate he didn't even want to imagine.

"What's the problem?" One of the HTs stood in the doorway.

"It's him." Danny told the man. "H-he...passed out. I think he has a brain bleed or something from when one of your guys hit him. He needs medical attention, man. And fast. Otherwise, he's going to die, and then you guys will be ass out on a million smackers."

Easy, Danny. Don't make it seem too obvious.

"Seriously, man. You have to help him. I tried, but...I don't know. Maybe you can get him to wake up or something."

With a low curse, the man ordered Danny, "You. Go stand over there. And if you make any sudden moves, I'll shoot you."

"Yes, sir. Don't want to cause any trouble." Garrett could hear him shuffling to the other side of the room.

Though his eyes were closed, he sensed the HT moving closer, and it took every ounce of training Garrett had to wait for Brett to make his move.

Three...two...

A strangled gasp filled Garrett's ears, and when the door closed shut, he knew it was time.

With his eyes flying open, he turned his body in one swift motion, attacking with his full strength.

Brett was hanging off of the guy's back, his arms wrapped around the HTs neck in an impressive chokehold. Danny stood by the closed door in case anyone else decided to enter, and Garrett went for the HTs gun.

The M13 was strapped across the man's chest. Using a move he'd learned years before, Garrett grabbed the weapon with both hands, pulled the automatic rifle until the straps grew taut, and rammed the side of the gun into the asshole's face.

The crunch of bones was satisfying as fuck. So was the blood pooling behind the man's mask.

From the man's low moan and half-opened eyes, Garrett could tell he was close to passing out. Instead of waiting, he decided to help the guy out.

With expert hands, he unclipped the weapon from the strap, flipped it around, and slammed the butt of his gun against the man's temple.

See how you fuckers like that, bitch!

Giving Brett a nod, Garrett waited for the other man to let the HT drop to the ground before dropping to a knee, positioning his arms around the bastard's head just so, and giving it one fatal twist to the right.

The HTs neck snapped, killing the man instantly.

"Holy balls." Danny's jaw dropped. "That... was...*awesome!*"

"Yeah well, let's not start celebrating just yet." Garrett huffed out a loud exhale. "We still have to find the girls and find a way out of here."

"Guess you were telling the truth." Brett looked back at him with an unreadable expression. "About your job, I mean."

"I was." Garrett swallowed. "You good?"

Brett looked down at the dead man and nodded. "These

sons of bitches took my little girl. I hope every one of them rots in hell."

"Amen, brotha!" Danny held up his hand for a high five.

When Brett and Garrett just stared at him, the kid shrugged it off and gave one to himself.

If the situation weren't so dire, Garrett would've laughed. But this wasn't the time for jokes.

Now, more than ever, he needed to stay focused. They all did.

Rummaging through the dead man's pockets, Garrett pulled out the man's keys, cell phone, and a KA-Bar strapped to his thigh. Checking the gun's mag, he noted it was full before slamming it back into place.

"Okay, so what now?"

Garrett looked at Brett and stood. With the M13 held securely in his hands, he said, "Now we go find our girls."

After giving Brett and Danny strict orders to stay behind him, Garrett slowly opened the door and checked the hallway. Seeing that it was clear, he silently motioned for the other two to follow him.

Going right, he headed for a door at the end of the hall. Light filtered in from all four sides, which told him it was likely an exit.

They made it three full steps before a commotion erupted from the opposite side of the building. Having no way to know who or what had caused it, Garrett had no choice but to continue along the same path, toward the exterior door.

As much as he wanted to burst through every door until he found his woman, his training wouldn't allow it. He needed to get the other two men out of the building and to the trees, and then come back in search of Avery and the others.

Save the ones you know you can save. Everything else is bonus.

Rafe Owen's mantra rolled through his head as he led Brett and Garrett through the door and out into the evening sun. As the door shut, a bullet pinged off its metal frame. Missing Danny by mere seconds.

"Holy shit!" The young man's eyes grew wide. "That was really fuckin' close."

"Get to the side!" Garrett ordered, waving his arm toward the wall near the door.

Brett and Danny flattened themselves against the concrete blocks.

More gunfire ensued, but it all came from the other side of the door. Hope filtered its way into Garrett's chest, but he didn't dare assume it was his team who'd caused the chaos.

From his position on the other side of the door—the side facing the direction it opened to—he could hear booted footfalls as they made their way toward him. Garrett gave the other men a silent order to remain where they were.

Forcing his spiking heartrate to ease, he raised the rifle and slid his finger to the trigger. Then...he waited.

Muffled sounds whispered through the cracks in the door. A second later, it flew open, and a man dressed in desert camo appeared.

Garrett's finger twitched. He damn near pulled that trigger. But when the unknown tango turned his way, he realized it wasn't a tango at all.

He lowered his weapon, his shoulders falling with a sigh of relief. "It's about fucking time."

"I think the words you're looking for are *thank* and *you*." Digger let his weapon fall to his side.

"Damn, it's good to see you, brother." Garrett shared a half-slap, half-handshake—or, Dap, as the kids called it—before Digger pulled him in for a hug.

Also making their way through the door were Bones, Apollo, and...

Holy shit. "Boss?" Garrett blinked, shocked as hell to see Owens had joined in the fun.

"Don't look so surprised, Falcon." The man's British accent seemed too proper and out of place for this shithole. "I was pulling field duty when you were still a pimply-faced teenage virgin."

"Guess Shadow got my signal, after all." He ran a hand over his worn face.

"She did." Owens nodded.

"She also got in touch with a friend of hers." Bones joined in. "Tex something or other. Said they met a few years back but didn't go into details other than to say she trusts him and he owed her one. And since Tac-Ops 2 and 3 are both in the middle of active ops, Shadow cashed in the favor he owed her. Whoever he is, this Tex guy must be hella connected, because he managed to secure a team to come here and help us transport the hostages back to the States."

"What team?" Garrett looked to his boss for the answer.

"Delta." Owens spoke low so Brett and Danny didn't overhear. "Turns out their colonel and I go way back. So, these guys are solid, Falcon."

Of that, he had no doubt. Delta Force were badass motherfuckers.

"And the HTs?" Garrett looked to his team. "I'm assuming since we're standing out here like this, the threats have all been neutralized?"

"All down for the count."

It was all he needed to hear.

"The hostages are all locked in rooms inside." He squeezed past his boss and Digger. "I've got the keys."

One by one they began opening the doors and setting the hostages free. With each door that opened, Garrett and Brett looked for Avery and Jess. And with each one, they were met with disappointment.

The hostages, of course, were elated to know they'd be going home. But for Garrett and Brett...their fear grew even stronger.

"Where are they?" Brett demanded. "They should be here!"

Yeah, they sure as fuck should be.

"Who's they?" Apollo asked.

"Two of the female hostages. Avery Webb and a fifteen-year-old girl named—"

"Jessica Campbell," Brett blurted from behind them. Pushing his way through the crowd, he added, "She's my daughter."

"And they were both brought here, with all of you?"

"Yes." Garrett and Brett answered in unison.

"We've searched this place from top to bottom, Falcon," Apollo spoke up. "There's no one else here."

"Oh, God." Brett stumbled back to the wall between two of the rooms. His knees gave out, and he slid to the floor. "I've lost her."

"No." Garrett assured him. "We haven't lost anyone, yet." To the other hostages, he hollered out, "Listen up! We're looking for the woman who was with me and this man's daughter. They were the ones separated from the group when we first got here."

Several mumbled and some shook their head, but no one spoke up.

"Avery's twenty-eight, about this tall. Long, dark hair. Jessica's about the same height. Blonde. She's only fifteen."

Again, no one acted like they'd seen them since their arrival. Garrett's spirit damn near broke, and Brett's face crumbled with acceptance. But then...

"Wait!" A woman in her forties made her way up from the back of the group. "I think I heard them earlier."

"Where?"

"Down there." She pointed to a room at the end of the hall, opposite from where Garrett, Brett, and Danny had been held. "I was in the room right next to that one, and I heard them. A man went in about an hour after we got here. It sounded like he'd taken one of the women out of the room for a little bit before bringing her back."

"She's right." A man came up beside the woman. "I was in the same room, and I heard it, too."

"Okay, but they're not there now, so—"

"Because another man came back and took them both."

"When?" Garrett stepped forward. "Where did he take them?"

"About fifteen minutes ago. Right before all the shooting. I-I have no idea where they went."

"Fuck!" Garrett spun and slapped a palm against the nearest wall.

"Wait." Bones pulled his phone from his pocket and began texting someone. "Shadow's been keeping an eye on this area. Maybe her system saw them leave."

Jesus, he must be out of it. That should've been his first thought.

Less than a minute later, Bones had a response. "Got 'em." He relayed the message. "Shadow says they left the property seven minutes before we arrived and headed north in one of their cargo trucks. Male driver, two female passengers. They were tied up and put in the back of the truck."

"Seven minutes." Garrett's hope returned. "They couldn't have gotten far."

Taking over, Owens ordered, "Digger, you and Falcon go. Take the SUV. The two of you should be able to handle one HT."

I'll fucking handle him, all right.

"I want to go, too!" Brett shot to his feet.

Garrett understood the man's need to get to his daughter, but he wasn't about to put a civilian at risk more than he already had.

"I'm sorry, but no." He shook his head. "You need to stay here."

"The fuck I do."

"Brett, listen to me. Digger and I are trained for this shit. You're not. Let us take the risk."

"But Jess—"

"Is going to be all right," Garrett promised him. "Now, you trusted me before. I need you to trust me with this."

Brett's watery gaze locked with his as the man said, "She's my life."

"I know." Garrett put a hand to his shoulder and

squeezed. "And I'm going to get her back. I'll get them both back."

Turning toward the building's nearest exit, Garrett passed by Digger and said, "Let's go."

"Yeah, don't mind us!" Bones' southern drawl was thick as he hollered out from behind them. "We'll just hang out here. Get to know each other a little bit. Maybe play some Bingo or Go Fish."

Digger chuckled at their teammate's joke, but Garrett was too focused on the task at hand to even crack a smile. The bastards who'd caused this whole mess were all dead...except one.

And that man had made a huge fucking mistake when he took Avery and the girl away. Right now, he was driving that truck thinking he was free as a goddamn bird.

He was wrong.

Because Garrett was coming after him. And when he and Digger caught up to him—because they *would* catch him—there'd be serious hell to pay.

Hang on, baby. I'm coming for you.

CHAPTER 15

Avery sat in the back of the truck and prayed.

After waking up with a pounding headache and a throbbing jaw she was surprised hadn't shattered, she and Jess had comforted each other the best way they could.

With Avery's prompting, Jess had told her all about where she lived and what her family was like. That she had a younger brother, Josh, who'd gotten the flu at the last minute and had to stay home with their mom.

Then Jess had started to cry because she blamed herself for what had happened. She'd told Avery that her dad had wanted to reschedule the trip, but—according to Jess—she'd acted like a total brat and had thrown a fit. Eventually talking her parents into having her mom stay home and tending to Josh while Jess and her dad went on the cruise.

Avery had promised her none of this was her fault. She'd also did her best to convince the poor, scared girl that her dad would never blame her for anything that had happened.

Then Avery had shared her own story with the sweet girl. She'd told her all about her parents and Alex. What it was like growing up in a small town in North Carolina, and how moving to the big city had terrified her.

To pass the time, Avery tried to explain to Jess what her job was. But it didn't take much to realize the girl was confused at best, disinterested at worst.

But that was fine, because anything was better than focusing on where they were and what would happen to them if they weren't rescued.

And then the man came and took them away.

It wasn't the one who'd taken her before. That man had been cocky and so completely full of himself. This guy... the one driving the truck... he was the one who'd come into the room after, yelling at Marcus for touching her.

And right now, he looked like he'd been hit with a thunderstorm of emotions.

Sad—Avery could've sworn the guy had been crying. Pissed off at the world—she could totally relate. But the thing that struck her most odd was how utterly and downright terrified he'd looked when he'd been shoving them into the back of the truck.

But he was one of the bad guys. An important one, from the way he'd shouted orders to the other men before they left.

And ever since then, Avery couldn't help but wonder... who or what could scare a man like that?

"Where do you think he's taking us?" Jess asked from the other side of the truck.

The vehicle hit a bump, and Avery winced when her head bounced off the inner wall. "I don't know."

"Wherever it is, it can't be good."

No, Avery supposed it wasn't. But what could they do? Their hands were tied—both literally and figuratively. And they were stuck in here with no way out.

The truck hit another bump. One so big, Avery felt her ass fly off the bed's floor before slamming back down.

"Ow!" she failed to hide the pain the hard jolt had caused.

Jess's worried eyes rose to hers. "You okay?"

"Yeah, I—"

One of the trailer's double-doors creaked open. Not a lot, just enough to let a sliver of evening sun into the dark space.

"That last bump must've popped it loose," Jess pointed out the obvious.

"Yeah…" Avery let the word linger. Her wheels began to spin as quickly as the ones carrying them over the dirt road.

"What?" Jess picked up on her change in demeanor.

"I have an idea." She looked back at the pretty blonde. "A way to escape. But you're not going to like it."

The young girl looked at the open door and back to her. "If you're thinking we should jump and make a run for it, you're right. I don't like it." Jess glanced at the door again. "But if it means getting away from that asshole and finding help for my dad, I say…let's do it."

Pride for a girl she'd just met warmed Avery's heart.

With a smile, she awkwardly pushed herself to her knees. Doing her best to keep her balance steady, she slowly made her way closer to the back of the truck.

Jess got to her feet with the grace and ease of a teenage girl, and Avery made a mental note to take up yoga if—no *when*—she got back home.

The fleeting thought that yoga would also help limber her up for Garrett crossed her mind, but she pushed it away for now. She needed to focus because...holy shit, the road was passing by in a blur.

Fear crept its way in.

This was crazy, right? It wasn't like this was the movies. She sure as heck wasn't a stuntwoman. And Jess...God, Jess was just a baby compared to her.

The seeds of doubt began planting themselves in her mind. Filling her brain with everything that could possibly go wrong.

They could land on their heads and break their necks. They could survive but break their legs and be unable to run. The driver could spot them from his sideview mirror, and slam on the breaks and catch them.

Oh, God. I don't think I can do this.

But as quickly as the thought came, another one took its place. Not one of her own, petrified creation. No, these were Garrett's words. The ones he'd spoken to her when they were on the bridge...God, was it just that morning?

You're stronger and more daring than you give yourself credit for. And if you need proof of that, all you have to do is look at us.

His words proved true then, and they were true now. She could do this. She *had* to.

If she didn't...

Avery turned to Jess who looked even braver and more determined than she was.

Though they'd only just met, like Garrett, Avery felt a sort of bond. One they'd forever share thanks to the horrific circumstances that had brought them together.

You can do this, Aves. Jess is counting on you to do this.

"Okay." Avery gave the girl a nod. "This is probably going to hurt."

There was no *probably* to it. They were traveling at least thirty miles an hour, so would it hurt? Definitely. Could they end up with broken bones? Maybe.

But a broken arm or leg would still be better than whatever horrors awaited them if they sat on their asses and did nothing.

You've got this.

That voice was her sister's. And both she and Garrett were right. She *was* stronger than she gave herself credit for. And she *could* do this.

"You ready?" She looked to Jess.

The brave girl gave her a nod. "Ready."

"Make sure you curl yourself inward and start rolling as soon as you hit."

She had no idea if it was good advice, but it was something she'd picked up from one of the action-adventure romance books she'd read last year.

It had worked for the hero and heroine in that story. And as she pushed the door wider with her shoulder to give them both room, Avery prayed it would work for them, too.

"Okay, on the count of three. One...two...three!"

Avery squeezed her eyes shut and forced her feet to push off the truck's metal floor. Jess let out a tiny squeal as they both took air.

And for a split second, they were weightless.

The unforgiving ground was like concrete as they hit.

Pain ricocheted through Avery's body from the hard impact, her right side taking the brunt of the fall.

Her shoulder, ribs, and hip felt as though they'd been smashed with a giant sledgehammer, and every last molecule of oxygen was pushed forcefully from her lungs.

But they'd done it. They were free.

Curling into a ball proved to be a difficult task with their hands secured behind their backs, but still, they rolled.

When they finally came to a stop near the side of the road, Avery took precious seconds to catch her breath and make sure she hadn't accrued any life-threatening injuries.

Her chest heaved with its efforts to suck in some much-needed air. Though it took her a moment to gather her bearings, she was able to do a quick assessment of her limbs and other parts necessary to begin running.

"Are you...okay?" She turned to look at Jess.

Amazingly the resilient teenager was already pushing herself up to her feet. Dressed in cutoffs and tank top, her hair was full of dust and tangles, and her arms, legs, and one of her cheeks were a bit scraped up.

Other than that, from what Avery could tell, she was fine.

Thank you, God!

"Holy crap!" The bedraggled girl blew out a breath. "I can't believe we just did that!"

"Me...neither." With a wince, it took Avery a bit longer to rise to her feet. Still wearing nothing but her one-piece suit, she felt like every inch of her exposed skin was already beginning to bruise.

Definitely going to feel that for a few days.

Shooting the fading truck a quick glance, Avery nearly cried in relief when she saw it still driving away.

Motioning to the grass, she said, "Come on. We need to keep ourselves covered as much as possible in case he notices we're gone and comes back."

Fighting past the pain in her battered body and the unprotected soles of her feet, Avery walked over rough dirt and rocks as they made their way into the field.

The grass was thicker here than the fields she'd seen from their early morning bus ride, but still didn't conceal them completely. Still, it was better than nothing.

Running as fast as they could back in the direction from which they came, Avery kept her eyes peeled for any signs of life. A house, a car...something that would give them a chance to find help for Garrett and the others.

Several minutes later, she heard it.

A motor. Not rough and clunky like the truck they'd jumped from. This one sounded smoother. Newer.

"There!" Jess yelled. "Hey! Over here!"

She was at the side of the road before Avery could stop her. Jumping up and down, she did what she could to catch the driver's attention.

Avery swung her head back toward the oncoming vehicle.

She could see the black SUV clearly now. Not only was it new, but it also looked official. Like ones she'd expect someone from the government to be driving.

Or a drug dealing mob boss who liked to cut people up for fun.

Fearing it was the latter and cursing her enjoyment of scary movies, Avery ran to where Jess was still jumping. "Jess, wait!"

Afraid this *was* like the horror flicks she'd seen—the ones where the people escape only to flag down one of their captors—Avery yelled at Jess to come back into the grass.

"What are you doing?" Jess argued even as she followed her.

Shoulders burning from the strain, Avery dropped into a crouched position. "What if it's them?"

"What if it's not? My dad's back there!"

So was Garrett.

Shit, shit, shit.

They were at a crossroads. A giant one. And Avery had no idea which one to choose.

If these were the bad guys and she and Jess had just flagged them down, they were truly and royally screwed. But if it was someone else, someone who could help them get Garrett and the others free...

The vehicle skidded to a stop, and Avery's heart leaped into her throat.

Apparently, it didn't matter *which* road she would've chosen. Whoever was in that SUV had already seen them.

"Avery?"

She could feel Jess's muscles trembling next to her. Knowing platitudes would be useless at this point, Avery chose to keep quiet and bowed her head to pray.

A door slammed shut and then another. She held her breath as they remained silent and still. Maybe whoever it was couldn't see them, after all. Maybe the grass had hidden them better than she—

"Avery!"

Her eyes flew open, and her heart sang with praise.

"Garrett?" she whispered, unable to believe what she'd heard was even possible.

"Avery! Jessica! Where are you?"

Ohmygod!

Avery shot to her feet. Tears filled her eyes the second she found him.

"Garrett!"

His eyes grew round when he spotted her, his entire body lighting up with relief. "*Avery!*"

Garrett ran to her. She awkwardly made her way to him. And when they met near the side of the road, he damn near knocked her over with his strong embrace.

"Oh, God!" He squeezed her tightly. "Oh, thank God!"

"H-how did you...wh-where did you..."

She couldn't seem to formulate a sentence to save her soul. But it didn't matter. Nothing else mattered but the fact that Garrett was here.

"Let's get these off of you." Spinning her around, Garrett used a knife he'd gotten from who knows where to cut through the plastic ties with ease. "How did you manage to get away?"

"The truck's back door popped open, so we jumped."

"You *what?*" Garrett spun her back around, the look of shock on his face almost comical.

"It was our only shot at escaping." She offered him a tiny smile. "So, we took it."

With several mumbled curses, he handed the sharp weapon to a man she'd never seen before. Dressed in brown camouflage like the military wore, he looked to be about Garrett's age.

While he freed Jess from her restraints, she asked, "Where's my dad?"

The man cutting the ties at her wrists answered with, "He's still back at the warehouse with the others."

"Those men still have him?"

"No, honey," the stranger assured her. "We took care of them."

"You took *care* of them?" Avery looked up at Garrett. "What does that mean?"

Once again, the other man answered for him. "It means, they're no longer a problem."

"Look at me." Garrett's soft order had her following his command instantly. His eyes were filled with emotion she couldn't quite place as he leaned in and took her mouth in his. Keeping the kiss short, he pulled away just enough to rest his forehead against hers. "I thought I'd lost you."

"Me, too."

He lifted his head and brushed some hair from her face. "Are you hurt?"

"I-I'm okay."

Despite her answer, he began to gently run his hands along her body to check for possible injuries. "Did those bastards touch you?"

"It's just some scrapes and bruises," she promised. "Really, I-I'm okay."

It was the truth, as miraculous as it was.

Relief flooded his gorgeous eyes, and she thought he might kiss her again. Until he spotted the bruise on her swollen jaw.

"Ah, baby." He took extra care to rest his palm against the side of her face. His touch was feather soft, but his next words were positively lethal. "If he's not already dead, I'll fucking end him."

Not already...

"Garrett, what happened?" She glanced at the man standing with Jessica and then the vehicle before bringing her gaze back to his. "Who's he, and where are the other hostages?"

Before he could answer, the stranger looked at Garrett and said, "Falcon, man...I hate to break up this heartwarming reunion, but we really shouldn't be out in the open like this."

"Falcon?" Avery frowned.

A strange look fell over Garrett's handsome face. With a lick of his lips, he nodded and said, "That's what my team calls me. I'm Falcon. This is Digger."

His team? And what kind of names are Falcon and Digger?

Avery's head swam with a million new questions.

"I don't..." She shook her head and swallowed hard. "I-I don't understand. What's he talking about? What team?"

He gave her a smile that oozed with guilt. "Sweetheart, Digger's right. We need to get you and Jess the hell out of here before the man who took you realizes you're gone and decides to come back. I promise, I'll explain everything later."

"Okay." She gave him a slight nod.

After riding back to the warehouse where they'd been held, Avery had helped Jess find her dad. It was a tearful reunion for all, Avery included. Especially when Jess had left her dad's arms to rush over and give Avery a hug and tell her thank you.

All smiles and happy tears, the hostages were divided between four trucks. Three belonging to the hostage takers, or HTs, as she'd learned they were called, and another utility truck that was there when they'd gotten back to the warehouse.

All four of those vehicles were driven by an entirely different team. Avery had watched them closely as they'd shuffled everyone into their seats, deciding they looked and acted as she'd always imagined a special forces team would. Just like Garrett's team did.

Garrett has a team.

She still couldn't wrap her mind around that.

And it wasn't just *any* team, either. No, it was a group of hot, sexy, badass men who'd flown to the DR, stormed the warehouse, and taken out all the bad guys.

Well, almost all of them.

The man who'd taken her and Jess was still at large, but Garrett and the others had assured her that she and Jess were safe.

Avery wanted to believe him. A few hours before, she would've believed *anything* he said.

Now, she wasn't sure she could trust him at all.

Rather than riding in a truck like the other hostages, Garrett had insisted she ride with him in the SUV, along with the other three men on his team.

Wrapped in a blanket given to her by one of his guys, she sat next to him. He was unusually quiet, only talking when one of his buddies asked him a question. His hand holding hers the entire way, as if he never wanted to let her go.

When they finally made it back to the port at Amber Cove, she and Garrett were greeted with breath stealing hugs from Colt, who looked exhausted and heartsick with worry for his brother.

While the three were talking, Garrett and Avery were

asked to go with ship security, along with the other hostages. They were escorted back onto the ship using an entrance normally reserved for employees only.

Once inside, Garrett *did* let her hand go. Right after he explained they were all going to be separated so they could give their official statements to cruise security, members of local authorities, and a man Garrett had introduced to her as his boss.

Three long, grueling hours later, she'd told them everything she knew and then signed a non-disclosure agreement. One promising never to divulge what she knew about Garrett and his team to anyone without direct permission from Rafe Owens, Garrett's boss.

It wasn't a hard promise to make since she didn't really understand most of it, and no one had given her any specific details about who or what Garrett truly was.

Finally back in her stateroom, she shared a very emotional phone call with her sister before taking the longest, most amazing shower of her life. Then she'd gotten dressed and fell onto the bed.

And still, she was no closer to getting answers than she was before.

As she lay there, events from the days prior rolled through her mind. Memories assaulted her...glorious, wonderful memories. But there was one that kept coming back to her, no matter how hard she tried to ignore it.

Do you really sell insurance?

She'd asked Garrett that question while sitting at the beach.

I do. If you want, when we get back to the ship, I can show you my license.

Avery could still picture him squatted down before her

that day. So caring and attentive. He'd gotten her water when she'd become too hot. They'd laughed and talked... and kissed.

And then he'd looked her right in the eye and lied to her face.

Tears that had yet to fall poured from her eyes and onto her pillow. She tried to fight them at first, but it was no use.

It was all too much, and everything seemed to hit her at once.

Garrett's confusing betrayal. Being held at gunpoint and then groped by that horrible man. Jumping from a freaking *moving* truck. Thinking she was going to die...

It all came rushing over her in a giant tsunami of pain. And the only thing Avery could do was ride the wave. Until finally, blessedly, she cried herself to sleep.

CHAPTER 16

Exhausted to his bones, Garrett rode the elevator to his and Colt's floor, thankful as hell that he was alone.

What a clusterfuck of a day.

Leaning his back on the car's wall, he closed his eyes and drew in a long, deep breath before letting it out slowly. Just as it had every time he'd so much as blinked these last few hours, Avery's gorgeous face filled his mind's eye.

Only she looked different, now. No, that wasn't right. She looked exactly the same. But she'd looked at *him* differently.

Like he was a stranger. Someone she barely knew, rather than the man she'd made love to over and over again.

And he couldn't get that look out of his fucking head.

It was all there, in her eyes. Her beautiful, dark chocolate eyes. Every emotion she'd been feeling since the minute she'd heard Digger call him by his team nickname.

Confusion. Sadness. Betrayal.

He'd promised to explain everything to her but hadn't

wanted an audience for that particular conversation. So he'd waited.

When he and Digger had first found her and Jess in that field, he'd been so fucking relieved he'd damn near bawled like a baby. Hours later and he *still* hadn't gotten rid of the fear he'd felt speeding down that road in search of them.

After arriving at the ship, and his brief but emotional reunion with Colt, he'd been debriefed by the head of cruise security, a man Owens knew personally.

Of course, he knows him. Owens knows everyone who's anyone.

After that, he and his team, along with Owens, used their secured satellite phone to call the president—yep, that's right, *the* president of the United States.

It wasn't the first time Garrett and his team had been on a call with the powerful man. And, given what they did for a living, it wouldn't be the last.

Once they'd filled him in on what had happened, Garrett gave a written statement to the local police chief. He'd left out the part about the Delta Force team who'd aided in their transport back to the ship. Instead of naming names, he used vague words like 'additional team members'.

One of the reasons those guys were able to do the things they did was largely because of their anonymity. Garrett and his team wanted to do whatever they could to help them keep it.

As far as the other hostages knew, the Delta guys *were* part of their team. And there was no reason for them to think otherwise.

The elevator dinged and Garrett stepped out into the

large, carpeted space. Turning right, he headed down the hallway—to Colt's room.

He knew he should go to Avery first. Especially since Colt had met them out on the dock when they'd first arrived.

As lame as it was, Garrett admittedly was using his brother as an excuse to put off having to face her. Because Colt was his blood.

Sure, he'd be pissed about the lies and secrecy. But in the end, the guy would still love him, regardless. Because they were family.

With Avery, Garrett didn't have that same type of assurance. She could walk away free and clear if she wanted. But God, he prayed she wouldn't.

Reaching Colt's room, he lifted his hand and knocked. His brother opened the door, looking tired and worn, but not nearly as green as the last time he'd seen him.

Garrett braced himself. For a punch. A tongue lashing. Whatever Colt wanted to dish out, he'd take it in stride.

Fisting the front of Garrett's dirty ass shirt, he fully expected his other fist to come flying. Instead, he found himself being pulled in for a brotherly hug.

"So damn glad you're okay. Even if you are a lying asshole."

"Love you, too, brother." Garrett patted him hard on the back before pulling away.

Stepping into the privacy of the room, they let the door close behind them before talking again.

"You call Dad?"

Colt nodded. "Second I got the news that you'd been found, and you were okay."

"He doing all right?"

"Yeah." His brother shoved his hands into his short's pockets. "You know Dad. He's tougher than the two of us combined."

"That he is." Garrett ran a hand down his face and bit the bullet. "Guess I have some explaining to do."

"Guess so."

The two sat in the bedroom area—Garrett on the loveseat and Colt on the edge of the bed. And for the next thirty minutes, he told him everything.

How he sold insurance on the side as part of his cover. How he and his team travel the world saving hostages from bastards like the ones who'd taken them.

All of it.

"You could've told me, you know. Pops, too."

"I know. I could've asked my boss for permission, and he probably would've granted it. But I know how hard losing mom hit you and Dad. Me, too, but you were always her favorite, and Dad, well...Mom was his everything."

Just like Avery's mine.

"Owens seems like a cool guy." Colt smiled. "Bet that accent of his has the ladies pounding down his door."

"Not sure about that, but yeah. Rafe's a great guy to work for."

During their earlier meeting, Owens had given him the green light to fill Colt in on his job. The only formality mentioned was that Colt would have to sign the same NDA required of all Tac-Ops spouses—should any of them ever got married.

I want to be the first.

Six months ago, the thought of marriage would've sent him running. Now it didn't even make Garrett flinch.

Not anymore. Not since Avery.

"How's she doing?" Colt asked, as if the guy could read his mind.

"Shaken up." He leaned back against the seat's cushion and sighed. Raking a hand through his hair, he growled, "Bruised and scratched all to hell."

Knowing her perfect skin had been damaged because of those assholes filled him with a rage unlike any he'd ever known.

"I saw that when you guys first came back" Colt blew out a breath. "I'm afraid to ask, but…what happened to her?"

Garrett shared what he knew, which wasn't much. Mainly the incredible story of how she and Jess jumped from the truck in order to escape. Every time he thought about it, *pictured* it, his gut filled with so much acid he thought he'd puke.

"Damn." Colt shook his head.

"Yeah." It was all Garrett could think to say.

After a stretch of silence, his brother asked, "You two okay?"

"I don't know." And that knowledge fucking gutted him. "She's bound to be pissed at me for not telling her the truth about my job."

"Yeah, well…I can relate."

Garrett's lips curved with a small smile. "I need to go see her. Explain why I couldn't tell her everything before. Make her see that everything else was the truth. How I feel about her, and all that."

"Yes." Colt rose to his feet. "You do."

"I just hope she understands, so we can…"

"What?"

"Be together."

"So this thing with her…it's not just a vacation fling?"

"Not for me." Garrett's answer was instant. "And before today, I really felt like it was more for her, too. Now, I don't know what we are."

I don't know if we're anything, *anymore.*

"Well, brother. There's only one way to find out."

"Yep." Garrett pushed himself up off the loveseat. "Guess I'd better get to it."

"Guess so." Colt smirked as he walked him to the door. "I hear groveling helps with situations such as this."

Garrett snorted. "You know a lot of people who've been in this type of situation?"

"You'd be surprised." Colt opened the door with a smile.

"All right, man. I'll catch up with you later."

"Good luck."

"Thanks."

The walk to Avery's room seemed to take forever. With every step, Garrett went over what he wanted to say to her, searching for the perfect words to make her understand.

But when she opened her door and those red-rimmed eyes found his, he forgot every damn thing he'd planned to say.

So he settled for, "Hey."

"Hey."

The smell of coconuts and vanilla filled his nostrils like a soothing balm. Dressed in a pair of loose, khaki shorts and a white t-shirt, she'd obviously showered the day away. But now that her skin was clean of dirt and grime, that damn bruise on her chin looked even worse.

So did the scrapes and cuts on her arms and legs.

Garrett's back teeth ground together as he thought of all the ways he could kill the son of a bitch who'd hit her.

"You okay?"

"Yeah." He blinked. "Can I come in?"

Stepping to the side, Avery held the door open for him. Once inside, she shut it behind him and followed him into the room's main area.

He glanced at the suitcases stacked on top of the bed. "I guess they told you they were flying you and the others out soon."

She nodded. "Something about ensuring our safety and not wanting to risk us being accosted by the other passengers on board. I guess the cruise line is issuing us all a full refund, though. So that's something, I guess."

She sounded as impressed about that as he felt. Like a refund could make up for what any of them had gone through. Not that it was the cruise line's fault, but it pissed him off knowing the assholes were only offering it to help keep from being sued.

"Listen, Avery." He shoved his hands into his pockets to keep from grabbing hold of her and keeping her in his arms forever. "I need you to know I never lied to you."

"Garrett, please don't—"

"I *do* sell insurance," he insisted. "It's just not my main job."

"Clearly."

"I wanted to tell you the truth. I was planning on telling you and then everything went to shit."

"That's convenient."

"I'm serious." He *did* go to her then. "As soon as we got back from the excursion, I was going to call my boss and get permission to tell you."

"You have to ask permission?"

"Yes." He nodded with sincerity. "We do. Just like a lot of other covert agencies."

"I'm assuming he knows you're telling me now?"

"He does. Not that it matters, at this point. I mean, you saw the kinds of things my team and I do."

"So what are you, exactly? Some sort of mercenary for hire?"

"No." Garrett shook his head. "I'm a covert hostage rescue specialist. We use Travel Assurance as our cover, but my team and I...our main job is to locate and rescue people who've been taken captive by guys like the ones we dealt with today. We do a lot of classified missions the government doesn't want the public to know about. That's why we have a cover job. Keeps us hiding in plain sight, so to speak."

"That's how you got the gun on board the cruise ship."

It was a statement, rather than a question.

"Yes. My team and I have special permission from the president to carry concealed weapons aboard aircraft and seacraft of all kinds."

"The president?" She let out a disbelieving laugh. "This is insane. I mean...I've read about things like this. To be honest, I'm a little bit obsessed with stories where the heroine gets kidnapped and taken to some faraway place, and the hero rushes in at the last minute to save her. Part of me even used to wish that would happen to me, because in my mind I'd somehow romanticized it all. But this...this isn't romantic, Garrett. This is terrifying."

"I know." He put his hands on her shoulders. "Baby, trust me, I know. When that man ripped you from my arms today, I felt like I was watching my entire world disappear.

And when I finally got free and tried to find you, only to be told you'd been taken someplace else...God, Avery. I can't even *describe* the terror I felt thinking I'd lost you forever. But then, Digger and I came over that hill, and we saw you and Jessica standing on the side of the road, and I thought...I thought I've found my other half again."

"I felt the same way." She swiped at a tear that had fallen. "But then I saw you with that other man, Digger, and I...I don't know." Clearing her throat, she told him, "My sister was engaged to a man who kept things from her. I saw what the secrets and lies did to her. What they're still doing to her, and I don't want things to be like that with us."

"It won't." He vowed. "Baby, what that jerk did to Alex was unforgiveable, but this isn't even close to the same thing. You have to know that."

"I do." She pointed to her head. "In here. But here"— she tapped her chest—"I feel like a fool."

Christ. "You're not a fool. And I know this sounds crazy, and my timing is shit. But I promised you the truth, and that's what I'm giving you. Avery, the truth is I l—"

A loud knock came from the door, making Garrett want to punch whoever was on the other side.

He was a hair's breadth away from saying the most important words of his entire life, and someone knocks?

You've got to be fucking kidding me.

"I-I'd better get that."

"I'll get it."

After almost losing her today, he wasn't taking any chances. With his fists white-knuckled, Garrett walked to the door, swinging it open to see which asshole deserved to die.

When he saw the guy's face, his rising temper began to cool.

"Hey." Garrett greeted the other man. "Avery, this is Ghost. He and his team helped us at the warehouse today."

"I remember." She stepped closer.

"Ma'am." Ghost, the leader of the Delta team that had helped them with hostage transport stood in the hallway dressed in a crisp, clean Army uniform. "My men and I have been asked to escort you and the other passengers involved in today's incident to the airplane that's taking you back to the States."

Today's incident. How politically correct.

"I'll get my bags." Avery turned to head to the bed, but Garrett needed more time.

"Give us a minute, yeah?" He looked at the other man.

With an understanding tip of his head, Ghost said, "We're wheels up in twenty. Need to be on the road in ten."

"Just need a second."

"I'll be out here."

Closing the door, Garrett faced Avery again. With her bags in tow, she rolled them across the smooth carpet toward him.

"I guess this is it."

He swallowed down his emotion long enough to ask, "Is it?"

Avery's brown eyes softened. "Honestly, I don't know. I mean, I can get past the deception. You have rules and procedures to follow, and I get that now. I can even respect the fact that those are important to you, and you don't break protocol on a whim. But I guess this is all still just... a lot, you know?"

"I do."

But he also knew, if she'd give them a chance, they could work through it all...together.

"The team and I are flying out today, too," he told her. "But we've got a few things to wrap up here, first, so I'm not sure when we'll be landing back in Charlotte." *Just ask her.* "Can I call you later? Maybe we could meet for dinner tomorrow night, or..."

"Actually, I think..." Avery shifted the strap on her shoulder. "I think I need a little time. To process everything. I hope you understand."

"I do." He fucking hated it, but he did. "My number's in your phone, so...call me when you're ready. I promise I'll pick up if I can."

"Okay."

After a second's hesitation, Avery rose to her tiptoes and kissed him on the cheek. "Goodbye, Garrett. And thank you."

"For what?"

"Everything."

With no other choice, Garrett opened the door and watched her walk away under Ghost's protection.

CHAPTER 17

Two weeks later…

"KNOCK, KNOCK." Bones appeared in Garrett's office doorway.

"I'm busy, Bones," Garrett lied. "What do you want?"

"Nothin' much," the Texas native drawled. "Just that there's a smokin' hot brunette out front, and for reasons I will never understand, she's asking to see you."

He shot up out of his chair so fast the damn thing flew back and smacked the bookshelf behind him.

"That's what I thought. But I should tell you—"

"Out of my way," Garrett muttered as he pushed past the other man and headed down the hallway toward their office reception area.

"Falcon, wait!" Bones hissed as he caught up to him. "It's not who you—"

"You." A smokin' hot brunette who was most definitely *not* Avery Webb stormed toward him. "You're Garrett Morgan, correct?"

She looked familiar, but he couldn't quite place her. "Yes, I'm Garrett. How can I help you?"

"You can start by telling me why you haven't called my sister."

Oh, shit.

"Alex," he spoke her name out loud. He remembered her from the picture Avery had shown him. "You're Avery's sister."

"Damn right, I am." The pissed off woman crossed her arms and shot daggers at him from across the room. "Now are you going to answer my question, or try to BS your way through having ghosted her for the past two weeks?"

The handful of clients—actual insurance clients—who were sitting in the seating area waiting to be seen were staring at him as if they, too, wanted to hear his answer.

Behind him, Bones whispered, "I think I'm in love."

Clearing his throat, Garrett held out his arm and motioned back to the way he'd just come from. "I think we should talk in my office."

"I think that's a fabulous idea."

Storming past him, Garrett couldn't help but see what Avery had meant about them being different.

Physically, they had similar attributes. Alex was petite and lean, but curvy in an attractive, feminine way. She had dark hair like Avery's, but it was cut short in a sharp, straight bob.

The white blouse and gray pencil skirt she wore was conservative, but they'd been paired with a set of red stiletto heels that looked like they could be used as a deadly weapon.

He was reminded of another set of heels.

On an entirely different woman. One he missed with every breath of air his lungs pulled in.

Focus, dickhead.

A blaring difference between the women was how they handled their anger. Back on the ship, he'd known Avery was angry with him, but she hadn't come at him guns-a-blazin' like Alex was now.

She'd been almost quiet. Withdrawn. And it had broken his fucking heart.

Alex followed Garrett into his office. He'd hoped to meet her at some point. Let her see what a nice guy he was and how much he cared for Avery. All that 'meet the new boyfriend' stuff people did when they first started dating.

But this...this wasn't *quite* how he'd imagined that first meeting would go.

"Please." Garrett shut his office door. "Have a seat."

"I'll stand, thank you."

"Okay."

He walked to his desk but remained on this side of it, rather than sitting in his chair. A move like that seemed a bit pretentious and stuffy for his first chat with the woman he'd hoped to someday be his sister-in-law.

"She's miserable, you know."

Her words turned his stomach. "She is?"

Alex mumbled something about men being stupid before saying, "Yes. She is. So, I'll ask again...why haven't you bothered to contact her?"

"Avery said she needed time to process everything."

"Yeah, well...that was two weeks ago. Time's up."

He knew exactly how long it had been since he'd seen her. Down to the very last minute.

"I told her to call me when she was ready." He shoved his hands into his pockets and leaned his ass against the front of his desk. "I picked up the phone a million times, but I figured if she wanted to talk to me, she would've called. I just assumed she didn't want to see me again."

"She didn't." Alex didn't pull any punches. "Not at first."

Hope began to bloom inside his chest. "And now?"

"Now she spends her days drowning herself in work and her nights cuddled up to Gus."

Those hands came flying out of his pockets as Garrett straightened his spine. "Who the fuck is Gus?'

Alex's bow-shaped lips turned into a slow grin. "Her cat. But I'm glad to see your jealousy is alive and well. Means you still care."

"Of course, I still care." He frowned. "I wasn't trying to *ghost* your sister, Alex. I was trying to do the right thing and give her space like she wanted."

"I'm sure you were." Some of the heat cooled from Alex's dark eyes. "And I'm trying to do the right thing now by telling you she's a mess."

Garrett studied the other woman closely. Through all her anger and desire to rip his balls off, he also found sadness and concern.

"I take it she doesn't know you're here?"

"No, and she'll kill me if she finds out."

"It'll be our secret." He offered her a small smile. "And, for what it's worth, Avery's lucky to have a sister who cares so much about her."

"Thank you."

Now that it seemed as though he was out of the line of fire, he shifted from the defensive to the inquisitive. "You said she's a mess. Are you sure it's because of me? I mean, she went through a pretty traumatic experience."

"I know." Sadness filled her sister's eyes. "Those first few days after she got back, she had a rough go of it. She stayed at my place, which was good because she'd get these nightmares and wake up crying. I'd put on some coffee, and we'd talk them out. She told me everything that happened that day." Alex drew in a breath and said, "Thank you, by the way."

"For?"

"Risking yourself by going after her. You could've just gotten yourself and those other passengers back to the ship, but you didn't. You went looking for her. And if you and your teammate hadn't found her when you did, who knows what would've happened to her and that girl."

"I wasn't leaving until I found them." She needed to know that.

"That's what Avery told me."

"You said she stayed with you when she first got back. What about now?"

"She's back at her own apartment. I think the nightmares have subsided. She pretends to be okay, and...I don't know. Maybe she really is. Avery's a strong woman. A hell of a lot stronger than me."

"Funny." He grinned. "She said the same thing about you."

"Of course, she did." Alex rolled her eyes and sighed. "Look, I'm sorry I stormed into your place of business like this. I just—"

"Love your sister."

"Yeah." She smiled again. "I do. And from the way my

sister talked about you while she was on that cruise, I'm willing to bet you do, too."

Confession time. "I do."

Alex's smile grew wide. "That's what I was hoping to hear. I guess the only other question I have is, what are you going to do about it?"

Thirty minutes and one half-assed plan later, Garrett found himself standing outside Avery's door.

"You sure this is a good idea?" He glanced over at the woman who'd talked him into this hair-brained idea.

Alex simply shrugged and knocked on that door. "We're about to find out."

AVERY SQUEEZED the last of the water from the tips of her hair and tossed the towel across the edge of her tub. She should probably hang it up, but whatever. She'd do it later.

With no plans for the day other than going through her emails and returning a couple of calls, she decided to throw on her stretchy pants—or fat pants, as she liked to call them—and her favorite oversized t-shirt.

It was stained in a couple of places, and there was a hole just under the collar in one spot, but it had been her dad's, and she loved it.

That's not all you love.

A low growl built up from deep inside her throat. Damn it, she *had* to stop thinking about him.

Garrett Morgan was nice, funny, had a mouth made for sin and abs that went on for days. He was the kind of man who ran into danger, rather than away from it.

He'd done that for her and Jessica. He risked his life on

a regular basis and for what? For complete strangers. Who did that?

Heroes, Aves. Smart, sexy, amazingly selfless heroes.

Stomping to the kitchen, Avery went to the freezer and pulled out the tub of chocolate chip ice cream she'd bought the night before. Yanking her silverware drawer open, she grabbed a spoon, closed the door with her hip, and went into her living room where she unceremoniously plopped down onto the couch.

The first bite didn't help. Neither did the second. Nothing seemed to help ease the aching in her heart.

You could call him.

She could. She probably should. Yeah, she'd been upset about the whole secret agent job thing at first. But come on, what girl wouldn't?

No woman wants to be with a man who isn't completely honest with her. And okay, so his deception wasn't really that big of a deal. So he hadn't told her he worked for a government sanctioned company who went on super classified hostage rescue missions. So what?

They hadn't even officially declared themselves in a relationship yet. Did she really expect a guy like that to divulge top secret information to a woman he'd just met? Sex aside, had they sat down and talked about the future... their future?

No. They hadn't.

So why are you still mad at him?

She took another bite to keep from admitting the truth out loud. Because if she were being honest, Garrett wasn't the one she was pissed at.

No, if she didn't have a mouthful of delicious, creamy,

soul-healing yumminess, Avery would have to admit that *she* was the one she was mad at. Not Garrett.

He'd done nothing but treat her with kindness and a gentleness she'd never known with another man. Taught her about passion and adventure.

It was because of *him* that she'd gathered the courage to jump from that damn truck to begin with. And what had she done in return?

I walked away.

Shoving another giant bite of ice cream into her mouth, Avery thought about the countless times over the past two weeks that she'd picked up the phone to call him. The numerous texts she'd typed out and then deleted because she was too chickenshit to follow through.

Truth be told, Avery was afraid after the way she'd left things between them, that he'd decide she wasn't worthy of his love and reject her.

So instead of calling or texting, she'd spent the last two weeks trying desperately to forget him. But she was finally beginning to realize that no amount of ice cream—chocolate chip or otherwise—was going to fix what felt broken inside her.

There was only one thing that could heal a wound that deep. One man. She just had to find the courage to pick up the damn phone and call him.

And she would. After a few more bites.

Filling her spoon again, she'd just put the next helping in her mouth when someone knocked on her door.

Alex.

Avery dropped the spoon into the round, cardboard quart container and pushed herself off the couch. With the ice cream in tow, she began walking to the door.

Mouth filled with the freezing cold dessert, she did her best to talk around it.

"Go away, Awex. I awready tode you, I don't wanna go out wi you tonight." Avery opened the door and, sure enough, she found her sister smiling back at her.

"Nice outfit."

"Thanks." Avery ignored Alex's obvious sarcasm and swallowed the final remnants of her bite. "Now, go away."

She started to shut the door, but her persistent sister threw up a hand to stop her. "I'm not here to talk you into going out."

Relieved, Avery sighed. "Then why are you here? Because as much as I love you and appreciate what you're trying to do, I'm also not up for one of our sisterly heart-to-hearts."

"Good." This seemed oddly pleasing to Alex. "Because I didn't come for that, either."

Avery frowned. "Then why are you here?"

"For him."

Alex reached for something out of Avery's line of sight. A second later, in one sudden, breath-stealing moment, Avery found herself staring into the eyes she'd dreamed about every night since coming home.

"Garrett?" She blinked, half-expecting him to disappear.

He glanced down at the tub of ice cream in her hands and then back to her. "Hey, sweetheart."

Avery opened her mouth to say something more. Something profound and wise and...yeah, she had nothing.

So instead of saying anything, she grabbed hold of her sister's arm and yanked her into the apartment. "Give us a second."

Then she slammed the door in Garrett's face.

"What are you doing?" Alex scowled at her.

"Me?" Avery's voice rose two octaves. "What about you? What the hell is he doing here?"

"I knew you wanted to see him, but I also knew you were too damn stubborn to call him yourself. I saved you the effort." Her sister shrugged. "You're welcome, by the way."

"Are you kidding me right now?"

She's your sister and you love her. Don't. Kill. Her.

Avery spoke through a set of clenched teeth when she asked, "Why didn't you at least give me a heads up?"

"What, and ruin the surprise? That's kinda the whole point here, Aves."

"Alex, *look* at me. I'm like a cross between a drowned rat and the poster child for Losers Anonymous."

"You're not a loser." Alex chuckled.

Avery wished there was a mirror close by because she was certain there was smoke shooting out of her ears. "Never said I *was* one...just that I *looked* like one. But thanks for that."

"Honey, listen to me." Alex's tone softened. "That man out there couldn't give two shits about what you're wearing or whether or not your hair's done. He just wants to see *you*."

"How do you know?"

Her sister crossed her arms and raised a pointed brow. "Because I know misery when I see it. And believe me, that man out there? He's as miserable as you are."

"Really?" With a quick glance at the door, Avery bit her lip and tried not to feel happy about that fact. She didn't want Garrett to be miserable. She just wanted...

Him.

"That's what I thought." Alex went to the door. She opened that door, and then she said, "Now that my work here is done, I'll leave you two lovebirds to figure all your shit out." To Garrett she turned her tone serious long enough to give him a parting, "Hurt her, and I'll rip your balls off and shove them down your throat."

"Understood."

"Good." Her sister shot her a parting smile. "Call me later."

Avery was still trying to figure out what the hell just happened when Alex hollered a belated, "I expect details!"

Mortified, she closed her eyes and hung her head. "Yeah." She glanced back up at him. "So that's Alex."

"We've met." His eyes twinkled with humor. "She seems…"

"Certifiable?"

Garrett chuckled. "I was going to say very protective of you."

"*Over*protective you mean." She stepped to the side and held out her free hand. "Would you like to come in?"

He motioned toward the now-melting ice cream. "Only if you plan on sharing some of that."

A smile tugged at her lips. "I'll get another spoon."

One empty quart later, and they'd made it through the awkward stage of their reunion. The whole 'How ya been?' BS that people used to procrastinate saying what really needed to be said.

Like a band-aid Aves. Just get it over with, already.

"Garrett, I—"

"I wanted to—"

Avery smiled when they both started talking at the same time. "You go."

"Nope. You."

"Fine." She filled her lungs, releasing the air slowly to buy herself even a second more. "I'm sorry."

Confusion and shock filled Garrett's blue eyes. "For what?"

With a chuckle, Avery stood and grabbed the empty ice cream container. "Where do I begin?" Filled with nervous energy, she walked to the kitchen to throw it away. "For starters, I shouldn't have jumped at you about the whole job thing. I also shouldn't have pushed you away like I did." She returned to the living room but remained standing. "And I should've called you before now."

Garrett's expression was impossible to decipher as he made his way across the room to her. She'd been so busy worrying about her appearance she hadn't taken the time to notice how *he* looked.

And damn.

Talk about suit porn.

Wearing black dress pants, a white button up, and a black suit jacket, the man looked good enough to eat. And the way he was staring back at her was...

"I'm a mess," Avery blurted randomly.

His steps never faltered as he continued moving forward. "You're beautiful."

"You don't have to toss out lines, Garrett." She ran a hand down her damp hair. "I know exactly what I look like. Something else I should probably apologize for."

"You don't need to apologize for a damn thing, Avery." He stopped inches from where she stood.

His familiar, masculine scent blanketed her the way it

had when he'd first walked in. Her fingers twitched at her sides with the need to touch him. To feel his arms around her and know she hadn't destroyed her chance of having a future with him.

"You have nothing to apologize for, but I do."

"No—" She started to shake her head, but he cut her off.

"Please, just…let me say this."

Avery nodded. "Okay."

"The second I realized how I felt about you, I should've called my boss and gotten permission to tell you. So, while I couldn't tell you at first, I should have given you all the facts sooner. You never should've found out the way you did."

"H-how much sooner are we talking?"

The corner of his lips curved in a boyish grin. "I knew after that very first kiss that you were it for me. As crazy and unbelievable as it seems."

"It's not crazy." Avery took a small step forward. "I felt it, too."

His eyes locked with hers. "I should've called you before now. To be honest, I was afraid you'd hang up on me."

"I'd never do that to you."

"It was stupid." He shoved his hands into his pockets. "I've been stupid."

"We both have." Avery blinked at the sudden moisture forming in her eyes. "I've missed you." The confession escaped with a whisper.

"God, Avery." Garrett reached a tentative hand toward her face. When she didn't flinch away, his lungs expelled what sounded like a sigh of relief. "I've missed you, too. So much."

She leaned into his touch. "Garrett…"

"Sweetheart."

Avery wasn't sure who moved first. It didn't even matter. She was finally back in his arms, and if she had anything to say about it, she was never, ever leaving them again.

CHAPTER 18

Eight days. It had been eight glorious, blissful days since she and Garrett had reunited. And boy, what she'd heard about makeup sex…

Holy multiple orgasms, Batman!

Everything she'd ever read about makeup sex was true. And then some.

Garrett had spent that first night making her scream so loud Avery was sure her neighbors were going to call in a noise complaint. And they'd been nearly as bad every night, since.

Either he'd stay at her place, or she'd go to his. She'd cook them dinner or they'd order in so they could eat in their underwear and then hop right back into bed—or the shower—for another round of mind-blowing pleasure.

They both still worked, of course. They'd kiss each other goodbye in the mornings, then again when they'd see each other at night. For Avery, it was like she'd gone from missing a part of herself to feeling so full of love and happiness she thought she would burst from it.

Not that she intended to stop.

No, life was good. Better than good. And she had a feeling it was only going to get better.

Avery smiled as she entered the parking garage located next to the building she'd just been in. One of the bigger companies she'd done some work for had called her this morning, asking if she'd come by and help show their new tech guy the basics of her accounting program they'd recently purchased.

Apparently, their former tech person just up and quit without so much as a notice, so no one had been able to train this new guy on the innerworkings of the set-up. Since she had the afternoon free, Avery had been happy to come by and do it.

Her heels clicked across the pavement as she made her way down the ramp to the level where her car was parked. Normally, she parked on the street, because let's face it... parking garages are just plain creepy.

But the street crews were out doing their monthly cleaning, so she'd had to settle for parking in here.

Avery's phone began to ring from inside her purse, making her jump. Damn, she thought she was getting better at that. She had been better. Especially this past week.

It'll take some time, sweetheart. You just have to give it time.

Those had been Garrett's sweet, caring words to her when she'd woken them both up that first night he'd stayed with her. She'd been having a dream—a nightmare, really.

They'd been back in that warehouse and that man was taking her from him again. She'd been kicking and screaming like she had that day, but in her dream, when Garrett tried to help her, he didn't just get hit in the head with the gun.

He was shot and killed.

Through her sobs, he'd held her. Rocked her softly and whispered the most loving words she'd ever heard. Then he'd made love to her. Slowly building her up to that magnificent cliff, until they'd both gone over the edge together.

Pushing her irrational fears aside, Avery pulled her phone from her purse and picked up her pace.

"Hey, sis."

"What are you doing tonight?"

Avery smiled at Alex's typical non-greeting. "Having dinner with Garrett."

"Of course, you are. Don't you two ever come up for air?"

With a laugh, Avery started to feel around her purse for her keys. "I'm breathing right now, aren't I?"

"Surprisingly," her sister teased. "Fine. But I get you all to myself tomorrow night. I'll even treat you to dinner."

"Sounds good."

"Catch you later. Love you."

"Love you, too."

She'd barely ended the call when her phone rang again. This time, when she saw the caller's name, she felt a little flip in her heart.

The same one she got every time Garrett called. Or smiled. Or touched her like he had in the shower that morning.

"Hey, you," she answered with a smile.

"Hey, yourself."

Would she ever get tired of hearing that rumbly voice of his? Nope. She didn't believe she would.

"Where are you?" he asked. "Sounds like you're underground."

Avery laughed. "Because I am. I'm in a parking garage over on South Caldwell. I got an emergency call from one of my clients, and I had to come put out some fires. But I'm done and heading to the store to get stuff for dinner. Chicken and pasta sound okay?"

"Actually, that's why I'm calling. We had a thing come up at work, and I'm not going to be done until later tonight."

"Oh." She did her best to hide her disappointment. "That's fine. You coming over later, or do you just want to see what tomorrow brings?"

"I'd love to come over tonight, but it's looking like you'll be asleep before I get out of here. Want me to call you tomorrow? You can come to my place, and I'll cook for you, for a change."

"Okay." Avery smiled. "Alex just called and was wanting to meet up for dinner, so I'll call her back and let her know I'm free."

"Have fun. And tell her I said hey."

"I will."

"Be safe, sweetheart. I'll call you tomorrow."

"You, too. Bye."

"Bye."

Ending the call, Avery sent Alex a quick text with the change of plans. Her sister wrote back immediately with clapping emojis and instructions to pick her up in an hour.

Which was just enough time for her to go home,

freshen up, and change into something a little less "worky".

Avery slid her phone into her purse and pulled out her keys. Only a couple spots away from her car, she went ahead and hit the fob to unlock her doors.

And still, she was smiling.

It was ridiculous how utterly happy she was. Like deliriously, annoyingly happy.

This is it, Aves. This is what you've always read about. This. Is. Love.

They hadn't said the words yet, but she felt them. And for now, that was enough.

Lost in her blissful thoughts, she reached for her door and began to open it.

She should have been paying closer attention to her surroundings. She should have waited until she was locked away in the safety of her car to text her sister, instead of walking those last few feet with her head stuck in her phone.

If she had…if she'd been more aware of her surroundings, Avery would've seen the man coming up behind her. She would've seen him and been able to run or scream for help.

She could've called nine-one-one. *Something.*

But she hadn't seen him. Not until it was too late.

A gloved hand covered her mouth. Avery tried to break free of the enormous man's grip, but she was no match for his tight hold.

She felt a sharp prick on the side of her neck, followed by a cool, burning sensation. Avery didn't even have time to think. Not about Garrett or Alex…or *anything.*

Because whatever was in that syringe worked fast. Damn fast.

And her eyes had already closed.

"I THOUGHT we'd already decided not to work with the CIA anymore." Garrett looked at his boss for clarification. "You can't trust a fucking word those assholes say."

His teammates muttered their agreeance, and even Owens showed a rare smirk. But then their boss said, "You're not wrong, but in this instance, I don't know that we have a choice."

They'd been called in for a briefing on a situation, or rather an *anticipated* situation the government was preparing for in the Middle East.

And apparently, they were being asked to work in conjunction with the CIA.

"Falcon's right." Apollo spoke up. "Our specialty is hostage location and rescue. Why are they calling us in on this now, when there hasn't even been a single riot yet, let alone a hostage situation?"

"Because the powers that be want us to take a preemptive approach to this thing," Owens explained. "And frankly, given the evidence and chatter the CIA has picked up so far, I can't say I disagree. Now, I know we've been over all the intel once already, but I'd like to go through it again. Just so we can—"

Garrett's phone began to ring, cutting through whatever else Owens was about to say.

"Shit. Sorry, Boss." He glanced down and saw a number he didn't recognize. Tapping the screen, he sent the call straight to voicemail, then turned the sound off completely. "Thought I had it on silent."

"As I was saying, I'd like to go back over the intel to look for anything we might have—"

"Sir?" Ashely, their front reception manager, beeped in through the office's intercom system.

Owens visibly tampered down his frustration. "Yes?"

"Sorry to interrupt, but there's a call on line two for—"

"Take a message and tell them I'll call them back."

"Actually, Sir, it's for Mr. Morgan."

Garrett's ears perked up. "Me?"

"Yes. It's a woman and she sounds upset. She says it's an emergency."

"Did she give you a name?"

"Alex. Alex Webb."

Shit.

"I'll take it in my office." Standing, he shot Owens a glance and said, "Alex is Avery's sister. They were supposed to have dinner together, and—"

"Go." Owens nodded. "And let me know."

Heart pounding, Garrett tried not to overreact. Given the way Alex acted the first time she was here, it was quite possible her idea of an emergency was nothing more than a blown fuse or a flat tire.

But something in his gut told him this was more than that.

Not bothering to shut his door, he raced to his phone, picked up the receiver, and tapped the line.

"Alex?"

"Garrett? Oh, thank God. I tried c-calling your cell... your number was in her ph-phone, but you didn't answer, and—"

"Alex!" Garrett said the woman's name sharply. "I'm having a hard time understanding you, so I need you to take a breath and tell me what's wrong."

She sniffed, and goddamn it, that wasn't a good sign. The woman was crying. Like breath-hitching, couldn't hardly speak crying.

"She's gone."

Her whispered words came out so low, he almost thought he'd imagined them. "What do you mean, she's gone? Gone where?"

"I don't know." She started to cry again but cleared her throat and kept on. "We were supposed to meet for dinner almost two hours ago."

Made sense. Avery had told him she was going to make plans with her sister since he had to cancel theirs.

"When she was late, I didn't think much of it. But after an hour went by with no call or text, I got onto that one app that lets you track your friends or family…you know the one I'm talking about? We signed up for it together like a year ago so we'd always be able to find each other in case of an emer…gen…cy." She started to cry again.

"Alex, honey, I know you're upset, but I really need you to tell me everything you know."

Doing his best not to panic, Garrett scribbled notes on the back of an envelope as she relayed what she knew.

"When she didn't show up, I called her and then texted. I kept trying, but she wouldn't respond to either one. So, I looked at the app. It showed her in a parking garage uptown."

"Off of Caldwell," he nodded.

"Yeah." Alex sniffed. "How did you know?"

"When I called earlier, she was walking to her car."

But fuck, that was two hours ago. "Is the app still showing her there?"

"It is, but that's because her phone's still here."

Here? "Alex, are you in the parking garage now?"

"Yes."

"And Avery's phone is there, but she's not?"

"No." He could hear her fighting through another round of tears. "I found her purse and keys on the ground near her car. Her phone was still in it, and her driver's door was barely open. She's not here, Garrett. I think...I think someone took her."

Oh, God. I can't lose her again.

Forcing himself to focus, Garrett said, "Alex, listen to me. I need you to hang up and call the police."

"I already did. Right before I called you."

"Good girl. I'm heading to you right now, okay? So just stay where you are, and I'll be there as soon as I can."

"Garrett, I'm scared."

"I know, honey." His heart felt like it was being ripped out of his chest. "I am, too."

After telling her to text him with the actual address— there were several parking garages along that particular road—Garrett ran back to the conference room to fill Owens and the others in on what had happened.

"Avery's been abducted." He'd just blurted that shit out like it was nothing.

All eyes flew to his.

"What?" Apollo's dark brows became furrowed.

"Again?" Bones sounded as shocked as he felt.

Even Digger joined in with a "What the hell?"

But it was Owens who kept a cool head. "What do we know?"

After quickly relaying everything Alex had told him, Garrett informed his boss he was heading to her last known location.

Without even asking, the team got up to join him. Owens gave them a nod with the order to keep him apprised of the situation.

"Anything you need, Falcon." His boss gave him a somber look.

"Thanks."

And with that, Garrett turned to leave, knowing his team and his boss had his back. As always.

Several traffic violations later, he and the others were pulling into the garage where Avery had been when they'd last spoken. The area near her car was blocked by several Charlotte PD cruisers, as well as an unmarked department-issued vehicle.

Thankfully, Owens had a close working relationship with the department heads, so Garrett and his team were met with very little—if any—resistance when they arrived on the scene.

"Alex!" He ran to Avery's sister the second he saw her.

Unlike the feisty woman he'd met a little over a week ago, this Alex looked broken and lost as her face crumbled, and she threw herself into his arms.

"They have no idea where she could be."

"Shh," he did his best to console her. Meanwhile, he was struggling not to break down into a puddle of tears, himself. "We're going to find her, Alex. I won't stop until I find her."

"I know." She sniffed and pulled away. Wiping her face dry, she straightened her shoulders and said, "It has to be them, right? The ones who took you guys before?"

He hadn't thought the person or people behind their abduction in the DR would've risked following them to the States, but...Alex was probably right. Two abductions this close together couldn't be a coincidence.

"What did the police say?"

Alex relayed what she knew. She'd given her report. The cops had taken pictures of the scene, and were collecting evidence, including Avery's purse and phone. And they were going to access the garage security footage to see if they could get a look at whoever had taken her.

Other than that, all they'd told her was to go home and wait for their call.

"I can't just sit on my ass and wait for more evidence to fall into their laps, Garrett. We have to do something to find my sister."

"And we will." He promised her. To Digger, he said, "Get Shadow on the line. Have her access the cameras in here. See what she picks up."

With a nod, Digger got to work contacting Shadow. The man may be the team leader, but this job was personal.

Avery was *his* woman. His to cherish and protect. She was his future.

Damn right, he was going to find her. And then he was going to destroy the person who thought they could touch what was his.

CHAPTER 19

Avery sat in one of the jet's smooth, leather seats, her right wrist handcuffed to the armrest. She glanced down at the place where her skin was worn raw from her futile efforts to get herself loose.

Not like she had anywhere to go even if she could get free. Which she couldn't.

She'd come to a little over an hour ago with a splitting headache, a mouth that tasted like she'd been sucking on cotton, and a brain fog that was just now starting to lift.

Worst of all, there was a pain in her chest that wouldn't go away. Not one caused by whatever drug they had given her, but rather a heart that was being chipped away with every minute she got farther and farther from home.

She'd been left all alone in the jet's cabin area. Not once had anyone come back to check on her or make sure she hadn't gotten loose and jumped to her death. Of course, they probably assumed they were safe on that count.

Jumping from a truck was one thing. A plane? Not a chance in hell.

Avery thought about her sister, and her heart began aching again. Alex had to be a blubbering mess by now. Too much time had passed for her not to have realized what had happened.

Knowing Alex, she would've pulled up her phone's location on that app she'd talked her into getting. Then she'd probably call the police and…with any luck, Garrett.

Avery closed her eyes, hating how upset he must be. He was probably crawling the walls trying to find her. He and his team.

Please let them be out there, looking for me.

She had to believe they were. And after seeing them in action, if anyone could find her, it was them.

The jet jerked as its wheels skidded across the runway. Looking out the small, oval window, Avery realized she had absolutely no idea where she was.

Something that didn't bode well for her dreams of being rescued.

The door to the front of the jet opened, and a man she didn't recognize stepped out. He was big, really big. With dark hair, broad shoulders, olive skin, and a scowl that she somehow knew was permanent, he looked like Hollywood's version of a mafia hitman.

The man came over, released the cuff, and pulled her to her feet. With a gun pointed at her side, he motioned to the back of the jet where a door was already open and waiting.

"Move."

Too scared to argue, Avery did as she was told. When they got to the opening, she saw that it was a staircase leading down to the pavement below.

Gripping the railing as she went, Avery was hit with a wave of hot, humid air as she took each step with caution. They were pretty high up, which was scary enough, but add in her drug-induced state, the heels she was still wearing, and her fear from the gun pointed at her back, it was a wonder she could move at all.

When they got to the bottom of the steps, the man got a meaty grip on her upper arm—the same arm that had finally healed from the abuse it had taken by those jerks from before—and led her to a fancy black car that was parked across the tarmac.

The windows were tinted, so she couldn't see inside, but something told her whoever was behind all of this was in there right now, waiting for her.

Forced into the backseat, Avery barely had time to get her feet inside before the door was slammed shut and she was locked inside.

Her first reaction was to try to get out, but the doors had been childproofed. There was no way for her to escape.

A long ride and several tears later, the car stopped, and Avery was pulled free. She was taken by surprise when she found herself being led toward the biggest, most beautiful mansion she'd ever seen.

What the hell?

The big brute with the meaty hands took her around back. Once again, she found herself in awe of the gorgeous scenery.

Huge, beautiful palm trees set off to the side of an enormous inground pool. An intricate brick layout made up the patio portion where a set of decorative chairs and matching table awaited them.

If she wasn't completely terrified, Avery would find the place incredibly enticing.

A rough hand guided her into one of the two chairs. The man remained silent, his only form of communication the gun that was still pointed directly at her.

"Who are you?" Avery finally spoke up. "What do you want with me?"

The arrogant prick smirked but said nothing.

Before long, however, another man joined them. One she found vaguely familiar.

I know him. How do I know him?

Unlike the big brute next to her, this man wasn't dressed in an expensive-looking suit. Instead, he'd chosen loosely fitting dress slacks and a silky Hawaiian shirt.

Sunglasses covered his eyes, but Avery could still tell he was looking directly at her. Sizing her up, maybe?

Walking next to him was a third man. He was shorter than the other two, his attire much more casual. Wearing jeans, a short-sleeved button up, and sandals, he looked more like the pool boy than someone of great importance.

But Avery recognized him instantly.

Oh, God.

"You." Her heart slammed against her chest.

It was the driver of the truck. The one who'd tried to take her and Jessica away from the others. "See, Sal?" He slapped the man next to him on the shoulder. "She does remember you."

Avery's eyes slid back to the man in the flower-print shirt. She studied his face closely, too. A flash of memory hit, and just like that, she knew.

"You're the man from the warehouse," Avery told him. "You were there that day, too."

"You have a good memory, Miss Webb. This is something I tried explaining to Sal, here. But he didn't think you would remember me."

Both men walked past her as the one who'd just spoken led the other man—Sal—to the edge of the pool. Stopping, they turned around to face her.

"I was there that day. You are correct."

"You're the one from the truck." Avery licked her dry lips. Her pulse raced as her heart pumped adrenaline and fear through her cold veins.

"You see, Sal?" The man in the sunglasses spoke again. "You've always underestimated American women. I've told you time and time again, they are not just beautiful creatures. They're also intelligent."

"You're right, Emilio," Sal offered. "My apologies."

The man—Emilio—smiled and gave Sal a kind nod. "Apology accepted."

Then he pulled a gun from his waistband and shot Sal right between the eyes.

Avery jumped out of her seat, screaming as the dead man fell backward into the pool. The crystal blue water from before slowly turned to a sea of red.

"Where were we?" Emilio returned his gun to his pants and faced her as if nothing had happened. "Oh, yes. I was about to ask you about your job."

"M-my job?" Avery couldn't take her eyes off the floating corpse.

I'm going to be sick.

"Yes, Miss Webb. Your job." With a few snaps of his fingers, he tore through the macabre trance she'd been under and made a motion for her to sit back down.

Not about to argue with the man who'd just committed

cold blooded murder—right in *front* of her—Avery returned to her seat, her entire body trembling as she moved.

"Much better. Now, about your job."

"W-what about it?"

"You and your friends cost me a lot of money when you escaped. To be fair, it really was Sal's fault, but since he can no longer be of assistance, I'm relying on you to get me my money."

"I'll call my sister right now. We'll find you your ransom."

"Oh, dear Avery. May I call you Avery? I'm afraid a measly million dollars simply won't do."

Another random memory flashed. This one from the bus ride the morning of the excursion from hell.

Flags. Lots of political flags. And this man's face was on every single one.

"Emilio Garcia," she said more to herself than to him. "You're running for president of the Dominican Republic."

"Very good." The bastard smiled. "Now about my money. Ten million dollars, to be exact."

The air left Avery's lungs in a loud *whoosh*. "Ten million?" she managed to choke out. "I-I don't have that kind of money."

"No, but the companies who've purchased your accounting programs do."

More confusion set in. "You want me to steal ten million dollars from one of my clients?"

"No, of course not. I want you to steal ten million dollars, split between several of your clients."

This guy wasn't just a murderer. He was insane.

"I can't—"

"Oh, but I think you can." Pulling a folded piece of paper from the pocket on his chest, he unfolded it and handed it to her. "That is a list of your top five most lucrative clients. I want you to transfer a total of ten million dollars into these accounts—"he slid her a second piece of paper with a list of bank account numbers on them—"as quickly as you can."

"I can't do that." Avery shook her head.

"You can, and you will. If not, I'll send Felix here back to Charlotte. Only this time, it will be that lovely sister of yours he takes. He'll bring her here and then torture her in front of you until you've completed your task. You don't want anything to happen to dear, sweet, Alex now, do you?"

Ohmygod. He knows about Alex. He knows everything about me.

"Please. I'll do whatever you ask. Just don't hurt my sister."

"I'm glad to see we have an understanding."

Another man came outside. In his hands was a laptop, which he sat on the table in front of Avery. Then, with a tip of his head, Emilio dismissed him, and the man vanished back inside the house.

"You have complete internet capabilities here. However, I should warn you. I have another computer set up inside that is connected to this one. I can see everything you do as you do it. If you try to message someone or tell anyone where you are, I will know, and you will die. And then, I will find that sister of yours, and I assure you, her death will not be quick and painless."

Oh, God.

Avery swallowed down the bile rushing to the base of

her throat. "H-how do you expect me to get the money from these companies? I sold them accounting software. It's not like I have access to their actual accounts."

"But you can gain it, no? How is they say...you can do it...remotely?"

"Well, yes, if I can call them and speak to the head of their accounting departments, I might be able to get permission to gain remote access. But I'd have to have a really good reason to do something like that."

"Tell them you found a glitch. Or a virus. Something that could be detrimental to their accounts if it's not fixed immediately. You're a smart woman, Avery. I'm sure you will figure it out."

The man started to walk away, and Avery's mind spun. "Wait!" she hollered after him. "I-if I do get permission to take over their system temporarily, they'll be able to see everything I'm doing, too."

"You can freeze their screens before you begin, isn't that correct?"

Damn. He knew more about this stuff than Avery thought. "Yes." She had no choice but acknowledge the truth. "But—"

"Excellent. I expect the money to be in those accounts within the hour.

Avery glanced at her watch and shook her head. "That's not possible. It's past business hours. It's going to take time to contact these people. And I'll need a phone, in case they want me to call to explain why I'm needing access. If I can talk to them directly, it'll save us both a lot of time, rather than sending an email and waiting for a response."

"Fine. You can use Felix's phone."

"Why mine?" The big man spoke up for the first time. "Then these people will have my number."

"Trust me." Avery turned to him. "These people are accounting nerds whose sole livelihood depends on their accounts being active and in order. If I tell them there's a potential for a breach, the last thing they'll be worried about is the number that pops up on their caller I.D."

"You have until morning, Miss Webb. In the meantime, Felix will be with you if you need anything."

Yeah, because that's helpful.

Avery watched as Emilio Garcia walked away, giving her mere hours to finish a job she wasn't even sure she could do.

With her stomach churning and her body trembling, she did the only thing she could do and looked at the list. The faster she got this done, the faster this would be over.

You just saw him kill a man. He's not going to let you walk away after that.

Her inner voice had a damn good point. She needed to stall until she could figure out a way to let someone know where she was.

It was her only chance at surviving this nightmare.

Looking back down at the list, Avery skimmed the companies Emilio had provided. One was a trust company who'd been her client for the last few years. Another was an automotive retailer she'd only recently picked up but was a very lucrative business. There was a grocery chain that she'd worked with for the past several months, and then there was the last name on the list.

Travel Assurance.

Holy shit! That's it!

Travel Assurance was the company Garrett worked

for! They were also one of her newer clients. But they were huge and brought in a shit ton of money. It was one of the reasons the company's head of accounting had wanted to switch to her system. Hers was the most secure, up-to-date system on the market.

And God must be smiling down on her because she now had an excusable reason to call them.

But as much as it killed her, she had to wait. They were the last name on the list, and Avery didn't want to draw attention to them or herself by skipping the others and going straight to them.

So she'd have to wait and get through the others first. Or at least a couple of them. With any luck, they wouldn't respond right away, and she could just say she'd moved on to the next ones on the list while waiting for the others to get back to her.

It wasn't perfect, but it was all she had.

Hope rising in her chest, Avery got to work and began at the top of the list. She'd never been a good liar, but it was amazing what one could do when their lives were on the line.

The first company she contacted hadn't hesitated to give her access. She made up some BS story about a potential weak spot she'd discovered in the system that could leave the company vulnerable for hackers and the like.

Since that was a huge buzz word for accountants, Avery was able to gain access and transfer a fourth of the money to the first of Emilio's offshore accounts without detection. Then she moved on to the next company.

It was the same thing with them. They trusted her—because why wouldn't they—and gave her full access, even offering to pay her a bonus if she'd run a check like this on a monthly basis from now on.

Avery had declined, assuring them that wouldn't be necessary. One, because when they discovered what she'd done, her reputation and business would be ruined, and two, she'd probably be dead, so it wouldn't matter anyway.

The third company, the grocery chain, proved to be more difficult. They wanted a detailed list of the issues and said they'd look that over and get back with her in the morning. It wasn't an unexpected bump in her plan, and in fact, it opened the perfect opportunity for her to move on to her real target.

Travel Assurance.

Without bothering to try to contact them first, Avery pulled up the company's department contact lists on her screen so the big jerk behind her would think she was looking up the accounting number.

Picking up Felix's phone from where she'd sat it after the last call.

"Who are you calling now?"

"The last company on the list."

"What about that one?" He pointed to the grocery chain since she hadn't crossed it off.

"I'm waiting to hear back from them, so I thought I'd move on to this one to save time. Since your boss is in a hurry to get this done, I figured he'd appreciate the efficiency in not waiting around."

"Fine." He grumbled. "Make it quick."

Praying he didn't see what number she'd dialed—and that Emilio wasn't listening or connected to Felix's phone somehow, Avery took a chance and called Garrett's personal cell.

Then she held her breath and waited.

It rang once. Twice. Three times. She was about to hang up and try again when she heard a voice that was like music to her ears.

"Yes?"

"Mr. Young?" She purposely used the name of the man in charge of Travel Assurance's financial department.

"Avery? Oh, thank God, baby. Where are you? Are you okay?"

He sounded tired. Ragged. And almost as terrified as she felt.

Fighting back tears, Avery put on the performance of her life and kept with the plan. "Yes, Mr. Young. This is Avery Webb of Webb Designs. I'm so sorry to bother you after business hours, but it's come to my attention that there is a glitch in the system I sold your company a while back. It's nothing major, but it could leave your company vulnerable to cyber attacks if it's not fixed immediately."

"You can't let them know it's me. Got it. Are you okay?"

"Yes, Mr. Young. That's correct. I was recently made aware of this issue and wanted to contact you personally so I could resolve it as quickly as possible."

"Are you safe?"

"No, sir. This is something I have to do myself."

"Okay, baby. I'm reading you loud and clear. Just keep talking, okay? The longer you're talking, the better chances we have of getting a bead on your location."

"I understand. Sure, I'd be happy to hold."

Risking a glance at Felix's unmoving form, Avery shot

him a look that said she wasn't happy at all to be placed on hold, but she had no other choice. From the uninterested expression on his face, and the way he dismissed her by looking back over the property, she was pretty sure he'd bought it.

"Good girl. I know you can't respond since you're supposed be on hold, but I want you to know we're doing everything we can to find you. I don't know how the hell you were able to call, but I'm so damn glad you did, baby. I'm with the team, and Owens. I'm putting you on speaker. Okay, Avery. Give us as much information as you can."

"Yes, I'm still here, Mr. Young. Excellent. Okay, so here's what I need from you."

Avery rambled off some computer and accounting terms to throw Felix off even more. Then she started in with what she prayed Garrett and the others would understand.

"There are six preliminary steps I need to take. Possibly more, but I won't know until I get into your system. After that, there should only be two major changes that need to be made."

"Okay, baby. I have no idea what that other stuff was that you said before, but if I'm hearing you correctly now, there are at least six tangos that you know of plus the two main people guarding you. Is that right?"

Relief sent tears prickling the corners of her eyes. "Yes, sir. That's correct."

"Great, Avery. That's really good information. What else can you tell us? Do you know where you are?"

"No, Mr. Young. I'm sorry, but I can't come in. I'm actually out of the country on vacation." Avery forced a chuckle she wasn't feeling and added, "That's right. The

Dominican vacation I told you about before. I'm surprised you remembered."

"You're in the DR?" Garrett sounded upset by the news.

That makes two of us.

"Yes, it's beautiful here. Lots of palm trees. Oh, and the resort I'm staying at is this enormous, white mansion with a gorgeous pool, and—"

"Enough!" Felix yanked the phone from her hand.

Avery started to turn toward him right as his fist slammed into the side of her head. Pain exploded inside her skull as her chair toppled over, and she fell with it down to the unforgiving brick patio.

White stars flashed before her eyes, and Avery may have moaned as she fought to remain conscious.

"You were trying to tell them where you are!" he loomed over her and growled.

"I was making…conversation," she groaned again. Pushing herself up onto her knees, she took a moment to stop the world from spinning before righting the chair and sitting back down. "That man is a talker." She huffed out a breath. Putting a hand to her already-swelling eye, she said, "He would've thought something was up if I had been short and impersonal. I didn't want him getting suspicious."

Felix pocketed his phone and tapped the table next to the computer. "You just worry about getting your shit done."

Praying the call had lasted long enough for Garrett's team to trace her location, Avery ignored the pain in her cheek and eye and did as she was told.

At least she got to hear his voice one last time. That was something, right?

Of course, it wasn't the same as being with him. Seeing and touching him. But for Avery, in her most terrified moments, it had been everything.

CHAPTER 20

"Falcon, man…if you don't marry that woman, I will."

Garrett looked Bones square in the eyes and said, "Oh, I'm marrying her."

Right after he found the son of a bitch who took her and killed him and whoever had just hit her. Because he'd recognized the sound of flesh hitting flesh and had heard her soft moan of pain right before the phone call abruptly ended.

Whoever you are, you're a dead man walking.

"Goddamn right, you're marrying her." Bones grinned from ear to ear. "Seriously, man. That was some impressive shit right there."

The former Marine was right, and the others in the group agreed. Avery had impressed the hell out of all of them with her quick thinking and cool demeanor.

Most women, hell most *people* he knew who'd been abducted twice in as many weeks would be falling apart well before now. But not his Avery.

Avery, the woman who'd been scared to climb down a

fucking ladder, had not only jumped from a moving truck, she'd also just passed along vital intel that would help in her own location and rescue.

And she'd done it brilliantly.

If he wasn't already head over ass in love with the woman, that moment right there would've done it.

"You guys there?" Shadow's voice came over the speaker in the center of the table.

"We're here," Owens answered her. "Tell me you've got something."

"I've got something," the mysterious woman answered. "A whole lot of somethings, actually. Sending you her coordinates now."

Their phones dinged simultaneously with the incoming location. Just as Avery had said, she was back in the DR.

"Property belongs to one Emilio Garcia."

"The presidential candidate slash drug lord we talked about a while back?" Garrett frowned.

"Yep." Shadow confirmed. "And the phone call your girl just made originated from his personal residence."

The room erupted in several what-the-fucks and groans.

"Shit." Apollo shook his head and looked at Garrett with concern. "If that's true, we're going to need more manpower than the four of us."

"He's right." Digger chimed in. "If Garcia is as bad as they say, he's going to be armed to the teeth. If Avery saw six guards, plus him and another one working closely with him, there's bound to be at least six more on the other side of the property."

"But Tac-Ops Two and Three are both still out of the country working other shit," Bones pointed out.

"Which is why"—Owens entered the room—"I've already got another team gearing up to meet us there."

"Which team?"

"Remember the Delta Force guys who helped us with hostage transport?"

"Ghost and those guys?" Garrett piped up.

Owens nodded. "Just spoke with Colonel Robinson. He's given them the green light to head back to the DR to help us get Avery back and take down Garcia once and for all."

"Hell, yeah!" Bones cheered. "I liked those guys."

Garrett did, too. And while he hadn't expected to be working with them again so soon, he was more than willing to have an extra set of guns. Especially if it meant getting Avery the hell out of there and bringing her back home, where she belonged.

"Let's gear up, boys." He stood and headed for the door.

His teammates followed. But when he got to the door, Garrett stopped and turned to face them. Taking precious seconds Avery didn't have, he addressed the entire group as one.

"In case I forget to say it, thank you. Avery, she's…important."

"We know, brother." Apollo squeezed his shoulder. "She's with you, that makes her one of us."

The flight back to the DR was the longest of his entire life. Garrett kept watching his phone, praying Avery would call again. Not that he really expected her to after the way their brief conversation had ended.

He felt heartsick knowing there was a chance they wouldn't get there in time. He wasn't blind to that fact, and his years in the Army and with Tac-Ops had taught him to be realistic. But he'd also seen miracles happen and people who should've died in the worst of ways make it out with barely a scratch.

So, Garrett focused on that. He *counted* on that. Because for him, with his Avery, there was no other choice.

As promised, the Delta team was armed and ready by the time they got to the rendezvous site. They were positioned a mile out from Garcia's property line.

Since they'd only worked together briefly before, and that was just a simple hostage transfer, Owens had provided them with basic intel on each operative prior to boarding the plane to come here.

Garrett and the others knew each man's call sign, rank, field specialty, and training. But because this was an op— the most important one of Garrett's life—they gave up precious seconds so Ghost could run through a quick introduction before they headed out.

Gotta know who has your six, and which six you need to cover.

"Let's get to it, so we can get what we came for and get the hell out." Ghost took command of the conversation. "This fine-looking gentleman is Hollywood." He pointed to the dark-haired operative to his right. "The big guy to his right is Beatle, next to him are Fletch and Blade, and that big guy over there is Truck. And this"—Ghost slapped the chest of an extremely tall man on his left—"is Coach."

"Will there be a test afterward?" Bones feigned concern. "'Cause I'm better with faces than names."

The group chuckled at the man's joke, but Garrett was too hyped up to laugh.

"All right," he took over. "Now that introductions are over, let's go over the op one last time. This one needs to be perfect, gentlemen."

"Copy that." Ghost gave him a nod. "You lead, we'll follow. And trust me when I say, every man on my team understands exactly where you're coming from on this."

"He's right." Trucks deep voice rumbled through the warm night air. "We've been where you are, brother, so we know what's at stake."

Coach chimed in next with, "Our orders are to treat this as your op, but we're also treating your girl as if she were our own."

Hollywood, Beatle, Blade, and Fletch each gave him a solemn nod. It was all the confirmation Garrett needed.

From this point on, these guys had their backs. More importantly, they had Avery's.

After running through the plan one final time, the two teams began their trek through the Dominican countryside.

Dressed in black to keep with the night's cover, they wore protective helmets and night vision goggles, bullet resistant vests, and gloves. Between the ten of them, they had enough firepower to take out a small village.

By the time they reached Garcia's mansion, they realized that was exactly what they would have to do.

"Delta, you positioned and ready?" Ghost asked his team through the coms.

"Affirmative," each man responded to their team leader.

The next voice over the coms was Digger's. "Falcon, Ghost, and I are taking the front. Coach, Blade, and Fletch have the rear. Beatle and Bones, you good to go on the east?"

"Affirmative," Bones responded for both men.

"Hollywood and Apollo, you good on the west?"

"Ready to rock and roll, boys," was Apollo's answer.

Ghost turned to Garrett. "You ready?"

Garrett pushed down his fear for the woman he loved and nodded. "Let's do this."

With his next breath, he took out the men standing guard by the front door with two succinct shots. At the same time, the others eliminated their marks, clearing the way for both teams to approach the residence without detection.

Thanks to Emilio Garcia's obvious arrogance, the man believed he was so untouchable, he hadn't bothered constructing any type of barrier between his mansion and the trees surrounding the property.

A dumbass move on his part, but it sure made their jobs a whole hell of a lot easier.

Moving in, Garrett, Ghost, and Digger took out three more men standing post toward the corners of the house. Almost as one complete unit, the two teams worked together to bring him that much closer to Avery.

Garrett was still kicking himself for not telling her his true feelings sooner. But if he got to her in time, if she was still in that house and she was alive…

It's the first damn thing I'm going to tell her.

Making as little noise as possible, the team entered the dark residence with ease. Garrett had noticed two lights on when they'd still been outside. One on the main floor, far west corner, and one on the second floor toward the center of the house.

Thanks to Shadow's computer genius, she was able to send them blueprints of the home prior to taking off in

Charlotte. That's how Garrett and the others knew the lit room on the bottom was Garcia's personal office, and the room upstairs with the light on was a guest bedroom.

If he was a betting man, which he normally wasn't, Garrett would say Garcia was in his office, and Avery was in the top bedroom.

But again, he wouldn't assume any of this. None of the men would. There was too much at stake to make assumptions.

The residence was surprisingly quiet with six tangos standing guard inside. On their end, Garrett took out one with a quick snap of the neck, Ghost used his KA-BAR to eliminate another, and Digger used a suppressor to take out the third with relative silence.

From the coms, they knew that Coach, Fletch, and Blade had taken care of any threats coming from their end. Within minutes, the ten men had met each other in the grand foyer.

Using hand signals alone, Ghost and Digger communicated with the others silently. Following the plan, Ghost, Garrett, and Digger headed upstairs via the main staircase. Apollo, Blade, Coach, and Fletch headed down the hallway toward Garcia's main office, and Hollywood, Beatle, and Bones took the second set of stairs at the far east side of the house.

One by one, the rooms were cleared. Even the two that were lit up.

With each new door they came to, Garrett felt his heart would fly out of his chest. And with each empty room, he was met with disappointment.

The house was empty. No sign of Avery or Garcia.

"Fuck!" Garrett lifted his night goggles and stared back at the others. "Where the hell are they?"

"I don't know." Ghost shook his head. "We've checked every last inch of this place, inside and out. There's no sign of them any—"

An engine roared to life from the east side of the property.

Son of a bitch.

"The fuck?" Bones scowled as all heads turned in that direction.

Headlights filled the foyer, and Garrett was thankful they'd already taken their night visions off.

"They must've been hiding in one of the vehicles," Blade stated the obvious. "We looked as we walked past, but...I don't know. We must've missed them, somehow."

"He's not getting away," Garrett started for the nearest door.

He hadn't come this far...gotten this close...only to lose her, now.

"Garcia must've heard us coming," Blade pointed out the obvious. "He's using her as fucking leverage!"

The one silver lining in this unexpected turn of events was that Garrett knew, even without having seen her, that Avery was still alive.

If Garcia had killed her, they would've already found her body. The only kill they'd found that wasn't one of theirs was a man floating on his back in the pool.

And from the look of things, he'd been dead several hours.

All ten men ran in the direction of the headlights. They got back outside just in time to see an SUV spinning around and speeding off.

With the moonlight shining through the back window, Garrett caught a glimpse of Avery's terrified face staring back at him. Her hands were pressed against the window, and she was screaming his name.

"Motherfucker!" he growled.

"Here!" Hollywood yelled from the driver's side of another SUV. "Dipshit left the keys in the ignition!"

As luck would have it, it was an Escalade. Seating capacity of seven, but enough room in the back to squeeze three more.

Sending up a quick prayer of thanks, Garrett sprinted toward the running vehicle. He didn't bother to see who was following him. He already knew.

His team. Ghost's team. He trusted them all to have his back.

Since Hollywood was already behind the wheel, Garrett jumped into the passenger seat while Digger, Fletch, Ghost, Blade, and Coach filled the seats.

Lifting the back hatch, Beatle, Apollo, and Bones hopped in and held on tight, their legs dangling over the back bumper as Hollywood spun the vehicle around, spewing gravel as they went.

"Where the fuck does he think he's going to go?" Apollo asked.

"Who the hell knows?" Hollywood put the gas to the floorboard and drove like a boss. "Wherever it is, he won't get far."

The chase continued for several minutes. The men tilting side to side as Hollywood maneuvered the SUV along the same path as the vehicle in front of them.

At one point, Garrett feared they'd lost them, but his

fears were put to rest when they turned a curve and spotted Garcia's taillights once more.

"There's a river up ahead," Ghost informed them. Looking down at his phone, he added, "A big one."

"Bet the fucker's got a boat," Bones piped in from the back.

Garrett's gut tightened with fear. If Garcia got Avery on that river, she was dead.

Sure enough, five miles and a shit ton of burned rubber later, they pulled into a parking lot near an impressive boat dock at the river's edge.

Garrett was out of the SUV and running toward the shadowy figures before Hollywood had a chance to put the damn thing in park.

Weapon up, he yelled at Garcia and the other man with him to stop. They didn't.

Dragging a fighting Avery with him, Garcia continued down the long, wooden path as the other man turned and opened fire.

"Garrett!" Avery screamed his name as the shot went wide.

"Shut up!" Garcia jerked her around like a rag doll.

Garrett's jaw clenched, a murderous rage filling his veins with ice. He'd never wanted to kill someone more than he did in that moment, but he couldn't risk it.

The way Garcia was holding her put her directly in his line of fire. And if he did try to take the shot and hit her instead of Garcia...

Put that shit away, man. She needs you to be the trained operative you are.

His subconscious was right. Pushing everything aside, Garrett let his emotionless operator mask fall over him.

Garcia made a sudden turn, he and Avery disappearing between two docked boats. The other man got off three more shots before vanishing behind them.

With a quick assessment of the layout, Garrett made a last-minute decision. One he prayed wouldn't cost him everything.

While he and the others continued dodging Garcia and the other hidden man's flying bullets, he hopped onto one of the nearby boats and silently climbed to the top. He spotted Garcia and the other man in seconds.

They were forcing Avery onto the large yacht next to him. One with too many fucking places to hide. He needed to take them out now, before they got her inside.

"I've got the guard," Apollo's low voice came through the coms.

A second later, a shot rang out, and the man who'd been protecting Garcia fell.

One down, one to go.

With Garcia in his sights, Garrett did a lightning-fast assessment of the situation to determine whether or not he was good to shoot.

He wasn't.

Fuck! "Hold your fire," he spoke only to the teams.

With his gun at Avery's head, Garcia pulled her toward the back of the boat near a section with no railing.

"Put your weapons down, or she's dead!" the once-powerful man yelled.

Garrett was already off the boat, his boots hitting the wooden dock before the man had uttered the first word of his threat.

"Let her go, Garcia!" he ordered. "It's over!"

"No! It's not fucking over! I'm going to be this country's next president!"

"No, you're not." Ghost appeared beside Garrett.

With the other men surrounding him, supporting him, Garrett tried reasoning with Garcia one last time.

"Look around you, Emilio. There's only one way this ends, and that's with you dropping your weapon and letting Avery go."

"No." Garcia held onto his fucked-up reality. "She's going to get me my money! She *owes* me that money!"

Garcia filled a fist with Avery's hair, causing her to cry out. Barely resisting the urge to kill, Garrett allowed himself to really look at her for the first time since finding her again.

She was scared to death, and her left eye was nearly swollen shut. But she was staring back at him with more faith and love than he ever deserved.

Garcia shifted his feet, the move giving Garrett a different angle than before. A *better* angle.

His heart gave a hard thump inside his chest.

"I've got a clear shot," he spoke low enough Garcia couldn't possibly hear him. With those five words, he let the others know of his plan.

To Avery, he asked, "Do you trust me, baby?"

Without a second's hesitation, she answered with a shaky, "Y-yes."

It was all he needed to know.

Clearing his mind and calming his breaths, Garrett aimed his weapon, slid his finger to the trigger, and said another prayer as he emptied his lungs and took the shot.

The bullet hit Garcia between the eyes. He started to

fall backward, and for a split second, Garrett thought his moment of terror was over.

Then he heard Avery scream and realized the dead man's fingers were still tangled in her hair.

As Garcia fell over the edge of the boat, he took Avery with him.

"Avery!" Garrett sprinted down the dock and dove into the water after her.

He was ready to drown if it meant saving her. But it turned out that wasn't necessary.

She'd already saved herself.

"Garrett!" Avery coughed as she swam toward him. "Oh, my...God!"

"Avery!" He grabbed hold of her and squeezed her so hard he was surprised she didn't break.

"Is it over?"

"Yeah, baby." He closed his eyes and held on tight. "It's over."

Remembering his earlier vow, he pulled away just enough to tell her, "I love you."

Water dripped from her long, wet eyelashes as she stared back at him in shock. "What?"

"This isn't even close to how I imagined saying that to you for the first time, but I don't want another second to go by without you knowing. I'm in love with you, Avery Webb. And I want to spend the rest of my life showing you just how much."

"I love you, too." She started to cry but then stopped herself. Brushing several wet strands from her face, she said, "Wait. Did you just ask me to marry you?"

Garrett smiled. "Yeah. I guess I did."

"Just making sure." She pressed her wet lips to his. "And the answer is yes. A million times, yes!"

The audience neither realized was there, clapped and cheer with congratulations. But Garrett paid them no attention. He was too busy kissing his fiancée.

Hours later, after dealing with the local police, *again*, Garrett and the others were finally free to go.

Thanks to the unlimited connections Owens had, including the U.S. president, both Tac-Ops and Delta had been cleared of any wrongdoing. In fact, they'd been assured the unnamed special ops teams who worked together to protect the people of the DR would be dubbed heroes in tomorrow's papers.

But Garrett didn't care about any of that. The only thing he cared about was that Avery was safe, and they were on their way back home.

Ghost and his team were also on a plane, although they hadn't said where they were headed, and Garrett knew better than to ask.

He did exchange numbers with the Delta leader, because yeah. Once you've shared an experience like the one they'd just had, that created a certain bond that you never really wanted to let go.

With a heartfelt thanks and a promise to invite them to the wedding, Garrett had said his goodbyes to the special ops badasses, and the two teams had parted ways.

"I knew you'd come for me." Avery's soft voice rose from where she lay against his chest. "I knew, if anyone could, it would be you."

"I'll always come for you, baby." Garrett kissed her on the top of her head. "Although, I have to say, I'd love it if you never got kidnapped again."

"Same." She chuckled before whispering, "It's amazing the difference a day can make, huh?"

"Yeah." Garrett had been thinking the same thing.

He'd woken up yesterday happier than he'd ever been. Then in the middle of it all, his world had been torn apart. But by the end, with the help of his friends—both new and old—it had been sewn back together.

And now it was stronger than ever before.

EPILOGUE

Six months later…

"I NOW PRONOUNCE you husband and wife. You may kiss—"

Garrett didn't wait for the preacher to finish. He was already kissing her. *Dipping* her. And Avery didn't mind one little bit.

"Get it!" Colt hollered from his spot as Garrett's best man.

Even the preacher and Rafe Owens, Garrett's stoic boss, couldn't hold back their laughs.

Avery chuckled against Garrett's lips, loving that she hadn't just gained a husband, but also the best brother-in-law a girl could ask for.

And, though no one could ever replace her father, Garrett's dad had already proven himself a darn good substitute.

Kenneth Morgan had beamed from the front pew

throughout the entire ceremony. Avery suspected she'd start getting questions about grandbabies soon, as Garrett had the last few years.

But she was fine with that.

They'd already discussed kids, and as of last month, they were officially trying. This wasn't news they'd shared with anyone yet. Not even Alex.

Avery would tell her sister, and probably soon. But for this first little bit, she liked the idea that she and Garrett had something that was just theirs.

Cheers and whoops from the small crowd filled the church where Avery and Alex's parents had exchanged vows fifty years ago to the day.

When she'd told Garrett about her idea for that to be their wedding day, too, he'd kissed her wildly and told her he loved the idea.

Alex was on board, too, and as the Maid of Honor—and Avery's only bridesmaid—she'd taken care of almost every part of the planning. Of course, she'd made several checklists.

None of which included kissing a hot guy.

But Avery was kissing one, anyway. And since Garrett was her husband, she'd get to kiss him whenever she wanted to…for the rest of their lives.

"What do you say, Mrs. Morgan." He stood them back upright. "You ready to party?"

Losing herself in his crystal blue eyes, Avery smiled wide. "That depends, Mr. Morgan."

"On what?"

She raised a brow. "On whether or not you can keep up."

Without any warning, Garrett bent down and scooped

her into his arms. Avery squealed, then tossed her bouquet of white roses behind them. Looking over her shoulder, she laughed when she saw her sister catch it.

Avery gave her hilariously horrified sister a wink as her newly pronounced husband carried her back down the aisle and out of the church as if she weighed nothing.

A barrage of hollers and high-pitched whistles blared from the men of Tac-Ops, as well as Ghost and his gorgeous wife, Rayne.

Avery had met the woman briefly before the ceremony, and they'd instantly clicked. When Avery had commented on that fact, Rayne had simply laughed and told her it took a special kind of woman to love men like theirs.

Speaking of...

Avery glanced at Garrett's handsome face as he moved them down the church steps with grace and ease. Her heart felt so full she thought it would explode from the love she felt for this man.

He was every fictional hero she'd ever read about. But he was real.

And he was hers.

ETHAN "APOLLO" McAllister stood at the bar and watched the happy couple dance. He ignored the feeling in the pit of his stomach, chalking it up to bad liquor rather than the jealousy he refused to acknowledge.

He didn't want to get married. Hell, he wasn't even *dating* anyone right now. So, what did he have to feel jealous about?

Fucking nothing.

It wasn't like his dating history was any less fulfilling than the next guy's. The women from his past had been nice enough. They'd enjoyed each other's company and had fun while it lasted. And when it ended, they always parted on friendly terms.

But that was the thing. It always ended.

As nice as those women were, none of them had ever made Ethan want what Falcon had found with Avery. He never imagined himself getting down on one knee or watching any of them walk down the aisle toward him.

Not because of anything they'd done. Truth be told, he wasn't sure why they hadn't sparked that special feeling deep inside.

You know why.

A woman's face flashed through his mind. A gorgeous, curvy, blonde with eyes that sparkled when she laughed and dimples that drove him crazy with the urge to kiss them.

Nope. Not going there.

He couldn't go there, even if he wanted to. Which he didn't.

Because those dimples...those curves...they belonged to a woman Ethan couldn't have. A woman Ethan shouldn't want.

And that same woman's lips...those full, luscious lips. Yeah, those belonged to a woman he never should've kissed.

Ignoring the voice—and woman—filling his head, Ethan took another sip of his Crown and Coke and continued with his people watching until his glass was empty.

When there was nothing left but ice, he tossed his cup into the trash and slipped away unseen.

But later, in the privacy of his own bedroom where no one was around to judge him, he let his mind wander back to that same woman. And when he laid his head on his pillow, he let himself pretend—for just a moment—that she belonged to him.

Instead of his best friend.

Want more from Anna Blakely's Tactical Operations Series? Keep watching for **Ethan's Obsession** (Tac-Ops Book 2) coming January 2022!

ABOUT THE AUTHOR

Author Anna Blakely brings you stories of love, action, and edge-of-your-seat suspense. As an avid reader of romantic suspense herself, Anna's dream is to create stories her readers will enjoy and characters they'll fall in love with as much as she has. She believes in true love and happily-ever-after, and that's what she will always bring to you.

Anna lives in rural Missouri with her husband, children, and several rescued animals. When she's not writing, Anna enjoys reading, watching action and horror movies (the scarier the better), and spending time with her amazing husband, four wonderful children, and her adorable granddaughter.

FB Author Page: facebook.com/annablakely.author.7
Blakely's Bunch (reader group): https://www.facebook.com/groups/354218335396441/
Instagram: https://instagram.com/annablakely
BookBub: https//www.bookbub.com/authors/anna-blakely
Amazon: amazon.com/author/annablakely
Twitter: @ablakelyauthor
Goodreads: https://www.goodreads.com/author/show/18650841.Anna_Blakely

facebook.com/annablakely.author.7

twitter.com/ablakelyauthor

instagram.com/annablakely

amazon.com/author/annablakely

WANT TO CONNECT WITH ANNA?

Newsletter signup (with FREE book!)
BookHip.com/ZLMKFT
Join Anna's Reader Group: www.facebook.com/
groups/blakelysbunch/
BookBub: https://www.bookbub.com/authors/anna-blakely
Amazon: amazon.com/author/annablakely
Author Page: https://www.
facebook.com/annablakelyromance
Instagram: https://instagram.com/annablakely
Twitter: @ablakelyauthor
Goodreads: https://www.goodreads.com/author/show/
18650841.Anna_Blakely

Taking a Risk, Part One (Jake & Olivia's HFN)

Taking a Risk, Part Two (Jake & Olivia's HEA)

Beautiful Risk (Trevor & Lexi)

Intentional Risk (Derek & Charlie)

Unpredictable Risk (Grant & Brynnon)

Ultimate Risk (Coop & Mac)

Targeted Risk (Mike & Jules)

Savage Risk (Eric & Riley)

Undeniable Risk (Ryker & Sophie)

Bravo Team Series

Rescuing Gracelynn (Nate & Gracie)

Rescuing Katherine (Matt & Katherine)

Rescuing Gabriella (Zade & Gabby)

Rescuing Ellena (Gabe & Elle)

Rescuing Jenna (Adrian & Jenna)

There are many more books in this fan fiction world than listed here, for an up-to-date list go to www.AcesPress.com

You can also visit our Amazon page at:
http://www.amazon.com/author/operationalpha

Special Forces: Operation Alpha World

Christie Adams: Charity's Heart
Denise Agnew: Dangerous to Hold
Shauna Allen: Awakening Aubrey
Linzi Baxter: Unlocking Dreams
Jennifer Becker: Hiding Catherine
Alice Bello: Shadowing Milly
Heather Blair: Rescue Me
Misha Blake: Flash
Anna Blakely: Rescuing Gracelynn
Julia Bright: Saving Lorelei
Cara Carnes: Protecting Mari
Kendra Mei Chailyn: Beast
Melissa Kay Clarke: Rescuing Annabeth
Samantha A. Cole: Handling Haven
Lorelei Confer: Protecting Sara
Anne Conley: Redemption for Misty
KaLyn Cooper: Rescuing Melina
Janie Crouch: Storm
Sarah Curtis: Securing the Odds
Jordan Dane: Redemption for Avery
Tarina Deaton: Found in the Lost
Aspen Drake, Intense
KL Donn: Unraveling Love
Riley Edwards: Protecting Olivia

PJ Fiala: Defending Sophie
Nicole Flockton: Protecting Maria
Alexa Gregory: Backdraft
Michele Gwynn: Rescuing Emma
Casey Hagen: Shielding Nebraska
Desiree Holt: Protecting Maddie
Kathy Ivan: Saving Sarah
Kris Jacen, Be With Me
Jesse Jacobson: Protecting Honor
Silver James: Rescue Moon
Becca Jameson: Saving Sofia
Kate Kinsley: Protecting Ava
Rayne Lewis: Justice for Mary
Heather Long: Securing Arizona
Margaret Madigan: Bang for the Buck
Trish McCallan: Hero Under Fire
Kimberly McGath: The Predecessor
Rachel McNeely: The SEAL's Surprise Baby
KD Michaels: Saving Laura
Lynn Michaels: Rescuing Kyle
Olivia Michaels: Protecting Harper
Wren Michaels: The Fox & The Hound
Annie Miller: Securing Willow
Kat Mizera: Protecting Bobbi
Keira Montclair: Wolf and the Wild Scots
LeTeisha Newton: Protecting Butterfly
Angela Nicole: Protecting the Donna
MJ Nightingale: Protecting Beauty
Victoria Paige: Reclaiming Izabel
Anne L. Parks: Mason
Debra Parmley: Protecting Pippa
Lainey Reese: Protecting New York

KeKe Renée: Protecting Bria
TL Reeve and Michele Ryan: Extracting Mateo
Elena M. Reyes: Keeping Ava
Deanna L. Rowley: Saving Veronica
Angela Rush: Charlotte
Rose Smith: Saving Satin
Lynne St. James: SEAL's Spitfire
Dee Stewart: Conner
Harley Stone: Rescuing Mercy
Sarah Stone: Shielding Grace
Jen Talty: Burning Desire
Reina Torres, Rescuing Hi'ilani
Savvi V: Loving Lex
Megan Vernon: Protecting Us
LJ Vickery: Circus Comes to Town
Rachel Young: Because of Marissa
R. C. Wynne: Shadows Renewed

Delta Team Three Series
Lori Ryan: Nori's Delta
Becca Jameson: Destiny's Delta
Lynne St James, Gwen's Delta
Elle James: Ivy's Delta
Riley Edwards: Hope's Delta

Police and Fire: Operation Alpha World
Freya Barker: Burning for Autumn
B.P. Beth: Scott
Jane Blythe: Salvaging Marigold
Julia Bright, Justice for Amber
Anna Brooks, Guarding Georgia
KaLyn Cooper: Justice for Gwen

Aspen Drake: Sheltering Emma
Emily Gray: Shelter for Allegra
Alexa Gregory: Backdraft
Deanndra Hall: Shelter for Sharla
Barb Han: Kace
EM Hayes: Gambling for Ashleigh
India Kells: Shadow Killer
CM Steele: Guarding Hope
Reina Torres: Justice for Sloane
Aubree Valentine, Justice for Danielle
Maddie Wade: Finding English
Stacey Wilk: Stage Fright
Laine Vess: Justice for Lauren

Tarpley VFD Series
Silver James, Fighting for Elena
Deanndra Hall, Fighting for Carly
Haven Rose, Fighting for Calliope
MJ Nightingale, Fighting for Jemma
TL Reeve, Fighting for Brittney
Nicole Flockton, Fighting for Nadia

As you know, this book included at least one character from Susan Stoker's books. To check out more, see below.

SEAL Team Hawaii Series

Finding Elodie
Finding Lexie
Finding Kenna (Oct 2021)
Finding Monica (May 2022)
Finding Carly (TBA)
Finding Ashlyn (TBA)
Finding Jodelle (TBA)

Eagle Point Search & Rescue

Searching for Lilly (Mar 2022)
Searching for Elsie (Jun 2022)
Searching for Bristol (Nov 2022)
Searching for Caryn (TBA)
Searching for Finley (TBA)
Searching for Heather (TBA)
Searching for Khloe (TBA)

The Refuge Series

Deserving Alaska (Aug 2022)
Deserving Henley (Jan 2023)
Deserving Reese (TBA)
Deserving Cora (TBA)
Deserving Lara (TBA)
Deserving Maisy (TBA)
Deserving Ryleigh (TBA)

Delta Team Two Series

Shielding Gillian
Shielding Kinley
Shielding Aspen
Shielding Jayme (novella)
Shielding Riley
Shielding Devyn
Shielding Ember
Shielding Sierra (Jan 2022)

SEAL of Protection: Legacy Series

Securing Caite (FREE!)
Securing Brenae (novella)
Securing Sidney
Securing Piper
Securing Zoey
Securing Avery
Securing Kalee
Securing Jane

Delta Force Heroes Series

Rescuing Rayne (FREE!)
Rescuing Aimee (novella)
Rescuing Emily
Rescuing Harley
Marrying Emily (novella)
Rescuing Kassie
Rescuing Bryn
Rescuing Casey
Rescuing Sadie (novella)
Rescuing Wendy
Rescuing Mary

Rescuing Macie (novella)
Rescuing Annie (Feb 2022)

Badge of Honor: Texas Heroes Series

Justice for Mackenzie (FREE!)
Justice for Mickie
Justice for Corrie
Justice for Laine (novella)
Shelter for Elizabeth
Justice for Boone
Shelter for Adeline
Shelter for Sophie
Justice for Erin
Justice for Milena
Shelter for Blythe
Justice for Hope
Shelter for Quinn
Shelter for Koren
Shelter for Penelope

SEAL of Protection Series

Protecting Caroline (FREE!)
Protecting Alabama
Protecting Fiona
Marrying Caroline (novella)
Protecting Summer
Protecting Cheyenne
Protecting Jessyka
Protecting Julie (novella)
Protecting Melody
Protecting the Future
Protecting Kiera (novella)

BOOKS BY SUSAN STOKER

Protecting Alabama's Kids (novella)
Protecting Dakota

New York Times, *USA Today* and *Wall Street Journal* Bestselling Author Susan Stoker has a heart as big as the state of Tennessee where she lives, but this all American girl has also spent the last fourteen years living in Missouri, California, Colorado, Indiana, and Texas. She's married to a retired Army man who now gets to follow *her* around the country.

www.stokeraces.com
www.AcesPress.com
susan@stokeraces.com

Made in the USA
Columbia, SC
05 June 2025

58950587R00183